A PLACE IN TIME

A PLACE IN TIME

Norma Hill

The Book Guild Ltd
Sussex, England

First published in Great Britain in 2002 by
The Book Guild Ltd
25 High Street
Lewes, East Sussex
BN7 2LU

Typesetting in Baskerville by
SetSystems Ltd, Saffron Walden, Essex

Printed in Great Britain by
Antony Rowe Ltd, Chippenham, Wiltshire

A catalogue record for this book is
available from the British Library

ISBN 1 85776 627 X

CONTENTS

1

A Saxon Village

Gudrum was feeling perplexed. He had come on a hunting foray into Fyllwood Forest with his friend Engel, and was usually full of pride at his hunting prowess, especially when he struck lucky and caught a deer, instead of the usual rabbits and hares that filled his mother's stew-pot. He stood disconsolately in a small clearing astride the young deer he had just killed, waiting for Engel to come up the path from the river.

Gudrum felt strange and out of sorts and he knew it was something to do with the way he had felt for the last two or three weeks whenever he had looked at Charis, the flaxen-haired girl who lived a few dwellings down from him with her parents and brothers and sisters at Fylton, his home encampment on the other side of the forest. Gudrum had grown up with Charis who was the same age, had shared his hopes and fears with her as with a sister, but just recently it seemed to him that the atmosphere between them had altered, from the old free friendship to a more cautious hesitant one. Gudrum sensed that Charis felt this too, because several times of late he had caught her unawares looking at him very strangely. A thousand or so years on in time he would have told himself he was a young man in love, but Gudrum was a Saxon lad living in the year 1042 and had different conceptions. All he knew was his strong animal desire to know Charis better, in a different way to friendship, mingled with protectiveness and tenderness at the same time. It was confusing because he had known her since they were children but had never felt this way before about her, or indeed any other girl, and there were plenty of other pretty girls in their encampment. Gudrum was a strong stockily-built youth of nineteen years, not over-tall, with light brown hair, and usually a merry outlook.

Engel came up the trail from the river and into the clearing, swinging a brace of freshly-caught fish. 'I saw Llew down by the river and swapped a hare for these,' he said as he placed the fish on the ground. Llew, or Llewellyn, was a good friend of Gudrum and Engel who always went hunting together. Llewellyn was a Welshman who lived at the side of the river below the great gorge of Goram which split the forest. He was older than the Saxon boys, and had lived there as long as they could remember, since they had been old enough to hunt in Fyllwood alone. No one had ever asked Llewellyn why he had strayed from his native land, whether it was from choice, or if he had been banished. They knew he had come by way of the big water that led from their river, and that he'd experienced a terrible journey in that treacherous water in his tiny coracle. The swift tides had landed him on sandbanks and several times he had thought his last hour had come. It was a story that he often told the boys while they sat in his small crude hut beneath the towering cliffs of the gorge, sipping hot broth. He also often told them tales of Goram the giant who had once dominated the gorge and they would sit fascinated listening to the Welshman lilting on with his Celtic talent for telling a good story.

Engel came up to Gudrum and his deer. 'Are you ill or something?' he asked. 'I should have thought you would have had this fella trussed up by now and ready for taking home. What's the matter, Gud?'

Gudrum smiled sheepishly. Engel was a good friend, but even to Engel he could not reveal these confusing feelings he was having. He stirred himself to action. 'We'll have him ready soon,' he said briskly. 'I had to look for some more strong vines to lash him to the pole.'

Engel looked at him quizzically but kept his mouth closed. He knew they had come well prepared with plenty of strong vines to plait a rough twine. They lashed the deer to the pole, packed their hunting bags and set off through the forest to Fylton and home.

The next morning Gudrum was about earlier than usual. His mother Melia, and two sisters, Marye and Frieda, were still asleep behind their awning as he crept out from the family hut. He had decided what to do about Charis and his feelings for her. He had thought long and hard about it overnight and knew it was the only answer. He would marry Charis. He would establish a family of his own, and he would care for her and protect her for the rest of her life; they would be joyously content. His heart beat fast at the thought of the future. He had no doubts that Charis felt the same way as he did. He knew her well enough to know that. In the manly fashion consistent with his upbringing he was now going to do something about it. He felt much happier now that he had made up his mind. He had no father to turn to for advice, for his father had been killed by a giant boar in the forest when Gudrum was but twelve years old. He remembered his mother Melia's grief and the trembling pale faces of his sisters. They had clung to him, Marye and Frieda, and he knew that he was to be the provider for this family now, young as he was. The neighbours and his father's brother had helped a great deal until he was a little older and able to go hunting further afield in the forest for two or three days' duration with Engel. The community had been good to his family and in the early days after his father's death there had always been fish and meat left at their doorway whenever relatives or neighbours had been on hunting trips. The Saxon community of Fylton had been well taught the basic Christian virtues by the priest Athold who lived down the slope to the south-east of them in the tiny chapel of St Whyte, a wooden building with a wattle roof.

It was to Athold that Gudrum hurried now. He sped down over the sheep pastures to the tiny lane leading to

3

the chapel. The birds were singing joyfully to the morning and he even spied a cheeky magpie, the early sun glinting on its wings, as he made his way purposefully down the lane. At its lowest point the pathway was crossed by a stream. It was April and there had been a lot of rain so the stream was in full flood as he leapt across the stepping stones, and a couple of young otters scampered away at his approach as he went up the bank towards the little chapel building about thirty yards away. Athold was astir and greeted him warmly. They went inside and Athold drew out a crude bench from the back of the dark gloomy interior. It took Gudrum a few minutes to accustom his eyes from the bright sunlight outside, for the chapel only had a few slits in the walls to provide light. The brightest thing about the building was the shining cross at the eastern end on the simple altar.

'Well my son, what brings you here this morning of the spring?' Athold asked.

Gudrum came straight to the point. 'I'm of a mind to wed a young maid from Fylton.' There, he had said it!

Athold smiled wisely. 'Is it Charis?' he asked.

Gudrum was surprised that his feelings for Charis had been so obvious, and then he realized that marriage to her would be the obvious conclusion to anyone who had known them both from birth. He said to Athold, 'Yes, it is Charis. I wanted to bring the matter to you first, Brother. Do you think it is a right idea?'

'Well, you certainly do, my son, to come racing to me with the sunrise. I see nothing against the thought. You are young and strong, you will work hard to raise a family in a good manner. Does Charis wish it?'

'I haven't spoken with her yet, but I know she will, I feel she will!'

Athold smiled benignly. 'Then go to her, young Gudrum. I shall be happy to bless your joining!'

Gudrum leapt up. 'My thanks to you, Brother!' He raced down the lane, over the stream and up the slope to Fylton. The encampment was awake and busy now.

'You were an early one this morn!' his mother remarked as she stirred the large pot of breakfast gruel.

Gudrum stared at Melia; did she guess his heart's feelings? He said, ''Twas a lovely morn, I felt like a mouthful of it before a taste of this excellent gruel!' He snatched a quick taste of the breakfast pot with a wooden spoon while she was turning away momentarily.

His mother laughed and pushed him away fondly. 'Get away with you, lad, 'tis not ready awhile!' Gudrum had recovered his usual merriment.

During the morning he sauntered, and almost swaggered, past the dwelling of Charis. He felt new confidence after his talk with the priest. As if in unspoken answer to his presence Charis came to the doorway to fetch something. She glanced across and smiled, noting his pausing.

'Hello Gudrum, no work to do? I have lots to do. You can help me if you like!' she jested.

Charis was a fine weaver of cloth and was also skilful at cheese-making from the herd of goats that her mother kept. Gudrum cleared his throat and laughed lightly, 'Women's work!' he said, 'but I'll see what you're making.'

He had previously seen her mother go to the goat patch and he knew her brothers and sisters were out picking herbs. He stepped inside. The hut was neat and clean and her work lay half-woven on the loom. She stood hesitant and shy, for she had never seen Gudrum in this mood before. Her flaxen hair shone brightly in the firelight and Gudrum was lost. He became bold.

'Charis . . .'

'Yes?'

He had never seen her eyes look so blue. 'Charis, we have known each other long since. I would like to know you better. Charis . . . I want you for my wife.'

He stole a look at her. She was smiling quietly. 'Gudrum' was all she could manage through her blushes. She and Gudrum had grown up and played together, and there had always been ease between them as with brother and sister. Now this was suddenly changed for Charis. True, she knew that lately he had been looking at her in a different way and she had thought about him constantly, but now this was different, he had declared himself.

'Well?' Gudrum ventured gently.

'Oh yes, Gudrum, I want to be your wife but . . . we must consult my family.' Her father Erich was away beyond the hills seeking lost sheep. It was her father she was thinking of.

'Bless you both, that's good!' Erich said, when Gudrum and Charis approached him a couple of days later.

Gudrum's mother smiled when he told her the news. She did not seem surprised. 'Charis is a good maid, she'll be right for you,' she said.

Thus it was that Gudrum and Charis began their short courtship, and it was in the month of May when the hawthorn trees were in blossom that Brother Athold joined them in matrimony. Gudrum felt he was the happiest man ever as he took the hand of Charis and led her from the chapel into the sunlight. She wore a plait of wild flowers in her flaxen hair, skilfully made that morning by her sisters. This deftness came naturally to a family adept at weaving and the like. The robe Charis wore had been finely woven from the wool of her father's sheep and dyed bright yellow with saffron. The crocuses from which they processed the dye grew in abundance about the edge of the forest of Fyllwood. Gudrum wore a fine new sheepskin jerkin, and Engel had cut him some fresh leather laces to hold his shoon and grace his calves.

Their neighbours and kin had built Gudrum and Charis a brand new hut not far from his mother and sisters, of good wood from the forest. There was little else but the hut the day they got wed, but the young couple soon had it looking less sparse. Charis's mother had given her the loom she loved so much, and some wool, and her father had provided them with a few healthy young sheep to start a small herd. Gudrum's mother, widow that she was, was happy to present them with a couple of goatskins she had put by, and started off their larder for them with a large goats' milk cheese. Gudrum and Charis were full of joy in their new life and creating their home, and made a visit to Hendrig the potter who lived at the foot of the hills to the south of Fylton, for some pots and basins. Charis paid for them with some fine woollen cloth she had made, and she also wove a merry-looking rug of many hues for their floor. She was clever with dyes and had an eye for a good pattern.

Because he was so busy establishing his household, Gudrum did not have much time to go on long hunting trips with Engel. A few short afternoon sorties into the forest or away across the southern hills were sufficient to keep the pot going for day-to-day needs, and he did not forget the pot of his mother and sisters. Engel missed his friend, but tagged on to others for lengthy trips into Fyllwood and beyond, and whenever he returned he always left food at the door of his friend. Charis, whenever possible, went out to tend their sheep, or she would go berrying with her sisters and the sisters of Gudrum. Sometimes she would help to tend her father's sheep or assist Gudrum's mother Melia with her few goats and the tedious process of cheese-making.

The summer wore on and they were happy days. By mid-September Charis knew that she was with child. The older women fussed over her in her early sickness, but she soon recovered and acquired a healthy glow about her young cheeks. Gudrum felt very proud, and now that winter was coming upon them he knew that he must away to the forest for a few long hunting trips to stock up his larder against the dark cold days that would soon be here, for he had a family to feed now. Off he went with Engel again and they came back each time burdened with meat, to skin and dry and smoke and store. One particularly fine doeskin Gudrum laid by to use as a cover for the baby. He tanned it truly and well, and when he had finished it was as soft as a baby's ear. Charis also had been busy. She had woven the finest woollen piece imaginable and had carefully fashioned a tiny shift and hood from it, and in the long winter when

7

the days were cold and the ground was frozen, Gudrum built a sturdy wooden cot to hold his son.

He had always thought of the baby as being a son, and he was proved right. In the month of March his son was born and they named him Davold. He was a lively infant, strong of limb, bright of eye and with a lusty cry. The priest Athold made the journey up from the chapel to bless the child with water. He sat by the goodly log fire sipping warm gruel and listening to the rain against the dwelling of Gudrum and Charis. They had made a fine union, these two. The warmth and love and comfort around him was evident, and not for a long time had he rued his single state so much. He sighed and gathered his garments about his thin ageing body as he bade his farewells and set off down the track to the chapel of St Whyte.

Gudrum and Charis prospered with hard work, and five years after they were married they had added to their dwelling so that it was three times the size of the original one. Their few sheep had increased to a modest flock and Charis had regular orders for her fine weaving and creative unusual patterns. Little Davold now had a younger brother and a baby sister, Luther and Cara, who were every bit as healthy and happy as he. They were a happy Christian family and old Athold would often pay them a visit, when Charis would provide him with a meal and the comfort of their hearth. There came a time however when Athold's visits were less frequent. His bones ached to walk up over the slope to Fylton, and he became breathless with too much exertion, although he was able to visit Gudrum's mother Melia in her last earthly hours and to say a blessing over her. Gudrum's son, Davold, was thirteen years of age at the time. Davold was beginning to accompany Gudrum on his hunting trips to the forest to learn the skills necessary to keep the family pot supplied. Engel very often went with them. Engel had been joined in union with a merry lass by the name of Ailsa, the daughter of the potter Hendrig. It was a great disappointment to Engel and Ailsa that although they had been together nigh on nine years there were no babies.

One certain day in August when Davold was just past fifteen years and when the year was 1058, Gudrum and Engel together with Davold set off for a trip to Fyllwood. They struck across country in a north-westerly direction, as Gudrum had long promised his son that he would take him to the great gorge to meet Llewellyn the teller of tales. Llewellyn was getting no younger and many times had asked Gudrum to bring his son that he might see the boy. Davold was blue-eyed and flaxen-haired like his mother, taller than his father, fleet as a fox on his feet and swift and sure with a bow and arrow. He had inherited his father's happy nature and he laughed and jollied with the older men as they penetrated deeper into the forest. Davold also had a quiet mystical side to his nature which sometimes troubled Gudrum. He did not want the boy to be too troubled with deep thoughts and grow up to be a dreamer, for it seemed to Gudrum that although his son was outwardly cheerful and showed remarkable prowess in all the manly skills, this did not satisfy the boy, and Davold had always seemed older than his years.

It was a goodly stride from Fylton to reach the edge of the river, but the day was fine and they had their animal skins with them to wrap in and sleep; indeed they intended to sleep near Llewellyn's shack. Gudrum was looking forward to a meal of fresh fish. There was a stiff breeze blowing down the gorge and off the river and it was making him feel hungry. As Llewellyn lived near the river he ate fish mostly as his staple diet, and he certainly knew how to cook them in a tasty way with herbs and flavourings. As they rounded the bend near the river Llewellyn's shack came into view. Gudrum, long used to noting changing signs as a way of survival in the forest, saw immediately that there was no smoke coming from the shack's crude chimney. Engel noticed it too, and in unspoken unison they quickened their pace. Llewellyn was lying on his back inside the hut, blood oozing from a wicked-looking gash on his forehead. Some of the blood was black and dried, and Gudrum knew he must have been lying there helpless from at least the day before. Llewellyn was barely conscious. They hoisted him on to his crude trestle bed and covered him with skins for warmth as he was pale and coldly damp with shock. They sent Davold for water to bathe the wound, collected some wood and soon had a fine fire going. Llewellyn recovered a bit then, and was able to talk a little after they had warmed some gruel and fed him.

' 'Twas some evil dwellers from 'cross the river did this,' he moaned. 'They rowed across and I thought they were friendly. I've seen them on the river before. They were from top of the hill on t'other side of the gorge – a place called Cliff Town. There's a very winding zigzag track there that leads right down to the river, just like our valley of the nightingales on this side.'

In spite of his concern for the old man, Davold was enthralled; all this talk of other people and other settlements across the river stirred his imagination. All he knew of the world was Fylton and the forest, the southern hills, and the dip where old Athold lived in the chapel of St Whyte. For the first time Llewellyn noticed him.

'So this is your young fellow!' he said to Gudrum.

'That's right,' said Gudrum, and to Davold, 'Davold my son, at last you meet Llew, one of my oldest friends!'

Davold was fascinated with Llewellyn. His father had told him that Llewellyn came from the other side of the big water into which the river flowed, and he felt curious to know more about the Welshman, and how he had settled here. As fate would have it he was to hear Llewellyn's story sooner than he thought. Llewellyn seemed to respond to their caring and after a while they were able to ascertain from him exactly what had happened. He had seen the men from Cliff Town on the river yesterday, and invited them to come and share his fish. There were four of them. They had landed but instead of waiting for social niceties they had knocked him on the head with a club and pro-

10

ceeded to ransack his humble little shack for anything they thought worth taking. They had stolen some skins and dried fish and also a pot of beans, but when he came to this point in the story Llewellyn chuckled with glee and reached down into some sort of pouch concealed under his sheepskin tunic. He drew out a bright golden object. It was round and had a large creature inscribed across the front. It was pierced through the top and was held on a fine strong leather thong. Davold drew in his breath. He had heard about gold and he knew he was seeing gold now. It was so shiny!

With his next breath Llewellyn chuckled again and turned to Davold. ''Twas providence you came this day, young Davold. 'Twas providence this sacred medal was saved and protected for you. I am getting to be an old man and I have long promised myself that Gudrum's eldest son should have this, my birthright!'

Davold gasped and Gudrum was really surprised now. Engel could only stare. 'Your birthright, Llew?' Gudrum queried.

Llewellyn grinned. Some of the old twinkle had returned to his eyes. 'Ever since you were a young lad of your son's age I've felt like a father to both you and Engel,' he turned to look at Engel, 'but you have not been blessed with issue and this is a birthright from father to son. You have been my true friends, but in all these years you've never asked me why I came from my land of the mountains, though I doubt whether I would have told you before; it has been a sore story with me. My father was a King.' He paused and saw the wonder in all their eyes. 'Yes, the King of the Caerdragon valley!'

Davold was enraptured.

' 'Tis true. It was many years ago, but I was the light in his eye, the tune in his heart. There was discord over a maiden. She was the daughter of the King of Penrilligan and I loved her truly, but her father and mine were mortal enemies and could never countenance our match. My father wanted me, nay ordered me, to join with another maid, an ugly one compared with my lovely Bronwyn, and I would not. Then my beautiful Bronwyn, because she could not join with me, threw herself from the top of a mountain. It broke my heart, indeed broke everything I had ever been or wanted to be. I renounced my title and my right to succession to be the King of Caerdragon. It broke my father's heart also, but in his sadness he was still a proud and proper man. Before I left he gave me this, my medal, as fit and right for the son of a King to wear. It is my birthright; you see it has the sign of Caerdragon upon it.' He rubbed his thumb across the image. 'My father said I might have a son one day. You Gudrum, and you Engel are the nearest I've ever come to having sons, and now that Gudrum has a son it is fit that he should hold the medal for Davold till he is full-grown. It is of finest Welsh gold and priceless.' There were tears on Llewellyn's cheeks now.

Davold was speechless.

Gudrum said, 'I don't know what to say. To think you are of royal birth! I feel really honoured. And what is more, Llew, all these years I never even ventured to guess at your poor sad story.' He put his arm around his son. 'I will certainly keep it for young Davold.' He scratched his beard thoughtfully, 'D'you know I've only ever seen our King of Wessex once, and that was in the distance.'

Llewellyn smiled wanly, 'Kings are made by people. Friends we choose.' He looked approvingly at Davold. 'You have a fine young man here. I am happy he is to wear the medal. He looks like a King's son, he will feel like a King's son!'

Davold indeed was tall, straight-limbed and had a fearless air about him. For now however he stayed quiet with wonder.

They stayed longer in Fyllwood than they intended, for they wanted to make sure that Llewellyn was quite well before they left. He was philosophical when they attempted to persuade him to move away from his lonely patch and live a little nearer to friends. 'I've lived here this long, I'll die here now,' was all he would say.

When they arrived back at Fylton, Gudrum and Davold were eager to show Charis the medal. 'I believe it's what they call a dragon!' she exclaimed excitedly, examining the beast engraved on the gold, 'I've heard of Welsh dragons.'

'Of course!' said Gudrum, 'Caerdragon . . . that was his father's kingdom! I remember once Llew told us a story of a valley where he had lived and the dragon that had menaced it back in the mists of time, until a brave fellow from the valley slew it. Llew was full of such stories!'

Llewellyn was not to live long. Maybe it was the effect of the blow on his head that hastened his end or maybe subconsciously he felt that now his affairs were in order he could die in peace. One October morning in the year that Llewellyn had given Gudrum the medal to keep for Davold, a travelling person came out of the forest to Fylton and asked for Gudrum the Saxon. Gudrum was found and the traveller passed him the sad message that his friend Llewellyn was now dead. Gudrum knew that Llewellyn had long been friendly with the travelling people. This travelling man was named Lazarus and Gudrum had met him once or twice on his visits to Fyllwood. Lazarus was a trustworthy fellow and Gudrum knew that his words were true when he told him that 'Llew had a peaceful end and was took care of proper'. By that Gudrum knew that the travellers must have been with Llewellyn when he died and that they had buried him. He was glad the old Welshman had not died alone; and sad that there would be no more visits to his friend.

So it was that Llewellyn the teller of tales, the son of a Welsh King, passed from this world, but not before he had bestowed on a Saxon friend the gift of his birthright.

In time Davold grew to be even taller and a very handsome fellow. The first time he went into Fyllwood to hunt alone, Gudrum gave his son the medal of Caerdragon to wear. Gudrum had been told by a wise old woman in the village that these kind of necklets were supposed to have magical powers to protect the wearer from harm. Certainly no ill ever befell Davold. He seemed to live a charmed life

13

and by the time he was twenty years old he had become an expert hunter. Old Athold had long noticed the restless challenging spirit within Davold, more than that of an ordinary lusty young man. Once Davold had taken off on his own into the forest he started travelling to other places. Sometimes he went with others and was well-liked among the other young men in Fylton. Indeed everyone seemed to love Davold and he received more than his fair share of admiring glances from the young women. He was not ready to lose his heart just yet; he felt there were so many things to see and do. He was the only young man from Fylton who had travelled really far beyond the hills to the south. He had recently gone to a holy place with a high tor that some called Glastonbury. On his return old Athold had listened intently to Davold's story. He had been to this holy place many years ago and was anxious to glean all the latest news of the Brothers there, but Davold seemed to be more concerned with the rumours he had heard on his travels. It was the mid 1060s and the general talk was that some strong fierce tribe called Normans from over the sea in Gaul had quarrelled with the English King Harold, and were known to be threatening the land. Athold had often heard rumours of invasion from one quarter or another when he was a young man travelling around, and was not greatly impressed. People along the way always liked to give travellers something to talk about. In fact old Athold was rather annoyed that Davold should pay heed to such rumours, for he wanted real news of the church at Glastonbury. By 1066 when the Normans did come, Athold was dead.

2

The Coming of the Normans

The first Normans seen in Fylton were three men-of-arms who arrived on horseback one bright August evening in 1067. They wore strange suits of what appeared to be knitted metal and round helmets slightly pointed at the crown. The first one carried a standard with an unusually patterned pennant fluttering brightly in the breeze as he rode. They all carried shields also vividly designed, and the two following the standard-bearer carried fearsome long lances. They presented an unusual sight as they clattered into the Fylton encampment, and everyone turned out of their dwellings, albeit guardedly. Davold could not help pondering how many good Saxon lads these Normans had slaughtered, but outwardly he stood unafraid and stalwart outside his father's hut as they dismounted. Their tongue was quick and strange as they attempted with the aid of many signs and gestures to establish to the villagers that they were only in search of food and shelter. The inhabitants of Fylton were not over-keen to help these intruders, but there seemed to be no alternative – these men were the conquerors – and after quick consultation between themselves arrangements were made for them to stay in the dwelling of Marye, Davold's aunt, the former dwelling of his grandmother Melia. Marye had lived there alone since Melia had died, and Frieda his other aunt had long since married Henk, one of the village lads. It was felt that Gudrum and Davold were near at hand should Marye need assistance, but the Frenchmen were quiet and polite, although their clothes and their speech were strange. They seemed also to have Christian virtues as they crossed themselves devoutly before partaking of Marye's excellent broth.

Davold, unlike some of his compatriots, felt quite cool and logical about the coming of these Normans, although there was a certain natural resentment. His attitude was that the Normans had overrun his homeland, so it was best to try and accept it and make use of their presence. They certainly seemed to be well-educated much-travelled men. He was not to know of the pillaging and disturbances that had taken place in other parts, or to guess at the sequestration of land and property that was to come. All he knew was that these Normans seemed to be decent men, and the inborn curiosity that had previously taken him over the hills to Glastonbury and other places to find out all he could about other folk and the way they lived, was working away at him now. He felt stimulated and interested and wanted to know more about these Frenchmen and the land they came from. He subconsciously wanted to be pleasant to them. His father, Gudrum, was not so open-minded. He snorted and made noises at his son's interest in the invaders. To Gudrum they were enemies, a burden to be suffered, and Charis his beloved took the same view, as did Luther Davold's younger brother, but Cara his sister, like Davold, was interested and excited. She openly showed admiration for the authoritative strangers in their midst and made frequent fanciful excuses to go and see Aunt Marye despite her mother's admonishing glances.

Cara was very much a younger edition of her mother to look at, flaxen-haired, blue-eyed, pretty and intelligent. The Norman who appeared to be the leader of the group had established with them that his name was Jean d'Arcy. He threw appreciative glances back at Cara whenever he had the chance, and Davold was quick to notice this. This alarmed him, for he didn't want his sister to come to any harm. He tried to keep her out of the way of the Normans as much as possible. Davold had an instinctive feeling that there was an ulterior motive in the visit of these Normans;

something other than just needing bed and board for a few nights.

He was to find out part of their reason the next day when, quite early, he was hovering outside his Aunt Marye's dwelling. After eating his breakfast gruel the Norman, Jean d'Arcy, came outside and nodded to Davold. He crossed himself deliberately to indicate his faith, then threw open both arms and looked all around and then at Davold questioningly as if to ask something. After a couple of repeat performances Davold suddenly realized what the Norman wanted; he was asking if they had a Holy Dwelling. Davold's immediate reaction was caution. What did the Normans want with the chapel? Just as swiftly he dismissed his fears and made a quick decision. They appeared to be Christian men and this could not be bad, he would show them the Chapel of St Whyte. All three Normans accompanied him down over the pastures to the little chapel. Athold's successor, Brother Luke, was young and enthusiastic, but like Davold he was slightly cautious of the strangers. He gave them a blessing and they stayed long and looked searchingly around the tiny building with muttered comments to each other. To Davold it was as if they were taking in every detail of the building, for they were much longer with their visit that one would expect, and while they were looking and talking between themselves, Jean d'Arcy had a parchment with him on which he made marks from time to time. Eventually they signalled their goodbyes to the priest Luke, and set off back to Fylton. Davold was bewildered, but at the same time his astute brain was telling him that these invaders were endeavouring to find out all they could about the land they had conquered, even down to the chapels!

The Normans stayed a further night at Fylton and then, the next morning, with terse but genuine signs of thanks they mounted their horses and rode off purposefully in a northerly direction. The village heaved a sigh of relief and went back to its normal routine. It seemed to them then that the invasion was not going to disturb their way of life too much. However, during the next two years they had further occasional visits from Frenchmen, civilians as well as military men. Always the Normans took a keen interest in the village, the land, the crops and livestock, asking questions, inspecting the sheep, then suddenly one day out of the hills, back came Jean d'Arcy heading a troop of six men. He had picked up a few Saxon words by now and was able to make himself understood more easily.

What he told the Saxons did not entirely please them. The new King of England, the Conqueror, William, was anxious to have details of all land and settlements, buildings, churches, farms, over the whole length and breadth of the realm. He wanted to take stock in order to apportion out rewards to the French aristocrats and men-at-arms who had fought at his side. The Saxons looked at each other knowingly. This was what all the previous visits had been about – they were methodical, these Normans!

There was not a little consternation among the Saxon men when they gathered together in the village, as was their wont at the end of the day. There were varying opinions. Some fiery-hearted young men were all for rebellion and taking a stand here and now against the conqueror King and his men. The land their flocks grazed, the forest of Fyllwood, the river, the hills, were theirs by right. No foreigner from across the water was going to tell them where to take their sheep, or when they could hunt in the forest, or indeed if they could hunt in the forest at all according to some rumours. These things were their birthright; all the things they had done and known since they could remember, and their fathers and grandfathers before them. No foreigner could call this his land or alter their freedom to roam at will by apportioning off what he fancied! The young firebrands were for rebellion, but not right away; they were for planning and striking at what they felt would be the right moment. Others were for waiting to see how things turned out.

Davold was in deep turmoil. He loved his life, the land, the forest. Like the others he wanted to be free to roam as always, but the Normans did seem to be progressive fellows, and they were Christians. Perhaps they would not apportion too much land to foreigners. How could they tame the great wild forest that was Fyllwood? He was growing to like Jean d'Arcy very much, and Jean seemed to be a fair-minded man. What was more, Davold was very conscious that his sister Cara was becoming very interested in Jean in an entirely womanly way. His instincts told him that any kind of liaison between Jean and Cara would be greatly frowned upon by his father and mother, and his heart was sick within him at the thought of the trouble that would be caused within the family by any such attachment; not only the family, but also the rest of the village, especially his hot-headed friends.

As he sat with his fellow countrymen he did attempt to point out a few good things about the Normans, such as the fact that they were obviously of the Christian faith, also well-educated and wise in the ways of the world. Beyond the comprehension of most of his village friends, Davold thought, but he wisely kept this last idea to himself. He went on to say that as the Normans knew of much, far beyond Fylton, surely they could help and teach, and enhance the lives of the Saxons with their knowledge,

His friends listened in silence, some nodding and agreeing a little, and some with growing irritation, like Felix the potter's son, younger brother of Ailsa, Engel's wife. Felix spoke up impatiently.

'You always were a dreamer, Davold. You always did want something beyond your reach. That's why you're always off beyond the hills seeking out strange places. 'Tis all very well to be educated and know about the world but,' he shook his fist passionately, 'we're talking about our very lives and the way we live being changed by someone we don't know who has no right to be here anyway. We're looking at the plain truth; our land'll be took if we don't stand hard against these tyrants!'

Davold could not answer this tirade. How could he explain to them what he felt? He couldn't even explain it to his own father. He felt deeply that there was something greater to be reached for, something beyond his life in Fylton. He knew he was a bit of a mystic. 'A dreamer' Felix had called him, although he did not feel that this was necessarily a bad thing. Nor was he ashamed of his thoughts. This was why he had spoken out, tried to make them see his point of view. Perhaps he should have become a priest, for religion had always been strong within him, and yet it was a deeper wider religion he felt than the outlook he had observed in both old Athold and Brother Luke. He had always treasured the seeds of thought that it was right to fight fearlessly for the greater good of all and to put away selfishness and bigotry. He believed that there was much to be learned from the world beyond Fylton, and no matter who or what they were, he felt a kinship with all men. He could clearly see Felix's point of view, but all that Felix knew was Fylton; he had spoken as he felt a loyal Saxon should. Davold just went on sitting there thoughtful and silent, and the others in their simple way felt he had been dealt with, crushed with criticism.

A little later as Davold strolled alone, still contemplating, by the edge of the forest in the evening cool Jean d'Arcy joined him. 'Thank you for your kind thoughts,' he said in his hesitant Saxon.

Davold stopped in his tracks, 'You heard?'

The Norman nodded gravely, 'Yes, mon ami. We meet it, the hot anger, everywhere in the land. It is to be expected.'

Davold was cautious, He admired Jean but he was still a loyal Saxon.

'I'm no lackey,' he said staunchly.

Jean answered quietly, 'I know. It's difficult for you.'

The friendship that was to last for the rest of their lives had begun.

In the difficult years that followed it was as if a permanent blight had settled over a once-contented Fylton. The land surrounding it, including Fylton, was under the jurisdiction of an Order of Augustine Brothers from the Abbey of the

Blessed Mary at Keynsham, a place to the south-east of Fylton, and the tiny chapel of St Whyte came under the Abbot's patronage.

Jean d'Arcy was destined to stay permanently at Fylton and become the Lord of the Manor (although he was not officially designated to this position until the year 1086). Davold had rightly seen that Jean was indeed a fair man, for Jean exercised his discretion to the limits to ensure that the Saxons were treated in as decent a fashion as possible with the allocation of land. Jean had been officially promised by the monarch a large acreage of land just below the hills, which included the dwelling of Hendrig the potter and his fiery son Felix. Hendrig's wife had died many years before.

When it became known about the granting of the land to Jean d'Arcy there was great anger and outcry from Felix, and he decided to take the law into his own hands. He very cunningly lay in wait for Jean one dark evening as Jean rode back alone from Keynsham, where he had been conferring as usual with the Abbot and Brothers on points of administration. Felix leapt upon Jean and unhorsed him just as he had crossed the stream below the chapel, and had slowed his horse before galloping up over the pastures that led to Fylton. There had been a bitter and bloody fight between the two, ending with a half-drowned very battered Felix being hauled along behind Jean's horse, hands tied, feet stumbling. Apparently in the process of the fight Jean had knocked Felix into the stream and held him there until Felix had given in. Jean had a black eye and a gashed arm but otherwise was all right. There were inevitably some among the Saxons who said silently, 'Well done Felix!', but in Jean d'Arcy they could see they had a hard man as well as a fair one. After all he was one of William's soldiers.

Jean was angry. The next day he gave Hendrig and Felix an ultimatum. They could either forget the whole business, stay on the land to pursue their potters' trade as usual and pledge their liege to him as he was to become Lord of the Manor – for there had never been any question of them being put out of their dwelling – or else they could pack up and move on if they still felt rancour. They chose the latter, but Davold knew without a doubt that in this new era of the Conqueror, every scrap of land was systematically being accounted for, and Hendrig and Felix would find that wherever they went there would inevitably be a Norman in charge.

This show of strength by Jean quietened down a lot of the undercurrent of rebellious talk that had been prevalent with some of the Saxons from Fylton. He was a true Norman, trained in soldiering, disciplined and clear-cut in his judgement. No half measures with Jean d'Arcy. After this incident Fylton seemed to settle down and became less restless. They realized too that they were fortunate to have Jean as their Lord. The travellers who passed through the forest from time to time, told hair-raising tales of some villages where the Lords had dealt out tyranny and death to all rebels. Felix would not have been let off so lightly elsewhere.

Jean was very busy with his plans for the extension of the chapel of St Whyte to make a new Norman church. The Abbot at Keynsham was keen to do this for the people of Fylton. The Abbot had told Jean it was the Conqueror's wish that the Normans build as many churches as possible in this land he now ruled, and indeed Jean had heard it said everywhere by his Norman compatriots that this was to be so. King William was practical in his ideas, for he knew that with the full co-operation of the churches his new dominion would be less arduous to rule. His Archbishop of Canterbury, Lanfranc, had advised him well on this.

The plans for the building of the new church now occupied practically all Jean's waking hours. He knew he would have to import some Norman labour for the building he had in mind, as the Saxons were good with wood but not so skilled with masonry. The Monarch had given Jean d'Arcy *carte blanche* to get on with the job, and Jean set about doing this with typical Norman thoroughness. His friendship with Davold the Saxon had grown to such an extent that he used Davold as a trusted confidant in his plans. Jean recognized in Davold the broadness of vision and clear-headedness that had often been mistaken by Davold's friends as dreamy and high-minded. Davold, in return, was as always thirsty for knowledge of the world beyond Fylton, and regarded Jean highly for his fairness, his knowledge and his general knightly manner. He felt there was none better than Jean to help with the difficult task the Normans had set themselves in administering the land they had conquered. Jean was just one year older than Davold and Davold felt a strong bond of manly companion-ship with this young Norman that he had never felt with any of his countrymen.

Davold listened eagerly to Jean's plans for the new church and also the way the Saxon camp was to be organized in future. The Conqueror was still very concerned with finding out about the land, and Jean had hinted that there was to be a large record compiled which would give in detail all the holdings of the lands in the realm. Davold had learned from his previous talks with the Brothers at Glastonbury that a former Saxon King of Wessex, Alfred the burner of the cakes, had attempted to organize and record details of what were called "the hundreds". These represented one hundred hides, a hide being a portion of land owned by a particular family. When Davold had also told Jean the story of King Alfred and the burnt cakes Jean had been highly amused, slapping his thighs and saying, 'What a wonderful tale my friend. I must save this story for the Monarch. He does not have much jesting in him, but this might crease his straight face!'

Davold was impressed. 'You know the monarch that well?'

'But of course! I have known him since boyhood, he has always been a friend of my family.' He could have added, 'I fought by his side many times,' but the delicacy of the subject of killing Saxons was too great.

Jean did, however, tell Davold a little of the politics of William's determination to invade England. He told of Edward the Confessor's long sojourn in Normandy, and

Edward's promise to William, then Duke of Normandy, that he would one day inherit the throne of England as rightful heir. 'Then that upstart Harold stepped in,' said Jean. 'What could William do but claim what he thought was his true birthright?'

Davold nodded, but the Saxon in him secretly wondered what poor dead Harold's side of the story was, for William was not truly born of the realm he now ruled. However, in his typical logical fashion he put the matter from his mind. This was the here and now; the past was gone, and yet he yearned to know more of politics.

Jean's plans for Fylton were quite definite. For the present time he occupied, together with a manservant, the dwelling he had stayed in on his first visit to the village, as Davold's Aunt Marye, whose dwelling it had been, had died in 1071. Jean, however, intended eventually to build himself what he called a "Manor house" on the patch of land sequestered for him below the hills, from which Felix the fiery potter's son had so wildly departed. Jean and Cara, Davold's sister, loved each other, and had done so for a long time. Jean had told Davold so. Old Gudrum was still mildly antagonistic towards all Normans, and Davold knew that Jean was biding his time. Jean and Cara were still young, and Jean had great things to do. He had to re-organize the new church building as well as his own house. His plans for the rest of the village entitled each man to a specific plot of land, as well as there being common land for grazing of sheep, cattle or goats. The strips of land were generous, but Jean made it clear that he expected loyalty and service in return.

The conquest was finally completed by 1072. Southern England had been taken comparatively quickly, as happenings at Fylton had revealed, but in the north there had been strong pockets of resistance which eventually were quelled.

24

3

The Building of the Church

Jean busied himself constantly with the plans for the church, which he had decided were to take precedence over everything including his plans for a suitable manor house, and most of all his plans for marrying Cara. In his thorough Norman way it had to be first things first. He had sworn allegiance to the Conqueror, and King William wanted the church enlarged and altered quickly, so this must be done.

Jean had decided that the main bulk of stone to be used for the church was to come from France. When he had first confided this decision to Davold, the Saxon felt that Jean had not gone into the matter deeply enough. To Davold it seemed that it was going to be time-consuming, expensive and fraught with all manner of hidden problems, to ship stone across from Normandy. He told Jean as much, but Jean laughed quietly and clapped his hand on Davold's shoulder, his brown eyes twinkling with expectancy, and also the knowledge of his complete control of the situation.

'Mon ami, I have it all worked out. The stone for the church will be brought across quite easily. I also want stone for my own dwelling. We will land it at the head of the river and transport it to Fylton from there.'

Davold was still unimpressed.

Jean went on, 'It will be far cheaper to bring it across from my land. We shall use it as ballast for the voyage. What is more we shall pre-shape it as far as possible. There are many stonemasons in Normandy to do this.'

What could Davold say to that? Wise and self-taught as he

25

was, he knew nothing of ships. He did not have the faintest idea what "ballast" was, and like most Saxons he knew next to nothing about working with stone. He should have known that Jean d'Arcy, the thorough one, had thought all this through carefully. Davold looked at his friend admiringly, 'You are a clever one, Jean' was all he could say.

Jean continued with enthusiasm, 'Now, Davold, this will mean that I must travel across to my country to make some arrangements. I can think of none better than you to watch over Fylton whilst I am away. It will be a goodly three months.'

Davold was surprised, and yet he knew in his heart that if Jean was to leave the encampment for any length of time then he, Davold, was the person to be left in charge, not only because of his friendship and understanding with Jean, but because he was a Saxon and cooler-headed than most. He knew there would be, and indeed there were, some who jibed at him with remarks like "traitor" and "lackey-dog", and it hurt sorely, for Davold was proud of his Saxon ancestry, but on the whole, most of the villagers when they knew of the situation, appreciated Davold being in charge.

In line with Norman custom, Jean had instituted a new system of crop-sharing which seemed to operate quite well. Many of the villagers had wondered why they hadn't thought of this before. Before the Normans came there had been no single tangible authority to guide them. They had previously relied upon the few elders in the community for guidance, and major decisions were usually discussed during the evening gatherings at the end of the village. These meetings still took place, for Jean had, as always, very wisely and democratically felt that it was good for people to have free discussion and to air their views and grievances. This enabled him to get a measure of the way people were thinking.

It was at one of these evening gatherings, when Jean had been gone scarcely two weeks, that some news came to the ears of Davold that disturbed him greatly. One of the Fylton villagers had met a traveller in Fyllwood and heard the news that fiery Felix the potter was dead. The circumstances were that Felix, when he had left Fylton with his father Hendrig, had travelled in a north-easterly direction until he had come to a place called Horefelle. The people there had been friendly, they had needed a potter, and what was more there had not seemed to be any Normans living permanently at Horefelle. They had received visits, but there was no established person in charge at that time. The trouble had started when a Norman was eventually seconded to watch over the land at Horefelle. It was over two years since the potters' departure from Fylton, and old Hendrig had never really settled at Horefelle. He had been happy at Fylton and if it had not been for Felix he would probably have stayed, but things being as they were he'd had no option. He had always been apathetic about Horefelle, couldn't seem to work the same, and had eventually died of a kind of quiet despair, just before the coming of the Norman. This had been the last straw for Felix, and he had not reckoned on the temper of the Frenchman, which matched his own. There had been some dispute over the land, similar to the dispute with Jean d'Arcy, and Felix, foolish hothead that he was, got up to his tricks again one dark night, and waited for the new Lord of the Manor, whose name was Lucien. Again the simple potter had been trounced. He still had not realized that he was no match for a Norman aristocrat, trained since boyhood in the art of war and quick skirmish. Lucien had shown no mercy, and Felix had been swiftly executed the next day, his home and pottery sequestered, and his wife and baby turned out on to the common ground to fare as best they could, for not long after he had arrived at Horefelle, Felix had married a maid, Agnes by name.

Unfortunately Agnes had no immediate relatives at Horefelle. She had been orphaned as a child and brought up by an elderly aunt, who was now terrified of doing anything to fall out of grace with Lord Lucien, a Norman who was greatly feared, having made his presence and authority well-known to the Saxons of Horefelle since he had arrived. The aunt had managed to smuggle some scraps of food to Agnes and her baby son under cover of darkness, and Agnes had contrived some form of tent to shelter under. It was in this state that the travelling folk came upon Agnes and heard her story.

Davold was greatly moved, as were all the people of Fylton. The men kept saying 'We must do something about this!' But what? The compassion in Davold was telling him also to do something about the plight of this girl, unknown to him, and her baby, the offspring of Felix. He decided there were three courses he could take. He could go to Lord Lucien and ask him if he could bring Agnes and the baby to Fylton for shelter and sustenance. He could go and collect Agnes and the child secretly under cover of darkness, or else he could leave Agnes and the child to Lucien's mercy, and trust that when the weather became harsher (it was summer now) Lord Lucien would find it in his heart to give her back her home. After a little thought he decided on the first course. Better to face Lord Lucien than to go secretly. He was, after all, in charge of Fylton at this time, and Felix, in spite of his shortcomings, had been an old boyhood friend. As for the third option, Davold felt he could not leave the fate of Felix's wife and child to chance.

Next morning without a word to anyone, not even Gudrum, he mounted his horse and set off in the direction of Horefelle. He had a rudimentary idea in which direction it lay. Davold rode a lot these days. In previous times he had travelled mostly in the forest on foot, and had ridden an old packhorse only on his longer journeys, but the Normans rode everywhere on horseback. Their horses were well-bred, well-trained and swift, and Davold had been especially pleased when Jean, just before he left, had given him the horse he now rode for his personal use. Gudrum saw him go but did not attempt to show himself or ask his son where he was going, although he did think it might be something to do with the plight of Felix's wife. The boy's friendship with Jean did not entirely displease him these days, Like all fathers he was anxious for his son to be successful in the world, and he certainly seemed to be that. Davold was a son to be proud of whatever the older Saxons might say, and he was especially pleased that Davold had been seen by Lord Jean d'Arcy as the natural leader and organizer while he was absent. Gudrum prayed to God that whatever business Davold was about this day he would be protected in his pursuit of justice. Gudrum's mind went back to that day in the forest long ago when old Llewellyn had given Davold the gold medallion of Caerdragon. Davold was certainly living up to Llewellyn's conception of a King's son and a leader of men. Davold wore the medal constantly these days, and Gudrum had stroked his chin thoughtfully more than once and pondered on the fact that perhaps the old hag years ago was right, and the medallion did give its owner a charmed life!

Davold inwardly did not feel very charmed as he rode towards Horefelle. He reached there just after noon and went straight to the encampment, although he had already espied a pathetic-looking makeshift tent pitched on the common ground outside the dwellings. Outwardly he put on a brave face, and he made an impressive sight as he asked for a hearing with Lord Lucien. He stood tall and fair with an impeccable air of authority about him. He wore a rich cloth tunic of scarlet as befitted a deputy to Lord of the Manor. These days he had discarded the sheepskin of the Saxon, except in the depths of winter.

By contrast Lord Lucien of Horefelle presented a different picture as he approached Davold. He also was tall, but swarthy and bow-legged, and with a hooked nose that was far too big for his face. He was richly garbed, but this could not in any way conceal his ill form.

'What brings you here, my man?' Lucien asked, taking in Davold's appearance. The man was a Saxon to be sure, but he had the style of the Normans and he rode a Norman horse.

Davold cleared his throat and spoke out fearlessly. 'My Lord Lucien, I am Davold the Saxon, deputy to Lord Jean d'Arcy of Fylton who is at present on business in Normandy.

I have come to humbly ask you if I may remove to my protection the widow and child of Felix the potter. There are relatives of Felix at Fylton.'

It was true, for Ailsa the elder sister of Felix was married to Engel, his father's lifelong friend. Engel had not been at the gathering last night. He had been sick with the colic this last day or so, so knew nothing of the plight of his wife's brother's widow and child.

Lord Lucien set his lips, and his huge nose sank almost into his chin. His eyes were dark and coal-like. Having met the man, Davold could now fully understand Felix's fate. The man was a trained soldier, but he was also one who didn't like to lose.

''Tis mighty impertinent of you, Saxon, to come and meddle in my affairs. I understand that Jean d'Arcy also had trouble with the potter and sent him from his land. What would d'Arcy say to you being here now?'

Davold stood his ground. 'I truly believe Lord Jean d'Arcy would sanction my visit. The woman and child are not to blame for the man's misdemeanours. There must be some mercy!'

Lord Lucien laughed sardonically, but nevertheless he knew he had met a fair match. 'Then have it your way, Saxon. I do not care what happens to the woman. Take her and the brat out of my sight if you will. They are cluttering up the common land. The sheep can make better use of it than them!' He laughed at his own feeble jest and turned and strode away.

Davold was elated. He was also hungry and thirsty. Lord Lucien was indeed an ungracious man. He had not even offered a drink of hospitality, Davold thought, and he must have realized that Davold had travelled over hard and hilly terrain since the morning. He clattered across the common and as if in answer to his thoughts an old woman approached him with a pot of ale held carefully in both hands.

'God bless thee young Davold. I have heard tell of thee. God bless thee, for the wife of Felix is Agnes my niece, and

30

her left with the poor babe . . .' she broke off, crying in the way of an old woman.

Davold downed the ale and thanked her kindly. She pressed a chunk of bread into his tunic pocket, 'for the journey back. God bless thee once again for being such a fine Christian man.'

Davold was slightly embarrassed but he managed to say, 'Never fear, woman. Agnes and the babe will be well cared for.'

The surprise at Fylton when Davold arrived with the woman and child was quite something to see. Word was sent to Engel and Ailsa, and Engel was soon up from his sick couch to greet this new sister-in-law and his baby nephew. The childless couple were more than happy now in their middle age to have a child in their dwelling at last. He was a beautiful babe and Agnes had named him Oswald. He was fair of skin and had inherited the red hair of Felix. Gudrum and Charis were pleased and proud of this thing that Davold had done. He was indeed a fine young fellow to have for a son, and when they considered the harsh and cruel behaviour of Lord Lucien they also felt grudgingly honoured to have his friend Jean d'Arcy as their Lord of the Manor. This incident certainly put Davold back into favour with a few remaining rebels. Also Jean, when he arrived home at last, was greeted by the villagers with more warmth than usual. Although it was not consciously realized, they had started slowly to appreciate Jean, and integration was beginning to take place. Jean was immobile of face when Davold told him of the death of Felix, but he approved without doubt what Davold had done for Agnes and her child.

'Mon ami, you are a man of my own heart,' he said, catching Davold's arm, 'but come, I must tell you of my journey and the results of my endeavours!'

As usual Jean had it all worked out in his own inimitable way. He had engaged a master mason, Henri Gascoigne, to come with a team of three stone-masons to erect the new church. An architect had worked some rough plans for

31

them and the pre-shaped stone was to be shipped in the spring of the next year. It was now autumn, so they had all winter to finalize details. Local labour would be used for the ordinary stone wall work, and the wall stones would come from local quarry workings. The woodwork would be no problem, for Saxons were renowned for their woodworking and carving abilities. Davold caught Jean's enthusiasm. He was full of excitement and anticipation. This would indeed be a joyous task for all, the building of a goodly church.

Jean had gone to Normandy via London. He had ridden to London, a journey that had taken him over three days of hard riding, and there he'd had an audience with King William, and also Archbishop Lanfranc. They had put all things at his disposal, and the ship which was to carry the stone for Fylton would first sail round from London in the spring, to the river mouth by Fyllwood Forest. From there Jean would embark and sail down the great channel past the Cornish coast and on to France. He would not go empty-handed. The ship would be laden with timber from Fyllwood to trade when they reached Normandy. On the return journey Jean would not only bring back the stone as ballast, but he also planned a cargo of silks and fine cloth and furnishings. He had missed the civilized comfort of his home in Normandy and he was going to attempt to make Fylton a little more like the sort of thing to which he was accustomed, also knowing that he had it in his mind to build a fine manor house once the church was under way.

Davold listened in wonder and he was greatly surprised when Jean said, 'You also must come with me, mon ami!'

'But who will watch over Fylton?'

'Bless you Davold,' Jean slapped his back, 'I have fixed that. I can leave my cousin Francis, or Matthew, or both, in charge this time.'

Francis and Matthew were the two original companions who had ridden into Fylton with Jean that first day in 1067. They were noblemen like Jean and hoping for manors of their own some day, if William saw fit.

Davold remained silent. Francis and Matthew could have been left in charge when Jean went to France earlier, he thought. This was the measure of the man. Jean d'Arcy was a true manipulator of people, and in this case Davold knew without a doubt that Jean had deliberately left him in charge of Fylton to lessen the anti-Norman feeling that had still been beneath the surface with some of the Saxons – and it had worked. Jean had also wished to aid Davold in finding his own level with his compatriots. What else did Jean have in store for him with this proposed trip to France? Of one thing he was certain, Jean d'Arcy was a true friend and a good man, so he felt content to stay silent and not challenge Jean's motives. Whatever Jean did would be for his ultimate well-being and the well-being of Fylton, he was sure. Another thought he tinkered with was that Jean and Cara were still enraptured with each other. He wondered how Jean would eventually tackle this problem and appease Gudrum who, although he was now much more friendly towards Jean, was still thought to be antagonistic at the thought of his daughter marrying a Norman.

The winter passed, during which time Jean organized several forays into the forest to fell trees and cut the wood into manageable size for the hold of the ship which was to arrive in the spring. The people of Fylton were quite enthusiastic to help Jean with his plans, and were more than willing to cut timber to trade for stone for their new church. The new church was a good goal to work for. The day came in April when the message came to Fylton that the ship from London had arrived, the ship that was to take them to Normandy, and it was anchored off the mouth of the river. Like all his plans, the operation of loading the timber aboard worked smoothly for Jean, and almost half the village men turned out to help, making the long trek through Fyllwood, and wishing Jean and Davold "Godspeed" when they were eventually ready to sail on the tide. The captain of the ship was Pierre de Luc, a man in his late thirties, ruddy-faced, a skilled master of the sea, jovial and fond of his wine, which, thought Davold, all Frenchmen seemed to be. There was a crew of eight to sail the ship, and as always Davold was keen and curious to observe all around him. Once they had left the Cornish coast and the end of the land behind, Davold was not a little disturbed at the power of the waves which lashed and drove at the ship. Pierre de Luc, seeing his agitation, reassured him in broken Saxon, 'It's just a lively sea, not a bad storm!' Davold wondered what a bad storm was like if this was "just lively"! His stomach felt a bit queer too, but Jean reassured him he would soon be all right, once he had become acclimatized to the motion. He survived, and they reached Normandy without mishap.

Jean and Davold stayed in a local tavern for a couple of days while Jean despatched several messages to various people. One morning two riders turned up leading two fine horses and Jean said to Davold, 'We shall now ride to the house of my parents. It is a full day's ride, but the weather is fine, and we will stop for refreshment on the way.'

The house of Jean's parents took Davold's breath away. He had never before seen such a big dwelling just for people to live in. The ornate furnishings, the beautifully carved furniture, filled him with wonder. Jean's mother and father were kind people, and like most people they took to Davold instantly. He was given a chamber to himself and his every want was attended to by servants. Davold could see that Jean's parents were very high people in the land, but they were also very Christian people and even had their own private chapel, richly draped with tapestries, in a chamber set apart. Jean had a younger sister, Nancy, who could speak little Saxon but was willing to learn, although for most of the time she chattered away at Davold in her quick French way, and he did not have a notion of what she was trying to say. One morning she was jabbering away at him as usual and he was trying hard to understand and answer. She kept introducing the word "Colette" into every other sentence. He was soon to find out that Colette was a girl, and a friend of Nancy's.

When Davold first saw Colette he knew that this was the girl he had been dreaming of and looking for most of his life. He was now thirty-two years of age, and although many maidens had looked his way he had always been too busy to think about marriage. Now, although outwardly he was calm and courteous to her, inwardly his heart was pounding whenever he beheld her grace and beauty. She was very dark-haired, with flashing white teeth, even features, and lively brown eyes. Her charm and movement entranced him and he found it very difficult to act normally in her presence.

Jean and Davold were six months in France this time. It was October as they sailed up past the Cornish coast again, and Davold was full of joy. He had Colette beside him. Beside him for life, for ever. He had married her. While they had been in Normandy Jean had been absent from his parents' home for a lot of the time, making arrangements for the stone to be delivered to the ship by a certain date, and for Henri Gascoigne, the appointed master mason and his men to be ready to sail with him at the right time. Davold had Nancy and Colette for his constant companions while Jean was so busy, and his passion for Colette had not subsided. He had been overjoyed when he found she returned his love. Her parents had not been over-keen about the match. They too were people of high standing in the land, and the thought of their beloved daughter marrying a Saxon and leaving the land of her birth did not greatly please them, albeit Davold was a Christian, handsome, and a good friend of Jean d'Arcy's. True love won through in the end, however. Colette's parents were concerned for her happiness, and they did like Davold as a man; he must be someone of importance in England judging by the large gold medallion he wore about his neck. Also he was a friend of Jean's and they trusted Jean utterly. In fact both Jean's parents and Colette's parents had hoped that Jean and Colette would join in marriage one day, but it was not to be. Indeed Jean's mother had hinted to Colette's mother that there was a maid he had eyes for, waiting back in England.

Davold and Colette were married in the splendid local Norman church three days before they were all due to sail back to England. It was a beautiful ceremony and Davold's only wish was that his own kin could have been present, although he was not unaware that he would meet a great deal of comment and some opposition from his parents when he returned home with his darling Colette. Colette had a large handsome carved wooden box full of cloths and trinkets, and also innumerable skeins of fine wool to bring with her across the sea. She was very skilled at working at tapestries and had produced a couple of beautiful designs which hung as evidence of her skill in the church in which they were married.

They had an uneventful crossing to England under Pierre's expert navigation, and Davold's stomach did not feel so queasy this time. He also had time to make better acquaintance of Henri Gascoigne the master mason and the three Norman stone-masons who had been enrolled to help him. Henri Gascoigne was a quiet likeable man and Davold felt sure that he would be liked by the people of Fylton. As they sailed up the mouth of the river and home, Davold told Colette the story of Llewellyn who had lived on the banks of the river below the forest, and of the gold medallion which he now proudly wore for the son of a King. Colette was greatly impressed. She had known from the start that Davold was different, and this difference was not only because he was of another race. Through the eyes of love she had noticed avidly how other people reacted to Davold when first they met him, and the impression was always the same. Folk were instinctively drawn to him; he had this splendid aura of sincerity and straightness about him that shone out like a beacon. He was a very special man.

As expected Davold's parents were not greatly enamoured of the match, but suffered it, and were pleasant enough to their son's new bride. The heart of Charis softened, however, when she saw the fine tapestry work of Colette, and she warmed more to her new daughter-in-law, for Charis loved her own weaving and working with cloth. Colette was homesick although she tried to hide the fact from Davold. The house of Gudrum and Charis where she and Davold were lodging temporarily was very unlike the ordered luxury of Normandy, although by Saxon standards the dwelling of Gudrum and Charis was considered to be excellent. Davold, in his instinctive way, realized this and made a strong promise to himself that one day he would build his adored Colette a fine dwelling, perfect to her every whim. In the meantime he was very busy assisting Jean with the replanning of the church and the delivery of the pre-fabricated stone blocks to Fylton. There had been a lot of work involved when the stone was unloaded. They had plenty of willing hands from Fylton to load it on to the carts that would be drawn through the tracks of Fyllwood Forest but organization was needed all the time. Jean did not believe in overloading the carts or fatiguing the men, or indeed the horses. 'All in good time,' he answered, quietly confident, when Jacob, a Fylton man in charge of the loaders said to Jean he would 'Hurry the lazy rascals up!'. The whole operation was completed in ten days, and Jean and Davold bade their farewells to Captain Pierre, who promised to pay them another visit if and when his journeys brought him to the river mouth again. He had long wanted actually to sail up the Gorge of Goram, and Davold's tales had further inspired him. He had heard tell of the town of Brigstowe that was further up this river, where there was a wooden bridge. The name "Brigstowe" indeed meant "place of the bridge". It would not have been feasible, however, to have landed the cargo of stone there. Jean had made sure of that, as the river was not suitable at that point for bigger craft, and also the tracks to Fylton from Brigstowe were not good for transport. They were up hill and down dale all the way. Through the forest from the mouth of the river had been the best way. Not only did Jean have to organize the pre-fabricated masonry from France, but also the local quarry stone for extending the church walls. The work commenced in January in the year of Our Lord 1076, ten years after the Conquest, and everyone concerned knew it was to be a lengthy task.

Cara had been relieved to see her Jean back safely, and was also surprised and not a little envious of her brother and his pretty French bride, although she took to Colette immediately. She watched anxiously the reactions of her parents to Davold and Colette, although she knew that marriage for Jean and herself was a different proposition. She knew how obstinate her father was, but he could do nothing about his son bringing home a bride from Normandy. He had, however, officially to approve of his daughter marrying an invader, and this would not put Gudrum in a good light with his compatriots. Gudrum had told Cara many times that she was young as yet to marry and might change her mind, although he knew in his heart, and Cara knew it too, that this was only an excuse and he had been saying this always while all her friends were getting wed and having babies. Cara was only content in the knowledge that Jean would forever be the one for her. From Jean's point of view he was wise to the fact that Davold bringing home a French bride had unintentionally softened the pathway for him and Cara a little. Jean had made his caring for Cara obvious enough on many occasions, and felt that Gudrum was being too short-sighted. If Gudrum pushed his prejudice aside a little and looked at things as they were it would be a lot easier, for after all Jean d'Arcy was Lord of the Manor, he would make his home in Fylton for the rest of his days, and, more importantly, if he had a mind to he could wed Cara any day without Gudrum's approval. What was more he could have taken Cara without marriage and without a second thought, as was the custom of some Lords of the Manor, like the wicked Lord Lucien of Horefelle; word had it that Lord Lucien sampled a different village maiden each night! However that was not the way of Jean d'Arcy.

38

Jean and Cara were to be agreeably surprised, for finally one spring morning Gudrum, a little grudgingly, gave Jean his pleasure to marry Cara. This was six months after Davold had arrived home with Colette. A month later Jean and Cara were united in Christian marriage. The old Saxon church of St Whyte was but a shell where all the alterations for the extended church were being carried out, but Jean and Cara were so happy this mattered not a jot – they would have been married anywhere as long as it was hallowed ground. They were married by Brother Joseph. Brother Luke, the successor to old Brother Athold, had been moved on to another church. The new priest had come from the Abbey of the Blessed Mary at Keynsham. Brother Joseph was a jolly likeable man, and very enthusiastic about the plans for the new church. The community at Fylton got on very well with him and he ministered to their needs with friendliness and dedication. He was a learned equable man and spoke Saxon as well as French and Latin.

In addition to the fact that he now had a French son-in-law and a French daughter-in-law, Gudrum had to admit that Jean was a fine young man who was making a good job of enlarging the church. He also had the satisfaction of knowing that his daughter would want for nothing for the rest of her life. Charis was as thrilled as any mother would be at her daughter making a happy as well as a prosperous match. She too had softened a great deal towards Jean, through Davold's union with Colette. Colette was a skilful industrious maid and she had already started work on a beautiful tapestry for the new church, the like of which had never been seen before in Fylton.

The building of the new Church of St. Gregory, the name which was to replace that of St Whyte, a Saxon saint, was a long and arduous task, but soundly and lovingly undertaken by Henri Gascoigne and his fellow stone-masons. The Saxons from Fylton that Jean had engaged to help lacked both experience and skill at working with stone, but were willing and quick to learn. Most of the straightforward wall reconstruction was undertaken by the Saxons, who marvelled at the clever stonework and masonry of the Normans. The inner wagon roof of the church was also constructed by the Saxons, and here they showed their cleverness and skill at working with wood. Henri Gascoigne had a fine eye for design and an instinct for what was right in the actual construction, whether it be wood or stone, and handled the whole practical side of the operation with easy expertise. Jean d'Arcy dealt with the supply of whatever was necessary in labour and material, and he had very generous backing from the Abbot at Keynsham who responded liberally to every request that came from Fylton regarding the church. The original Chapel of St Whyte had been just a plain oblong building with hardly any windows, no window at the eastern end and a few narrow apertures along the side walls. The Saxons had a purpose for this, the idea being that everyone in the main body of the church could see the priest without any light from behind getting in the way. Henri Gascoigne put in small deeply-set windows on every wall to keep out the weather, but strategically placed to let in ample light. The new church was rebuilt in a cruciform shape in the traditional Norman manner, and still facing east in the tradition of all Christian churches. There was a porch on the north wall and this was a very fine example of painstaking stonework. The rebuilt church of St Gregory was finally completed in 1088, twelve years after Jean wed Cara, and at this time work was still going on for the building of their Manor house. The book of records that was to be called The Domesday Book had been instigated three years before in 1085, and in this record the Conqueror had gathered all details of the lands he now reigned over. The feudal system had been introduced all over the country, and all men below the Lords of the Manors owed liege to their Lords, as indeed the Lords owed liege to their Sovereign the Conqueror.

Fyllwood Forest was no longer the place where a Saxon could roam at will or kill the game to his own liking. William had introduced some strong new forest laws which curtailed spontaneous hunting for Saxons in all the forests of England. The only people who still seemed to roam free and ignore the forest laws were the travelling people, and they were like will o' the wisps, here today and gone tomorrow, always out of reach of the laws that bound others. Jean d'Arcy for his part knew that it happened, but very often turned a blind eye to the surreptitious unofficial forays into Fyllwood Forest by some of the young bloods from Fylton. There was still plenty of organized meat and game for the villagers but Jean realized wisely that the inborn habits of a nation do not die easily and overnight. As long as the law was not broken on a large scale he was content to look the other way.

After the church was rebuilt Jean had, as promised, built a fine manor house below the southern hills, on a piece of ground rising up from the lower church grounds. Although the church had been his prior commission, Jean in his energetic manner had managed most of the construction of his Manor house at the same time. During this time Cara had borne him first a daughter and then three sturdy sons. Davold had built himself a homestead on the edge of his beloved Fyllwood Forest, in the lea of the hills, about a mile east of Jean's Manor house. It was more of a farm than a strip of land, for Jean had been generous to his friend when the apportioning of land took place.

Jean was not entirely satisfied with the altered church. He had wanted to make more changes, but as fate would have it, this would be left to someone else more than a century later. On the day of the blessing of the new church by Father Roget, the Abbot from Keynsham, the Fylton inhabitants gazed in wonderment at the expertly fashioned stone and the unusual designs.

As he joined in the ceremony, old Gudrum felt a lump in his throat. His beloved Charis had died of a fever two years previously, but his family were all around him. Davold and Colette were there with their offspring; they had produced two daughters and a son. There were also Jean and Cara and their three children. They had named their eldest son Gudrum, and old Gudrum had been touched with

41

emotion at the time, stubborn Saxon though he was. He still showed his merriment on occasions though, especially with his grandchildren, but not so frequently now that Charis was gone. After the blessing Father Roget mingled for a while with the villagers and spoke of great approval for the new Church of St Gregory, which had grown from the small cell-like Chapel of St Whyte. He eventually departed for Keynsham on a fine black horse escorted by several Brothers of the Augustine Order.

The next time the village saw Father Roget was seven years later when a handsome new font was installed in St Gregory's. There had been quite a few marriages at Fylton and the natural consequence was infants and an increase in the population. Brother Joseph baptized the infants and had long wanted a new font. Now Father Roget had come again with the Brothers from the abbey at Keynsham to conduct a ceremony of blessing the new font. The whole village it seemed came to the blessing. Jean d'Arcy and his family were there of course, as was Davold with his wife and children. Jeanette, the only daughter of Jean, had married the son of Henri Gascoigne, the master mason, the year before, and was with child. As they stood in the church it seemed to Jean that the child of Jeanette and her husband would most likely be the first babe to be baptized in this font, and so it turned out to be, for Jeanette's child, a son, was born two weeks later. Jean felt that this was truly meant to be. What could be more fitting than that the grandchild of the men who had been instrumental in the rebuilding of St Gregory's – himself and Henri Gascoigne – should be the first child to be baptized in this new font? The child was named Gregory after the church and its saint.

It was not surprising that the whole of Fylton was in church for this special occasion, the baptism of the Lord of the Manor's first grandchild, and Gudrum, who was now seventy-two years old and not so sprightly, sighed as he made his way out through the porch into the sunlight. He was feeling his age, and there had been so many changes. Jean d'Arcy was just behind him with Davold, and as Gudrum turned to speak to Davold his attention was drawn to the unusual look on the face of Jean. He seemed unaware of those around him and was talking to himself, 'I have known since it was built that this will be a church for all time. It has been fashioned with love and care and skill and thought. May all those who worship here be blessed and prosper in the work of our Lord.' It was a benediction. Gudrum at that moment felt at peace with all men. He looked at Davold and his son nodded silently. He also had heard his friend's words, and he could not have put his own thoughts into better meaning. Thus spoke Jean d'Arcy, first Lord of the Manor of Fylton in the year of our Lord 1095.

4

The Crusader and his Liege Man

In 1087 the son of William I, another William, had come to
the throne. William II was nicknamed "Rufus" because of
his red hair. He was a harsh man without the wisdom of his
sire and he received great opposition from Anselm, Archbishop of Canterbury. In 1100 he suffered an unfortunate
death while hunting in the vast forests near England's
southern coast. Nobody was ever sure how accidental the
aiming of the arrow had been. There were many rumours.
Some said the happening was revenge for the harsh forest
laws, and some said it was a plot organized by his brother
Henry who had then become King. The fatal accidental
arrow was purported to have come from the bow of Sir
William Tyrel, one of the courtiers in the forest with Rufus,
but the mystery as to whether the event was accidental or
intentional remained.

A little more than a century later the Lord of the Manor
at Fylton was Sir David de Lyon. He was a short stocky man,
but he made up for his lack of height with an undoubted
imperialistic manner. In 1198 he had been Lord of the
Manor for nigh on twenty-five years, and his eldest son, also
David, had been quite a few years away at a Crusade with
King Richard, known as Richard Coeur de Lion, who was a
distant cousin of Sir David. In addition to his eldest son Sir
David had sired four other sons and three daughters, so he
had not been greatly disturbed for the continuation of the
de Lyon lineage when young David had announced his
intention of going off on this latest Crusade. David was a
fine strapping young man, for Sir David had been zealous

44

in rearing his children in a good Christian manner, and all his sons were endowed with a high sense of duty and possessed all the knightly virtues. At the same time they had been made well aware of the fact that they had been born into a superior position in life, and their demeanour when dealing with the liege men and villeins and serfs at their father's disposal was instantly commanding and demanding of respect.

Sir David had finally completed the work on the church that Jean d'Arcy had commenced in the last century. St Gregory's had even more of a Norman flavour now. Bright coloured chevrons of red and blue had been introduced into the stonework of the pillars and more pre-fabricated stone had been imported from Normandy. The wooden wagon roof had been extended and made higher, and this once more was done with skilled Saxon labour. Sir David had received plenty of support from Keynsham Abbey. In 1167 the abbey itself had been greatly renovated and enlarged.

In the eleventh century the Christian noblemen and military leaders of Europe were inspired with the idea of gaining Jerusalem and the Holy Places from Muslim occupation. The first Crusade set out in 1095 and lasted four years until 1099. The Crusade had been eminently successful, for Jerusalem was captured, other parts of the Holy Land sequestered and three Crusader states created. The fall of one of these states in 1144 caused Western Christendom to organize a second Crusade in 1147, but Saladin the Muslim leader defeated the Christian Knights in their attempts to win back the land and also recaptured Jerusalem. In 1189 a third Crusade was mustered, and this was led by Philip II Augustus of France, Emperor Frederick I Barbarossa and Richard I Coeur de Lion of England, but there were no conclusive results from this mighty effort, for the Holy Land remained in Muslim hands, although Messina and Cyprus had been captured. It was to this third Crusade that young David de Lyon had ridden off to join the King his kinsman, accompanied by Will Potter his manservant.

45

David had been away a long long time and there were times when his family thought he must be dead at the hands of the infidels, but the journey home had not been straightforward due to the fact that King Richard was held prisoner in Austria as a kind of political pawn. He was eventually released in 1194 by the Emperor Henry, after payment of a huge ransom. Rumour had it that the ransom was paid by a fervently loyal Englishman with well-lined pockets nicknamed "Jelly the Rich", who resided at Ealing Manor in Hampshire near the coast. Richard I reigned for ten years in England but he was a monarch who spent much of his time away from the realm. Although the Crusade and his imprisonment had taken him far away he spent a lot of time in France, for his mother had been Eleanor of Aquitaine, and he held titles to land there. As a result most of the monarch's business in England was managed for him by one of his senior ministers, Hubert Walter.

On this day in the month of June 1198 there was great rejoicing in the manor house at Fylton, for word had come that young David, heir to Fylton Manor, was returning from his travels after nine long years. Her first-born had always been the favourite of Lady Jane, Sir David's wife, and she had been both proud and sad when her son had decided to accompany Cousin Richard on his Holy Mission. David had four younger brothers, Rupert, Edward, Stephen and Philip. Their sisters were Anne, Eleanor and Isobel. Sir David's daughters were comely maidens, not greatly beautiful but worthy and ladylike, and their greatest passions in life seemed to revolve around their needlepoint work and the herb-garden. Altogether the de Lyon family was well-liked and respected by Fylton folk, and at this moment Lady Jane knew that everyone in the village shared the joy and anticipation of David's imminent return from this wearisome third Crusade.

Lady Jane remembered well the tales her father had told her of when, as a young man, he had gone on the second Crusade back in 1147. Her father had been Davold of Fyllwood, named after his grandfather. Until she married

46

Sir David in 1173, Lady Jane had lived at Fyllwood Farm, built and so named by the first Davold on the edge of Fyllwood, a mile or so hence from Fylton Manor. Her brother, Godwin, was now head of the household at Fyllwood Farm, and the gold medallion with the curious dragon figure engraved upon it which Godwin always wore, and which their father Davold had worn continuously as a kind of protection when he was away in the Holy Land, had originally belonged to the first Davold of Fyllwood, so the story went. Legend also had it that the first Davold had been a great friend of the first Lord of the Manor, Jean d'Arcy, who had come over with the Conqueror. Sir Jean had built their present Manor house and had also been instrumental in building their fine village church of St Gregory. Sadly Sir Jean had been struck down with a tragic illness and died soon after the birth of his first grandchild. His eldest son, Gudrum, had succeeded to the Manor and he had been a good and fair Lord like his father, but Sir Gudrum had only been blessed with one son, Edmund. Edmund had gone on the second Crusade with Lady Jane's father and had been killed. So, sadly with the death of Edmund, the proud lineage of the d'Arcys had died out. All of Edmund's cousins on his father's side had been female except for the Gascoignes, his Aunt Jeanette's family, and under Norman law a daughter's issue did not inherit.

In spite of the times she lived in, Lady Jane was something of a scholar, and she delighted in poring over the old manuscripts that were stored in the church. She knew that the first infant baptized in the new font that was installed some seven years after the church was rebuilt, had been Sir Jean's first grandchild, Gregory Gascoigne, the child of his daughter Jeanette. She knew so because she had read it in Sir Jean's own script, written just before his death. The new priest recently installed at St Gregory's, Brother Peter Gascoigne, was a grandson of this very same Gregory Gascoigne. Lady Jane had a keen sense of history as well as local family interest, and she was sad that none of her daughters shared her enthusiasm for scholarly pursuits. At this moment her heart rejoiced with the thought of the return of her beloved son David. David had always shown a gift for learning and for wanting to know about people and the world and travelling. Indeed it was this instinct as much as his knightly virtue that had sent him to the Crusade, for whether he realized it or not he carried the genes of his Saxon ancestor Davold, who had also been a seeker of truth looking beyond his native heath. Lady Jane looked forward greatly to long talks with David and news of his travels. She felt that if she had been a man she would have done the same as David – travelled, seen the world outside.

As she sat dreaming, there were distant sounds that indicated the approach of horsemen. Lady Jane hurried to the doorway, and there coming up the green sward that sloped down from the house were two horsemen leading two packhorses. She recognized the horsemen immediately as David and his manservant Will Potter. The rest of the family had also heard the horses and there was great hubbub and excitement as they all crowded to the door and spilled out to greet the safe return of this son of the Manor, this hero, this Christian Knight returning to the bosom of his family. His chain-mail looked the worse for wear, but his tunic with the scarlet Cross of St George emblazoned upon it looked crisp and white and he held the banner of de Lyon high before him. The banner was very imposing; two black lions, rampant, one facing the other. David looked much older and leaner, but well, and it was obvious that he was immensely proud and happy to be home. He had picked up a following of villagers on his way through Fylton, and bringing up the rear of this trail was Brother Peter Gascoigne come to give his blessing. David dismounted and his redheaded manservant Will, looking very perky but aware of his position, touched his forelock respectfully to the family and took the horses off to the back of the house to be stabled, followed by some of the village lads.

There was a great deal of hearty back-slapping, masculine laughter and hand-shaking with the men of the family, with young David's father, Sir David, flushed and excited and carrying on as if it was he who had been on the Crusade! David's sisters giggled and held their distance, and Lady Jane waited patiently. Presently he came to her and gave her a big hug. 'Mama, Mama!' was all he could say. He kissed his sisters dutifully, and after Brother Peter had given him a blessing they all went inside. A chamber had been prepared for David and after a while he retired to rest for an hour or so.

Later that evening after a magnificent repast of Fyllwood wild boar, cooked deliciously in the special way that old Marjorie, the family cook, knew, with special herbs and flavourings, washed down with large draughts of ale, the de Lyon family relaxed and settled down to David's tales of the wonderful and mysterious places he had visited. Even the dogs, stretched out lazily across the hearth with full bellies from all the table scraps, seemed to be listening to the young master's accounts. He had brought with him several bales of the finest silks, splendidly coloured pinks, mauves, yellows and greens, some most exotic perfumes which set his sisters shrilling with delight, and a bag of unnamed spices, aromatic and unusual, but very pleasing. There was a blazing log fire in the main hall, for although it was early June the nights went off cold at this time of the year. Lady Jane sat with her family and was content. David was safely home, the harvest looked like being a good one, and that very day Sir David had been approached by a neighbouring landowner about the arrangement of a marriage between Isobel, her youngest daughter and the landowner's son. Lady Jane felt elated at the prospect. Soon she could foresee grandchildren being dandled on her knee, plump and cherubic and playful. Also she thought the time would not be far hence when it would be advisable for David to seek a wife. Indeed more than advisable, it would be his bounden duty. David must sire a houseful of sons like his father to ensure the lineage of the de Lyons. The dying of the lineage of Jean d'Arcy, that splendid first Lord of the Manor, must not happen to this family. Across the fireplace, uncannily as if reading her very thoughts, David stretched out his legs, looked at his mother and said, 'And now I must find me a goodly wife and settle down.'

After the initial excitement of David's homecoming the de Lyon household returned to normal again and David, as the eldest son, set about seriously fulfilling his duties to the Manor. The liegemen were predicting a good harvest. The Manor at Fylton had always been well-run with plenteous patronage from the Abbey at Keynsham. With fair management the serfs and villeins worked hard and faithfully, and there was a tradition that after ten years or more of constant service a serf would be rewarded with a small strip of land of his own to cultivate. Most of the serfs at Fylton were young men, sons of bondmen or liegemen who had served their Lord of the Manor well and been apportioned their land strips accordingly. Will Potter, David's manservant, had been a serf, son of a bondman, Thomas the Potter, and in view of Will's service to his son at the Crusade Sir David had granted Will a strip of land adjacent to his father's strip. Thomas had his potter's hut on his strip although he grew produce as well. Thomas supplied the pottery needs for the whole Manor.

Will's father had often told him tales when he was young, tales that their ancestors back in the last century had lived as freemen close to where the Manor was now, and those ancestors had also followed their trade as potters back in those far off days. Will speculated on this now and again and wondered how his family would have been now if the Normans hadn't come, for Will knew also from his father that he was of pure Saxon stock. However he could not complain, for he had always been close to Master David who treated him more like a brother than a servant. He had also had a chance to travel to the Holy Land and through many parts of Europe, something he would never have done if he had not been the manservant of Master David. Will was a likeable man, tall of stature with merry blue eyes and a hearty laugh to match his bright red hair. Many a maiden at Fylton had glanced in his direction since his return, for it was known that in addition to the piece of

50

land, Sir David had rewarded Will handsomely with silver marks, and Will had also brought home with him some fancy silks, cloths and spices. Indeed he was regarded as quite a catch by many Fylton mothers and their daughters. Will, however, had other thoughts. He had long since struggled with and cherished secretly a desire for Eleanor, one of Master David's younger sisters. Of the three sisters she was the daintiest, and although she was no great beauty Eleanor had a sweetness of manner and wholesomeness of character which had always enchanted Will. They had played together often as children but as Eleanor had matured into a young woman and been made aware of her status as daughter of the Manor, social interaction with the sons of bondmen had not been encouraged. Away at the Crusade Will had not seen Eleanor for nine long years but upon his return his heart had stirred afresh at the sight and sound of her, and the fact that she was still unwed. He had no conception of how Eleanor felt about him, humble Will the servant of her brother David, but Will was an optimistic lad. Moreover his travels had broadened his views and this breadth of thinking contributed greatly to his lively hope in his plans for winning his lady. Thomas the potter, Will's father, who felt he knew his place in the scheme of things, would have been horrified if he could have read Will's thoughts. Proud and happy he was to have Will home again, but also he felt some underlying unease. He kept telling himself that the young fellow was unsettled, as one would expect after his time away, but Will had also told his father on several occasions since his return that he did not intend to follow on in the potter's craft. Thomas had been greatly disappointed at this news, although Will had a younger brother Cuthbert who would undoubtedly follow in his father's footsteps, but Thomas had always hoped that both his sons would eventually work the pottery.

The year passed by quite uneventfully. David took an active part in the running of the Manor and went on many hunting trips into Fyllwood Forest. He was a man of many parts, aristocrat, soldier, Christian, and a visionary; a man who had looked at the world around him, the world of people, animals and growing things. With his return he had not only brought silks and spices but also some seedlings of the cedar trees he had so greatly admired in the Holy Land. He had met and sought advice from an old Syrian gardener who knew about cedar trees and how to propagate them. He had had the thought that these cedar trees might enhance the meadows around his father's Manor. He loved the shape of their flat outreaching branches. In due course a few were planted in suitable positions around the house, and he had one small plant to spare that he decided to place about ten paces in front of the north door of St Gregory's. Brother Peter was in agreement, it would look good there. In years to come, long after young David and Brother Peter were gone, all the young trees would grow into the fullness promised in David's imagination, to provide beauty and shade on hot summer days to generations of Fylton villagers, whether they be weary labourers in the precincts of de Lyon land or churchgoers at St Gregory's.

In addition to the affairs of the Manor and the hunting trips into Fyllwood, David had also made several visits into the town of Brigstowe built on the river which ran past the lower slopes of Fyllwood. Brigstowe was a few miles north of Fylton, a well-defended place with a fine castle. The town had been there since the time of Alfred the Great in the latter part of the ninth century, and like Fylton had not shown a great resistance to the Normans. It was a pleasant town with good inns. Ships came up on the tide and were moored to the banks. They were then unloaded when the tide ebbed so that they were left dry on the mud. There was a wooden bridge which had been there for some time, but only small craft could navigate right up to Brigstowe Bridge and land right at the city gates. There had been a castle of sorts in Brigstowe before the Normans came, but the Conqueror had ordered that the existing castle be made much bigger and improved, with plenty of stables and better apartments. Before the Conquest the town had been under the patronage of the Saxon Earldom of Swegen. The only attempt to make a fight for Brigstowe had been back in 1068 by the heirs to the Earldom of Swegen who had fled to Ireland at the time of the invasion. In Ireland they had regrouped and acquired a fleet of ships manned by crews of wild Irishmen. They had sailed up the river through the Gorge of Goram hoping to retake Brigstowe by surprise, but they were firmly resisted and no more rebellious attempts had been made. After the Conquest the patronage of the town had been granted by William to Roger of Berkeley. Subsequently the town and the castle had come under the control of Robert of Caen or Robert of Gloucester as he was sometimes called. Robert had made further improvements to the already splendid castle, building a large keep with stone transported from Caen. Robert of Caen had died in 1147 and was succeeded by his son William of Caen. William's daughter had married Prince John, brother to King Richard, and the castle had been part of the marriage settlement.

David enjoyed the company of the Normans in Brigstowe and became a frequent visitor to William of Caen's residence. He made many friends among the young sons of other landowners who were also magnetized towards the town. It was somewhere different to visit and relax after the undertakings of land upkeep. It was also a centre for gossip from Court, and Prince John was often there, but David had no great liking for the King's brother who seemed to be a selfish and self-indulgent fellow. David, being a relative of Prince John and King Richard, was infinitely acceptable to all the other young bloods who patronized the inns of Brigstowe, for many of them had sisters of marriageable age and it was well known that David was seeking a wife. David was not in too great a hurry, he did not want a marriage of pure convenience, and he had certain visions of the type of maiden he would choose as a life partner. Fate did not keep him waiting too long. On one of his forays into Fyllwood Forest he met and became friendly with a young fellow,

Edgar de Lacey, son of a landowner from beyond the southern hills. The friendship prospered and, inevitably, after a while David was invited to the home of the de Laceys. They lived just north of Glastonbury in a pleasant manor house very similar to the house of the de Lyons. Edgar had no sister but two lusty younger brothers. The de Laceys made David very welcome and he agreed to eat meat with them that evening and stay for a night's lodging. It was an arduous journey back over the hills to Fylton and the November weather was inclement. As he sat at board with the de Laceys he noted a maiden demure and without much conversation among the lively brothers. Edgar's mother noticed his glance and said, 'This is the daughter of my sister. May I ask you to greet Anna, she is staying here with us, her kin are in London.'

Afterwards David could not remember what he'd said in greeting. He could only remember that he did not remove his eyes from Anna all evening. She was young, seventeen perhaps, and beautiful. Her light brown hair was wispy about her face and mainly plaited back in the Norman style. Her eyes were as blue as the sky and her skin as pink as a baby's. She wore a gown of blue silk to match her eyes. David fell hopelessly in love. Next morning he rode back to Fylton on air, a man besotted. Edgar was highly amused at first and then delighted when David told him how serious his intentions were, for David knew he had found the girl he wanted to marry. Further enquiries established that Anna was the daughter of Paul Duchesne, a man whose business took him to Court quite often. David was meticulous in his courtship. He visited the de Laceys frequently and the more he grew to know Anna the more he grew to love her. Anna was not always at her aunt's house. Twice that winter David made the long rough ride to London to see his beloved and her parents, who thoroughly approved of the wooing.

David and Anna were married one bright March morning in the year 1199 in the Church of St Gregory at Fylton. Brother Peter Gascoigne performed the ceremony, there was much rejoicing, and David felt he was the luckiest man in Christendom. It was the second wedding in the de Lyon family that year for Isobel, his sister, had married in January.

Will had not been idle while David was courting Anna. He had, like Lady Jane, an appetite for reading and learning the past history of Fylton from the many documents that were stored in St Gregory's church. For a man of his station Will could read quite well. David had taught him on many otherwise boring evenings during their travels together, and Will had been a bright and willing pupil. Lady Jane found Will in the church one day poring over a particularly difficult parchment and came to his aid. Thus a most unusual friendship was born. Lady Jane was happy to find a kindred enquiring mind. She had also hoped that David would have spent more time in this way, but since his return he'd had time only for the Manor, his hunting trips, his visits to Brigstowe and his pursuit of Anna. Sir David was a good man and she loved him, but he had no heart for history. 'I don't know why you should want to delve among all that old stuff' he would say if she mentioned that she had been to the church to read about the past. Therefore she welcomed the genuine interest of Will in the church parchments, which to her were very important.

They became very important to Will also, when one day he came across the story of Hendrig the potter and his son Felix written in the scholarly painstaking hand of Jean d'Arcy. The parchment was faded and worn but the whole story was there to capture the imagination as clear as if it had happened yesterday. The waylaying of Jean d'Arcy by Felix the rebel, Felix's banishment and eventual death, the subsequent rescue by the first Davold of Fyllwood of Felix's wife and child from the rascally Lord Lucien of Horefelle, with the happy ending of Agnes and her baby Oswald being returned into the Fylton household of Felix's aunt and uncle. This fitted in with the stories Will's father had told him, that their roots had always been here in Fylton. When he read the story Will could not help feeling even closer to the de Lyon family, for had not Lady Jane's ancestor, the first Davold, been the one to rescue Will's ancestor, the baby Oswald? When he showed Lady Jane the parchment and they went through it together he knew that she felt this kinship too. Lady Jane began to invite Will to talk with her in her rooms, and he was a willing guest. This way he would see more of his adored Eleanor and try to establish some kind of relationship. His one fear was that a marriage of convenience would be arranged with a local landowner by her parents, as with her sister.

When he did meet Eleanor he always tried to make a point of making her aware of him as a young man and not just as David's former manservant. When David got married, although he still lived at the Manor house as befitted the heir, he did not have much need of Will. Sir David had paid Will off with land and silver marks, but of course the two men were forever united in a relationship that had been forged in their shared experiences on the Crusade. Will had, at one time, played with the notion of approaching David about his cherishment of Eleanor, but somehow he could not bring himself to broach the matter. Although he and David had been as brothers at times, the underlying fact that he was a liege man was always there in the way. Not only that, David had been so preoccupied with wooing his own lady that Will had not found the chance for serious talk, although David, being so happy with his own state, would probably have done all he could to help. Thus it was that Will decided to approach Lady Jane. Will's visits to Lady Jane's part of the Manor house became quite a regular thing and he appeared to be well accepted by all the de Lyons. In particular he had noticed that Eleanor's glance fell very often in his direction nowadays. Also some of the natural pleasure they had shared at being together as children seemed still to be there, and he dared to hope. However, he had decided that if and when he spoke his thoughts, and Eleanor was not interested, then he would try to forget the whole thing. It would be a different matter if there was opposition from her father. Lady Jane, he felt, would be surprised but understanding. When Will did eventually speak of his love for Eleanor to Lady Jane she did not show unusual emotion.

'You two were always inseparable as children,' she commented, when Will had haltingly put his thoughts into words.

She went on to say that it was going to be a little difficult to get the idea into Sir David's head, but the main thing was, did Eleanor feel the same way about Will?

Will felt he had progressed a little. He knew that Lady Jane liked him, respected him, but Sir David was Lord of the Manor and his word was law. Will knew that he must now talk to Eleanor without delay.

He found her the morning after his talk with her mother, on the lower slopes of the Manor pastures. She had been picking some flowers. The morning was bright but sharp and her cheeks were rosy with the fresh air. She appeared pleased to see him and his heart skipped a beat as he observed her with his eyes of love. Her gaze dropped, and he knew in that instant that she was aware of his feelings. Her manner was easy though, as she greeted him, and he felt heartened as they strolled down towards the church. He dared to hold her elbow to guide her over a stony patch and felt her quiver. He knew then that she felt the same as he did. Hope gave way to joy and he stopped and turned her to face him.

'Eleanor . . .'

She smiled, 'I know, Will, I feel the same. We have always been meant for each other.'

He gathered her to him and he could feel her heart beating. She dropped her flowers.

'Oh Eleanor I have been wanting to tell you ever since my return . . .'

'I know, I know,' she said, 'and all the time you were away I said prayers for you as well as for David.'

''Twas the same for me,' said Will. 'Through the long years I dreamed always of returning to you. I want you for my wife. There will be difficulties but we will overcome them.'

They stood there for some little time watching the stream that splashed down from the hills, with the church a silent sentinel in the background. A couple of young otters were diving and twisting playfully in the clear water, and Will knew he would always remember this moment, it was so perfect.

There were difficulties, many difficulties, and it took the test of time, love, and another year; until Sir David gave his consent for Eleanor to marry Will the potter's son, former liege man of master David. Lady Jane had consistently and faithfully put the lovers' case before her Lord and Master. She pointed out that Will was from good Saxon stock, and Fylton stock at that. His forebears and Eleanor's forebears had been equals and friends. The lovers shared a common heritage. Lady Jane even related the story of Felix that she and Will had found in the church documents, of how Will's ancestor, as a baby, had been brought back home to Fylton by Davold, Lady Jane's ancestor, after the dastardly behaviour of Lord Lucien of Horefelle. Sir David, who was a good man at heart, had softened at that story, and a week or so later had consented to the union of his daughter with Will. After all, he told himself, Will was no ordinary village swain, and he liked the fellow well enough. He had been to the Crusade, he had served his son David faithfully, and come to think of it David treated him like a brother already! Will was also a scholar of sorts although he, Sir David, had no time for that kind of stuff. When Sir David thought about it and about some of the coltish young fools his friends and fellow landowners were forever parading before him as the father of marriageable daughters, he decided that Eleanor could not have done better. The young fellow would have to be given more land of course, but that could easily be arranged. His daughter could not possibly go to live on a couple of strips of bondman's land. Sir David, who held good sway with the present Abbot of Keynsham took it upon himself to obtain a fair parcel of land from the Abbot to the north of the Church of St Gregory, and undertook to have a handsome house built thereon for the happy couple.

Until the house was completed Will and Eleanor would live at the Manor. Quite a few of the inhabitants of Fylton had now moved closer to the church. Fylton village was on higher ground to the west, but more and more villagers were finding it better to live nearer the centre of things like the Manor house and the church. As in pre-Norman days this place was still called Whyte Church by some villagers, but others who had recently moved from the original Fylton went on calling their new home Fylton.

On the day of the wedding of Will and Eleanor there was great rejoicing. Will's family had been overcome with pleasure when the wedding had been arranged. Will, in his joy and with generosity, had given his land to his father. From the silks brought from the east Eleanor chose a pale primrose for the village seamstress to fashion into a wedding gown, somewhat more elegant than the simple home-dyed saffron gown that Gudrum's bride had worn over one hundred and fifty years before in the simple Chapel of St Whyte, which was now the Church of St Gregory. It was very fitting to fate that Brother Peter Gascoigne performed the marriage, although nobody present dwelt on this. However, if Jean d'Arcy, the main instigator in the building of the church, had been present at that very moment he would have approved greatly that Brother Peter, the descendant of his daughter Jeanette and her husband, son of Henri Gascoigne, master mason, builder of St Gregory's, was conducting the union of Will, descendant of Hendrig the potter, (fiery Felix's aberration counted for little in the larger scheme of things), and Eleanor, a descendant of his dearest friend Davold. The blood was good and there was plenty of good Norman and Saxon stock in both families.

Will stood tall and proud as he made his vows, his red hair shining like gold in the autumn sun, his suit of rich brown velvet emblazoned on the breast with the Cross of St George. Eleanor in her primrose silk and small coronet of gems denoting nobility, was demure but smiling, and Brother Peter knew without a doubt that there was true love in this match. When their house north of the village was finally completed at the end of the year, Brother Peter performed a blessing the day that Will and Eleanor moved in. They had decided to call it Whyte Cross. It was a delightful mixing of words to Will's eager scholarly perception – Whyte he chose for the ancient Saxon saint whose name once graced the original church at Fylton, Cross was symbolic of a Christian man who had served in the Crusade. Will had originally thought of the Red Cross he had carried so continuously during his time in the Holy Land, but his sensibilities instructed him that this was somehow too trite – hence Whyte Cross, and Whyte Cross House, a site where various successive dwellings would stand strong for centuries. Soon after they moved in Eleanor knew that she was to have a child. Lady Jane was very happy. David had just presented the family with an heir, a robust noisy baby called Robert. Anna had wanted to name the child John; this adaptation of the Norman 'Jean' was now used frequently and had become very popular since the advent of Prince John, but David would not hear of it. He heartily disliked Prince John, now King John, and the name had bad connotations for him. Isobel, his sister, was also expecting an infant. In the past couple of years three of Lady Jane's children had married, and her dreams of many grandchildren to fuss over and spoil were beginning to come true.

5

Sir Ralph and his Forest Bride

In the year 1199 news had travelled to the Manor house at Fylton that King Richard was dead. He was a remote cousin of David de Lyon although they had not seen each other in years. Young David of course knew the King well from the Crusade. Richard had not spent much time in England, and now Prince John had succeeded to the throne. When he became King, John divorced the daughter of William of Caen, and married Isabella of Angouleme, a girl of thirteen. He had, however, greedily retained control of the castle and town of Brigstowe which had been part of the original marriage settlement from William's daughter. Because of his divorce King John had been excommunicated by the Pope, and the reign of John was not looked back on with great pleasure. The crusader David de Lyon's dislike of the man was shared by many, and although John had been on the throne when the great document of freedom, the Magna Carta, had been introduced, this had been mainly at the behest of his barons. King John died in 1216 and was mourned by few.

The people of Fylton were not greatly interested in matters connected with the Crown. Year after year their lives were bounded by the events of their immediate community, and the presence and jurisdiction of the Lord of the Manor was the hub of things for them. In the late thirteenth century, in the year 1275, Edward the First was on the throne, and Sir Stephen de Lyon, son of Robert, grandson of David de Lyon the Crusader, was Lord of the Manor of Fylton. Sir Stephen was a merry fellow, fond of drinking and the games of chance to be found in nearby Brigstowe town, but the estate was looked after well enough. The village men knew him as an easy man, some dubbed him a fool for he was so easy at times, but life at Fylton was pleasant. Sir Stephen's best friend was his distant relative who lived at Whyte Cross House; his name was Edward Potter.

Whyte Cross House was situated alongside the rough track that led to Brigstowe. Edward was a steady man, and while Sir Stephen's wife, Lady Elizabeth, encouraged the friendship for the stability that Edward showed, Edward's wife, Ann Potter, was very disinclined to smile whenever Stephen came riding up the track and set off for town with her husband. Her fears were not for what her stalwart Edward might do, but for what Stephen would get up to, and how Edward might try, out of loyalty, to extract Stephen from trouble.

One early spring day in 1275 Ann Potter was in her boudoir happily stitching away at a dress she was making for her daughter when she heard the clatter of a horse in the courtyard below. She hurried to look through the narrow aperture that served as a viewing point, there to see Sir Stephen on his fine black horse, smartly clad in a bright green tunic and velvet feathered cap, calling for Edward. Edward appeared from the stables looking slightly surprised. The hour was near noon and not at all the usual time his cousin called to see if he would accompany him on one of his jaunts. Sir Stephen called merrily to Edward, 'Come on fellow! I'm off to Brigstowe to make a mark or two. Are you going to try your luck?'

Edward shook his head good-naturedly enough, but inwardly he was thinking, why was Stephen going to the wagering games at this hour?

Outwardly he said, 'Sorry cousin. Can't be done. I'm having trouble with one of my mares, and aside from that we're busy with lambing.' Whyte Cross had become a thriving farm since its building, and Edward was a good custodian of his heritage.

Sir Stephen showed a momentary pique as he frowned irritably. 'I can't persuade you? Surely you have your men to attend to all these things!'

Edward shook his red curls. He had inherited this Potter characteristic along with the farm. 'Sorry cousin. Another time.'

'So be it,' said Sir Stephen. He turned his horse and trotted off towards the track that led to Brigstowe.

Edward shook his head again as he went back to his sick mare. He was more than puzzled. Stephen had never called for his company at this hour before; it was very strange. Edward had, on many occasions, ridden with his kinsman over the Brigstowe Bridge into High Street where there were several taverns which offered games of chance. Once or twice out of sociability he had played a wagering game, but never for high stakes which Stephen was wont to do. What Edward did not know was Stephen's real reason for wanting to ride to town at such an hour. The betting men started business just after noon and Stephen was desperately anxious to try his luck at the first opportunity. The day before he had lost a considerable amount of money. In fact if he did not recoup his loss he was done for, it was as simple as that. He had told nobody, least of all Lady Elizabeth who was constantly chiding him for his numerous idle visits to town, and was only happy if she knew that Edward was accompanying him. She would have been surprised to know that nowadays Stephen went to town quite often without his cousin, for Edward only liked to visit Brigstowe if he had business to attend to, and to combine this with a drink or two in the taverns. Stephen on this day would dearly have liked Edward by his side. He would have made Edward his confidant for he desperately needed to tell someone of his plight. Outwardly he had portrayed the usual jolly fellow to his cousin and his pride had stopped him from pouring out his troubles when Edward had declined to accompany him. His hopes were high however as he reached the town and clattered over the bridge which was bustling with activity from the many tenements built thereon.

Luck was not with Sir Stephen that day. In the early hours of the morning of the next day there was loud hammering on the sturdy oak main door of Whyte Cross. Edward jumped from bed and hastened down the stairs, pulling on some outer clothing as he went. He opened the door to a distraught and urgent Sir Stephen.

'Cousin, cousin, can you help? My house is afire . . . the men are doing their best to quell it . . . thank God the family are safe . . . and the horses are being got out . . .' he gasped, losing his breath.

Edward could smell the burning now, strong and acrid in the cool night air. He called a quick explanation to Caroline who was well astir by now, as was the rest of his household, donned his boots, and ran to fetch his horse to go with Sir Stephen.

Edward had never seen such a sight as they galloped across the fields. The huge flames of the burning house stood out plainly in the moonless night, and before they had even got there he knew it was hopeless. 'But how?' he kept asking himself, 'But how?'

A large crowd of awe-stricken villagers had gathered a little way apart from the burning house. Indeed the whole of Fylton was awake this terrible night. Most of the young men were striving valiantly with the flames, but as Edward had first thought, it was hopeless. The fire had taken too great a hold and the Manor house was doomed.

A tearful Lady Elizabeth and her four children were standing back from the inferno. The liege men were trying hard with their chain of leather buckets but she too knew that her home was finished. Ralph, Sir Stephen's elder son who was just sixteen years old, stood with his arm around his mother attempting to comfort her. His two little sisters were sobbing fitfully while Piers his younger brother just stared and stared as the house crackled and burned fiercely before them. Sir Stephen had disappeared.

Edward was full of compassion and practicality. He went

64

to Lady Elizabeth. 'You must all come to Whyte Cross. We have ample room.'

Lady Elizabeth had snatched up a few precious possessions, as had the children. Sir Stephen was still missing. Edward found one of Sir Stephen's reliable liege men and together they hitched up a large cart to a couple of horses and piled Lady Elizabeth, her children, and the possessions they had saved into it. When they arrived at Whyte Cross Ann welcomed them capably with hot ale, clean beds and deep consolation.

Edward eventually found Sir Stephen at dawn-break, sitting at the back of the house, his head in his hands, his fine clothes blackened with smoke and muddied with grimy water. The house was just smouldering now.

Sir Stephen said wretchedly, 'What have I done? . . . Oh God what have I done? I just didn't want those usurers to get their hands on it . . . I would rather it burned to the ground . . .' He seemed to be talking in a kind of mesmerized self-address. 'There was no other way . . . no other way . . . Oh God I was a fool to stake the house . . . and in the end I not only staked it, I torched it, torched it! . . . the beautiful house of my ancestors . . . but I couldn't let those scheming rogues get their thieving hands on it could I? . . . it was better it was burned to the ground . . .' He broke off, unable to speak any more, full of anguish.

Edward was greatly shaken at this. He put his hand on Sir Stephen's shoulder. 'What are you saying cousin? What are you saying? I do not understand!'

That seemed to spring Stephen into action. 'Nothing, nothing Edward, nothing! . . . forget it! . . . promise me on your life you will not speak of this to anyone . . . I have said too much.' Sir Stephen was pleading now.

Edward promised, and for the rest of his life he was to speak of this incident to no one, not even his wife Ann. He was as good as his word, but forget it he could not.

From that day onward Sir Stephen was a broken man. He lived for another eighteen months, but guilt and subsequent ill-health took charge of him before he collapsed and died quietly one day in church, and went to face his Maker. There was a fine funeral for the Lord of the Manor and the Abbot and Brothers from Keynsham were in attendance. The Manor lands were unspoiled and Sir Stephen had half-heartedly conducted the business of the Manor from Whyte Cross while plans were made for a new Manor house to be built. Father Courtenay who was the present Abbot had not seemed over-anxious to help with the planning of the new building in Sir Stephen's time. It could have been that he had some inkling of the man's guilty secret, but once the funeral was over he approached young Ralph de Lyon, now the heir, barely eighteen years of age, with prodigious offers of help. Ralph was an admirable young fellow who had grown up a lot since the burning of his home. Indeed he had taken over quite a lot of the duties of administering the Manor in the last few weeks before his father's death.

Edward often wondered if Father Courtenay had known anything of Sir Stephen's frequent visits to Brigstowe and his wild habits. Certainly a man of the cloth such as Courtenay would not countenance such rash gaming habits, even from a Lord of the Manor. Edward was sure that young Ralph knew not, or could not even guess at the strange happenings prior to the fire, and if Lady Elizabeth knew she never gave the smallest hint that she did.

While the new Manor house was being built, Lady Elizabeth and her children continued to stay at Whyte Cross, although sometimes for a change they would go across to Fyllwood Farm on the edge of the forest to stay with kinsfolk. Young Sir Ralph, as he was now, loved hunting in the forest with his cousin from Fyllwood when his duties allowed it.

More and more of the people of Fylton were moving to land nearer the church, and Sir Ralph was encouraging this by giving new plots of untilled pastureland to his liege men. The church, in the last fifty years, had become the real centre for the Fylton community. No longer did the men sit and discuss matters of an evening at the end of the village, as they had long since the time of Gudrum. The original old village of Fylton seemed these days to be mostly populated by the older men and women, who only wanted to stay where they had always lived, in spite of the fact that most of their offspring had moved down east nearer the church. The priest at St Gregory's at this time was Brother Michael, an amiable portly man who loved his ale, but was for all that a good Christian. Indeed the church had become the centre of activity for ale-lovers in recent years. Brother Michael, with an eye on his own needs, allowed brewers of ale who wished to sell some of their surplus stock to carry out their business in the church grounds to the north, and on days when the weather was inclement the business was conducted in the shelter of the porch. The trade thrived as the villagers were glad to purchase their ale so conveniently.

At about the time the new Manor house was being planned, Father Courtenay and his Brothers had plans for extending the chancel of the church and young Sir Ralph was enthusiastic with the idea. His kinsfolk at Fyllwood Farm promised the loan of a couple of men to help with the labour. The head of the household at Fyllwood now was Bertram Blessed, a fine figure of a man, broad and blond and an excellent hunter. He was ten years older than Ralph, but they had shared several trips into the forest together, enjoyed each other's company, and Ralph appreciated the older man's wisdom and advice. He was particularly fascinated with the story of the gold medallion that Bertram always wore. Bertram had told him the story of how the medallion had been handed down from father to son since Saxon times, and it was well known that there was a good measure of Saxon blood in Bertram's family, although it was very puzzling to Ralph that the medallion bore what appeared to be a mythical Welsh dragon. Ralph was quite a scholarly young man and knew of such things. Bertram Blessed like Ralph was unmarried as yet. The descendants of Davold had been dubbed "The Blessed Ones" by Fylton folk, maybe because of the Caerdragon medallion and its mythical reputation for good fortune, and gradually through common usage the name Blessed had become theirs.

The new Manor house which they called Lyons Court was finally completed in 1279, and a splendid house it was. Larger than the former house, it had the finest stonework in the land, for Father Courtenay had many connections with experienced stone-masons and artisans, and had seen to it that the new young Lord of the Manor had every help in this direction. In return Ralph had provided very generous labour from his liege men towards the extension of the chancel and the eastern end of St Gregory's, together with a couple of men from Bertram's workforce to assist the stoneworkers. When the work was completed a joyous service of thanksgiving was held. Fylton village was truly becoming a good place to live, with such a fine church and splendid new Manor house. Now that most Fylton folk lived in this eastern stretch of the demesne, the old Saxon encampment away to the west had become increasingly dilapidated and deserted.

Once these two main projects were over, Ralph and Bertram found time for a few more trips into Fyllwood Forest. Ralph was quite unlike his father. He had no time for the town life, and his idea of a good time was a hunting trip into the forest with fine company such as Bertram, to sleep under the stars and cook his own meat once in a while. He loved to ride right through to the winding river and the big Gorge of Goram, to gaze in wonder at the huge cliffs and the trading boats that sailed up to the outskirts of Brigstowe. The people that wandered through the forest and all over the southern lands of the realm, the travellers, were often camped by the river, and several times Ralph and his kinsman had sat and learned to fish through watching these nomads at this spot. On more than one occasion they had conversed with some men from the other side of the river who lived at the top of the cliffs in a small community called Cliff Town. These men had light homemade boats of animal skin which they would carry on their shoulders down the steep zigzag pathway on the other side. They would launch their boats into the tide and fish to their hearts' content. The fish were plentiful and it was not a hard task. The men from Cliff Town had previously had a bad reputation for being thieves and desperadoes but had now grown orderly under the Normans. One day they offered the two strangers a chance to fish from their boats, and Ralph and Bertram had eagerly taken advantage of the offer. The Cliff Town men had no idea that these two men were a Lord of the Manor and a prosperous land-owner from beyond the forest, for Ralph and Bertram did not wear rich apparel for hunting trips, and Bertram usually wore his medallion beneath his linen except for special occasions, for he was not an ostentatious man.

The day they went fishing with their new-found friends from Cliff Town they landed back on their side of the river as it was getting dark, so they decided to settle for the night on the high grassy part of the bank. They had just finished eating the last of their fish when there was some kind of activity a little way along the bank. It was a travelling group arriving to camp for the night. They thought nothing of it until they heard the music, and by that time both Ralph and Bertram had rolled themselves in their animal skins and settled down for the night. It was a balmy summer evening, warm and scented with wild honeysuckle. There was a full moon, and the music seemed to match the occasion exactly. At first the friends were curious and then they were fascinated when they saw that there were a couple of maidens dancing to the reed pipes of the young men sitting around the fire. They had never seen anything like it. They arose and crept closer. One of the older men sitting at the edge of the group, whom they knew slightly from previous excursions into Fyllwood, saw them in the moonlight and beckoned them nearer. 'Come lads, come and join our celebrations! 'Tis a happy night for us this night of the full moon. A son has just been born to one of our families and we are very joyful, for they had four daughters but now they have a son at last!'

Ralph and Bertram joined the group. They were offered ale and herb cake and the celebrations went on and on with great gusto. The young maidens danced continuously as if they didn't know how to get tired, and their dancing was strange and haunting. Ralph particularly was very attracted to the younger one. They were two sisters named Maive and Rachel, and it was from Rachel that he could not retrieve his gaze. He was like a man mesmerized and Bertram teased him at first, until he realized that Ralph really had become very attracted and enthralled by this young maiden. There was no doubt about it, she was a beauty. Her sensuous dancing and the wild music had stirred the young blood in Ralph, who had of late been highly preoccupied with the running of his estate and the building of his house, not to mention the welfare of his mother who was not a strong woman in body or mind. It was therefore not surprising, Bertram mused, that Ralph should suddenly fall headlong for the charms of this maiden. So be it, he thought. If the young Lord of Fylton Manor, a virgin man, wanted to have a bit of fun with a wild nomad maiden, then he, Bertram, would turn the other way, and his lips would be sealed, for Ralph had far too long been concerned with practical things although he was of an age when he should be enjoying himself.

Ralph and Bertram sat and watched the dancing and celebrations until the early hours, and dawn was breaking as they returned to their camp. Ralph was quiet and pre-occupied. It was almost noon when they stirred, and the travellers' camp along the bank was full of bustle and activity. Ralph arose first and stretched and gulped in the fresh river air. He knew without a doubt what he was going to do. Regardless of Bertram's jibes and nudges he was going to woo Rachel properly. His heart sang and he whistled cheerfully as he rolled up his bed. After he had splashed and freshened up in the river he pulled his tunic over his head and buckled on his belt.

Bertram watched him warily. 'What goes with you this day cousin?' he asked.

Ralph laughed lightheartedly and his brown eyes sparkled, 'I'm off yonder, fellow, to call on that sweet one called Rachel!'

There was something in his tone that puzzled Bertram. 'To call on her! By all that's sacred I know she took your fancy, but think about it man . . . think about it! She's only a humble young maiden whose people are travelling folk, and you . . . you are Lord of Fylton Manor! You are going to call on her? You are going to court her? Why fellow you know you could have any wench you wanted back at Fylton, and here you are going like some great gawping ignorant serf to call on Rachel . . . think about it!'

Ralph became very cross at that. He knew what Bertram was implying – have his way with the maiden and decamp, but this was not the style of Ralph. Maybe this was a sudden short infatuation on his part, nothing like this had ever happened to him before, but he felt he must conduct himself properly. He was rather taken aback with Bertram's outburst. Bertram, whose opinion he had hitherto valued greatly.

He said to Bertram, 'I thank you not for your coarse comments. I am of a mind to woo the maid properly. Maybe something will come of it, maybe not, but I think cousin it is my decision how I go about this.'

This indeed was the Lord of the Manor speaking. Bertram grunted knowingly and busied himself by deliberately poking the ashes of the previous night's fire.

Ralph strode down to the encampment and made his way through the tethered horses until he found someone, a young lad fiddling with some tack. 'Where can I find the family of Rachel?'

The boy directed him and Ralph made his way carefully across the grass past the frames that suspended cooking pots of all shapes and sizes, to a brightly decorated covered cart that stood a little apart from the others. An athletic looking man of mature years with a shock of grey curly hair and deep brown penetrating eyes was standing at the entrance. Ralph recognized him as one of the merry-makers from the previous night.

Ralph approached boldly. 'You are the father of Rachel?'

The man nodded. 'I am Joshua, leader of this group. Rachel is my daughter.'

Ralph was undeterred. 'I have come to call on her. I greatly enjoyed the dancing last night, and I would tell her so.'

Rachel's father looked at him warily. 'Where are you from, young fellow?'

'From Fylton beyond the forest to the east,' Ralph answered civilly.

The older man hesitated, then said, 'Come inside then.'

These travelling folk were well-known for their hospitality and kindness to strangers, and Rachel's father was no exception, but at the same time he was puzzled and worried; what did this young blood want with his Rachel?

Rachel was even prettier in the daylight than in the moonlight, and just the most ordinary movement of her body was graceful and like a dance. Ralph was not disappointed. She showed a becoming blush when he bade her 'Good day' and asked if she would stroll around the encampment with him. She looked demurely at her father for approval. He nodded his assent, for he had decided that Rachel could not possibly come to any harm just being escorted around his neighbours' carts and tents.

Ralph was glad that he had ventured so carefully. He had heard somewhere that these nomadic maidens were very chaste and their virtue guarded jealously by their families. This would be even more so with the daughter of the leader of a travelling group. He was glad that he had called on Joshua in the proper manner. Rachel was a beautiful creature to be honoured and cherished and treated with respect.

They walked for a little while, Rachel talking hesitantly, mostly about her family, but after a little time her shyness left her and her true pleasant personality emerged. She was very knowledgeable about the forest animals and birds and plants. Ralph felt that she liked him too, for last night he had not been unaware of the long glances she had given in his direction whenever she thought his gaze was elsewhere. He walked her back to her parents' cart where her mother gave them each a steaming bowl of camomile tea, which Ralph found quite pleasant. Joshua was sitting outside with a few men; one of them appeared to be younger than the others. Ralph knew instinctively with a lover's heart that this young man was one who also had his eye on Rachel, not only by the way he had looked at her when they sauntered back from their stroll, but also by the way his dark eyes had flashed at Ralph himself. After the tea he bade the family and their friends farewell, but only received a grudging nod from the young man. He knew for certain then that he had a rival.

Ralph was not to be put off. His heart and mind were full of Rachel. He could think of nothing else as he rode back through Fyllwood with Bertram. He knew that he must see Rachel again and his thoughts were full of plans and strategies to find out where the travelling folk were going next. He fully intended to continue his courtship of this maiden who had won his heart. Bertram felt that Ralph was out of his mind and did not mention the subject again, but he had been curious and had watched all the proceedings from along the bank when Ralph had gone to call on Rachel. Bertram's perception was that Ralph would soon forget the girl, but he was to be proved wrong.

Ralph returned to his manorial duties light of step and with new endeavour. His mother noted the change in him and told herself that his trip to Fyllwood had been responsible for this new eagerness. By devious means Ralph had found out the direction in which the travellers' band had progressed after they left their riverside patch, and so it was that one evening late in July he turned up at their encampment which had been set up quite a distance to the east of Fylton, some twelve miles, and well past the lands under the authority of the Abbot of Keynsham, to whose dwelling he had supposedly ridden. This had been surmised by all those from Fylton village who had seen him set his course eastwards earlier in the day. The Lord of the Manor always had much business to discuss with the Abbot and Brothers and was habitually riding to Keynsham.

The travellers' camp was quite near to a place which had formerly been occupied by the Romans centuries before. The Romans had called it Aquae Sulis but the travellers knew it as The Place of the Springs or, as some called it, The Place of the Baths. Some of the residents called it just plain Bath. It was so called because of the natural springs which were there, some of them warm from the earth and reputed to have healing powers to those who bathed in them. It was altogether a magical place, being quite sheltered and almost completely surrounded by rolling green hills. The travelling people were encamped a little way up one of these half-wooded hills, which were plentiful with rabbits and small game. There was fishing too, for the same river that flowed through the Gorge of Goram between Fyllwood Forest and Cliff Town, flowed through the valley below their camp near The Place of the Springs.

The day had been very warm and Ralph was glad to accept the drink of cold herb tea that the travelling people offered him. He scanned the clearing and soon picked out the bright cart of Joshua. He strode towards it and as he did so Rachel emerged. For a moment when she saw him she was stunned, and in that instant Ralph knew that his hard ride had not been in vain. She recovered her composure quickly and greeted him pleasantly. Joshua her father came from behind the cart and greeted him also, but in a strange searching fashion. Ralph suddenly realized that he was lavishly overdressed in the sight of these people; they had always seen him before in hunting garb, but now here he was fully garmented in rich cloth as befitted the Lord of the Manor, complete with the insignia of the house of de Lyon emblazoned upon his breast.

Joshua spoke. 'You never told us young fellow that you were from a noble house.'

'It was of no real consequence to tell you so,' Ralph replied, and Joshua left it at that for the moment.

Ralph meant what he said in all sincerity. To him it had been of no immediacy. He had always been happy to meet and talk with the travelling folk, and he admired their forest lore and hunting skill. They owed him no allegiance. He could see that things might become very tricky, for in his mind was the idea to ask for the hand of Rachel. He wished now, in spite of Bertram's teasing which had later turned to disapproval, that he had confided in and brought the older man with him, and yet again thinking about Bertram's attitude he knew that Bertram would probably not have been much help. One thing he was certain of, he desired his dreams of wooing and winning Rachel to come true.

'What are you going to do for the night?' Joshua asked in his practical way, for he could not envisage Ralph riding all the way back to Fyllwood in the small amount of daylight that was left. Ralph looked as if he were in no hurry and would linger awhile. 'I have a spare cart you can use if needs be . . .'twould be a shame to crumple your fine cloth,' he fingered Ralph's tunic curiously.

'Thank you Joshua. I have my skins packed on my horse, but maybe I will try your cart at that! First though I have it in my heart to speak with you.'

Joshua did not look surprised. 'Come inside then,' he said gruffly.

Rachel was hovering and her father astutely assigned her a task with a neighbour.

When they were alone Ralph spoke straightly. 'I would wed Rachel if I could have your permission.'

Joshua cleared his throat. 'She is promised.'

Ralph's heart missed a beat, and then he remembered the surly young man on his previous visit to the carts. 'Promised?' he echoed.

'Yes. To Jacob, son of my neighbour. They have been promised since they were children.'

Ralph said determinedly, 'Can he really make her happy? She is a beautiful maiden, and I love her truly.'

'No doubt you do,' said Joshua, 'but Rachel is a child of the forests and fields, used to roving life and open air. What sort of life would she have with you, a fine young gent from the nobility, why she'd just be your plaything!'

Ralph grew angry at this. He stood up and knocked his fists together. 'No, no, Joshua, you do not understand. I love her truly and I believe she feels the same for me. Does she feel love for this . . . this Jacob, just because his father is your neighbour and they have grown up together?'

Joshua sighed. 'She is a humble forest girl, you are of noble birth, it could not work . . .' he paused suddenly, 'Tell me, where do you live exactly, and who is your family?'

Ralph stood his ground proudly. 'I am Sir Ralph de Lyon, Lord of the Manor of Fylton to the east of Fyllwood Forest.'

That piece of information really did shake Joshua. He had not expected this slip of a lad to be a full-blown Lord of the Manor. He had privately surmised that he was the son of a noble house, and no more. He sat shaking his head. 'It will not work, it will not work . . .' he kept repeating.

Ralph was in command of the situation now. 'Why not ask Rachel?' he said coolly, 'and if she refuses then so be it. I will ride away with the dawn and trouble you no further.'

Joshua shook his head, 'She is an obedient maiden, she will do as I counsel.'

'Is that fair?' asked Ralph, 'I can give her everything her heart could desire. She will want for nothing. How can you deny her that?'

Joshua eyed him thoughtfully then, this young richly-attired stripling, fully aware suddenly of what this could mean to Rachel, but caution rose to the surface again and he shook his head once more. 'What about your people, your kin? Will they accept you taking back a forest lass to be your Lady?' He laughed ironically, 'No, 'twouldn't be fair, she'd be a laughing-stock!'

Ralph spoke up strongly. 'On my heart I promise you, a laughing-stock she will not be! Rachel, beautiful and so full of grace and loveliness – who could laugh at such wonder? . . . and she will soon adapt. I will show her patience and understanding. She is, after all, the daughter of a leader of men, and well able to hold her head high. Indeed she will be able to teach my sisters a thing or two about seasonings and fine cooking, I'll warrant!'

Joshua marvelled at the optimism of this young nobleman. The chief was a fair man at heart. He had another daughter to be sure, although Rachel was special, she was his favourite. Should he let this young pup have his way? Should he put the choice to Rachel?

'Tell me, my young lord, do you swear to me that you are not playing around? You, who could probably have any maiden you chose among your own kind!

Ralph saw that Joshua was weakening. 'I swear to you by all that's sacred, I am a virgin man; I have never tampered with any maiden. I have been too busy overseeing my land since my father died when I was but eighteen years old. Rachel has captured my heart and I desire to wed her in a good Christian manner!'

So that was it, thought Joshua. That was why he was such a young Lord of the Manor. The fellow seemed honest enough, although he must be told about the manner of travellers' weddings. Outwardly he said, 'What's all this about marrying in a Christian manner? We have our own ceremony, I'll have you know!'

That heartened Ralph. 'Fetch her then. Fetch Rachel and let me ask her before your witness if she will become my wife!'

Rachel agreed starry-eyed. Joshua put all his arguments before her but she was steadfast, and as for learning that Ralph was Lord of the Manor of Fylton, she was surprisingly unastonished. 'He has no clumsy ways, I guessed he was of gentle birth' was all she said.

Joshua could only think that his daughter was as stricken with this disease of love as Ralph was.

'Believe you me Joshua,' said Ralph firmly, 'we will make a good match, and we will learn from each other.'

Joshua became resigned but he still went on muttering under his breath, 'No good will come of it, no good will come of it to be sure!'

News soon passed around the encampment of the match that Rachel was to make with the fine young nobleman. Jacob, to whom she had been promised, had covertly watched the comings and goings from Joshua's cart, and now his worst fears were realized. He too truly loved Rachel and had been dreaming of their wedding day this last few months. Rachel had, of late, not been all that forthcoming with him, and he had put this down to maiden shyness. He knew now that since she had met Ralph she had only had eyes for this stranger. The next morning Joshua approached Jacob's father and put the situation to him. Jacob's father felt disappointed for his son, but as he pointed out it would not benefit Jacob at all to have a wife who was yearning for some other man. There had been no firm promise that Jacob and Rachel would wed, but it had always been the hope of the two fathers that this would happen, and of course of Jacob too. If Ralph had not happened along, Jacob and Rachel probably would have wed eventually. Jacob felt very bitter and let-down, and watched out for a chance to talk to Ralph, He stormed up to Ralph angrily when the young lord was tending his horse.

'What right have you, a stranger, to come and take Rachel? She is promised to me . . . ME!' He beat his chest with fervour and was about to strike Ralph, but Ralph caught his arm, not unkindly.

'I'm sorry, Jacob, but she has chosen me. There is no more to be said!'

Jacob glowered and slunk off leaving Ralph feeling uneasy, but there was nothing he could do about it, and soon his mind was once again filled with thoughts of joy that Rachel was shortly to be his.

They had a colourful traditional forest wedding, and Ralph was deeply impressed at the solemnity of the ritual, especially when they came to the part where one of the elders cut both his and Rachel's wrists cleanly and expertly, and then tied them tightly together to signify that their blood was now forever mingled and they were as one. Joshua had given his daughter a beautiful white horse, and as they rode off together towards Fylton there were many well-wishers from the travellers to wave them off, although Rachel's mother wept silently and her father was still musing quietly to himself, 'No good will come of it.'

The sullen young Jacob showed himself too. 'Farewell Rachel. I cannot wish you luck. You have broken my heart, and your father's promise. For that you will not be happy!'

It was almost like a curse and Rachel shuddered for a moment, but soon recovered when one of the old women called out cheerfully, 'May you have many babes. May the sun never set on your happiness!'

The surprise at Fylton was equal to that at The Place of the Springs. Ralph's mother was not too pleased. How would this young wild and free maiden fit into the household? His sisters, however, were delighted and excited. This was something quite novel and different from their usual routine, and Rachel was very amenable. Bertram, when he knew, was shocked. 'I never thought you'd be so daft!' was all he could say, although silently he hoped it would be all right for Ralph. He was fond of his young kinsman.

After the initial excitement Ralph announced that they were also to have a Christian marriage ceremony, in the Fylton village Church of St Gregory, and Brother Michael officiated. It was not a sumptious affair, but important enough for most of the villagers to come to see their Lord wed. Rachel had willingly agreed to this for she was a pleasant lass and most people found her easy to get on with.

Ralph ordered some fine new clothes for his bride and she eventually got used to wearing heavier richer robes, but shoes on her feet were a different matter. She had run barefoot all her life, and for her feet to be suddenly cramped into the light little French shoes that Ralph had ordered from London was quite an exasperating experience. She would wear them for half an hour and then cast them aside, and it became quite usual to see the Lady of the Manor descending the staircase at Lyons Court with great style in her fine new dresses, but with bare feet. Ralph was highly amused at this. It only made him love his Rachel more, but there were the older women who whispered and gossiped about how unseemly this was. Rachel also spent a lot of her time in the open air in the gardens and meadows around the house, even when the weather was inclement. She had some difficulty in getting accustomed to living in a house.

At Christmas Rachel knew she was to have a child. Ralph was overjoyed, and even his mother became more approachable, plying her daughter-in-law with all kinds of special foods and treats, and advice. Rachel in her sweetness accepted it all, but had her own ideas about childbirth. She could not understand the fuss that Ralph's household was making about the expected event. At this time she missed her mother, for she knew that were she back at one of the encampments, when her time came, she and her mother or an aunt would have made off to the forest and delivered the babe swiftly and surely with the minimum of fuss. However, Rachel, loving Ralph as she did, made her own concessions to his way of life, and allowed all the trappings and fuss that accompanied the birth of a child of the Lord of the Manor, and a son and heir it turned out to be. He was a fine chubby boy, "A real good'un!" to echo the words of the village woman, Annie, who acted as midwife at most of the births in Fylton.

Ralph was highly delighted with his son and readily agreed when Rachel mentioned her preference for the boy to be named Joshua after her father, although there were more frowns from Ralph's mother. She wanted the child to be called Thomas after her father! A final compromise was reached by having the child baptized Thomas Joshua, but thereafter Ralph and Rachel referred to their son as Joshua.

On the whole though, with the birth of this son and heir, the de Lyon household and the village of Fylton settled down to the acceptance of Rachel in their midst. In fact as one sagacious liegeman put it, ''Tis a very good thing to mix the blood a bit!'

Rachel was certainly well-liked throughout the village, and did her utmost to uphold the traditions of the de Lyon household, despite her barefoot comings and goings. When she embarked on frequent excursions outside the house, from her desire to be in the fresh air, she grew to know quite a number of the village folk as they worked in the fields. She personally cultivated a wondrous kitchen garden patch, and grew vegetables and soft fruits which delighted the family cook, in addition to reviving and replanning the existing herb-garden with plants that produced most unusual flavours and seasoning. She sometimes went riding on her magnificent white horse, and Ralph often accompanied her on these rides, for he well understood her need to be in the open. The marriage was working well, there was no doubt about it. With true love they each understood the other's requirements,

One day in the spring when young Master Joshua was but eight months old, word came to Rachel that the travellers were in Fyllwood Forest again. She left her baby son with a maidservant and rushed to find Ralph to ask him to accompany her to the forest. She felt a great need to see her people again and tell them the news of baby Joshua. Ralph agreed willingly and they set off. One thing that Rachel had mastered and that was wearing riding boots. Ralph had commissioned the village shoemaker to make her a pair of riding boots of the softest leather he could find. The man had been very conscientious in his task to measure her feet precisely, and the finished boots fitted perfectly. Whenever she rode out with Ralph she felt very proud of her boots, and although she did not know it, it subdued quite a lot of the careless servant tittle-tattle of how she ran barefoot around Lyons Court.

As they rode lightheartedly into Fyllwood that day there

was no hint of the tragedy that was to ensue. They were making for the clearing by the river, for that was where her kinsfolk would be, and indeed it was a place that had happy memories, for this was where they had first set eyes upon each other. They had been riding along a rough track for about half an hour when Rachel espied a special wild herb that she needed for her garden. They both dismounted and Ralph bent to help her with it when suddenly there was a twang and a buzz and Rachel fell forward on her face, gasping and choking with an arrow solidly pierced through her back to her breast. Ralph bent frantically to support her and as he did so there was blood frothing at her lips as she struggled to breathe. Her eyes were wild with pain and fear like those of a trapped young animal, as she clung to him, and he knew without a doubt in that moment that she would soon be beyond earthly help. As he cradled her she attempted to speak: 'Ralph . . . you have made me . . . so happy . . . the babe . . . care for him well . . . you . . .' and then suddenly the life left her, his beautiful once so animated Rachel lay dead in his arms.

Afterwards Ralph could not remember how long he was there in the forest holding her to him. He was frozen in that instant of grief and horror. He was in shock. The forest stood in all its glory as usual, the same forest they had ridden through so full of joy a little previously, and yet it did not seem to be part of his perception any more. He was looking at his surroundings and yet they were distant, the forest sounds were faint as if coming from far away. He eventually forced himself to move and in doing so brought his senses back to reality. He tried to think, he must find someone to help. Would that he had brought a liege man with him. In fact he nearly had, and then had changed his mind and deemed it best that he went alone with his wife to see the travellers. That was it. He would find the travellers as quickly as possible, but wait . . . who had killed Rachel? Who had done this murderous deed? Why? Was he in danger? As for this last question he did not care, he felt he wanted to die too now that his beloved was dead. Somehow he got to the clearing and found the travellers. He had left Rachel lying where she had fallen and covered her with a horse-cloth. Her white horse he took along with him.

When Joshua espied him and the horse he knew with the quick intuition of his kind that all was not well. He ran to greet Ralph, and it did not take many halting words from Ralph for Joshua to realize what had happened.

'Oh my glory, oh my glory!' Joshua beat his chest with woe, 'Who would do such a thing? Who would do this awful thing?' He stopped with a sudden thought, and dashed across the encampment to one of the carts. He emerged holding Jacob by the scruff of the neck. Jacob was sobbing violently and making no resistance.

'I saw him come back a while since,' said Joshua, 'and I thought he was acting strange. I knew something had happened!'

Jacob spoke then. 'I never meant to hit her, on God's oath. I never meant to. I was aiming for him,' he looked at Ralph. 'He stole my maiden and I wanted to repay him for all the hurt he'd done me. I was only going to wing him. I never thought it would end like this!'

In spite of his grief and shock Ralph felt at that moment that he could willingly have struck Jacob down, killed him there and then with the heavy side-sword he always carried. He struggled to control himself. It was this embittered young man who had done the dreadful deed without a doubt. Jacob was grovelling at his feet now, 'Please, please forgive me ... I'll do anything, anything...' his voice faltered away as he saw how Ralph was looking at him.

'Nothing can bring her back. My wife, the mother of my child. Because of you my child is now motherless!'

At that Jacob beat the earth, and Joshua who had been listening to all this cried out with a loud voice, 'I knew no good would come of it. I told you no good would come of it!'

Quite a few travelling folk were now gathered around them, for the bad news had travelled swiftly. Rachel's mother was wailing, as were all the women, and presently a group of Joshua's friends led Jacob roughly away. Jacob made no resistance.

'What will they do with him?' Ralph asked.

'He will be properly punished. We shall hold our own court,' Joshua replied.

That sounded ominous and Ralph knew without a doubt that Jacob would be put to death.

They brought Rachel's body home to Fylton on a rough litter, quickly and deftly made from forest vines. Fylton was a saddened village that spring, and Ralph felt all the time as if he were living through a bad dream, but he kept having to tell himself that the dream was very real indeed. Joshua had accompaned him on the sad journey back through Fyllwood. 'I would dearly love to see the boy,' he had said when he had asked Ralph if he should accompany him to Fylton.

There were tears in the man's eyes when Ralph told him they had named the baby after him.

'What a wonderful thing it is,' he said through his tears, 'to have a future Lord of the Manor named after me.'

'You forget,' said Ralph realistically, 'you are a Lord of the Manor in your own style, for are you not the leader of your travelling group?'

In the years that followed, Ralph never remarried. His son grew tall and strong, a lad to be proud of. When Ralph died and he became Lord of the Manor he was every inch of what that role demanded. What Ralph had said of the travellers' leader was true, for young Thomas Joshua had in his blood the best of two cultures. Throughout his life he was greatly loved and revered by the villagers of Fylton for his strength of character and fairness of decision.

6

The Loss of the Medallion

It was in the year 1345 that Joshua the Just, as he was affectionately called by the villagers of Fylton, died. Fylton was very similar to the village it had been a century before. The Potters were still at Whyte Cross Farm, the descendants of Davold, the Blessed family, were still at Fyllwood Farm, and the de Lyon family were well represented at Lyons Court, but many changes were to come. Sir Joshua had left three sons, and the eldest boy, Thomas, was the new Lord of the Manor. The villagers at Fylton had become a well-integrated mixture of Norman and Saxon ancestry, and the earlier animosity towards the invaders had now almost dissolved.

The head of the household at Fyllwood Farm was Arnold Blessed, and it was he who now wore the golden medallion of Caerdragon that had been passed down through his family so constantly since the time of Davold. Arnold was a quiet man, rather taciturn of nature. He got on well enough with his neighbours at Lyons Court, and, because he knew not of it, and because the connection was remote and far back in time, he never thought of the de Lyon family as being kinsmen. Arnold's family were mainly of Saxon stock and yeomen of the land, and although they were friendly with the de Lyon family they regarded the people at Lyons Court as being quite different from them. Their lifestyle was different. The de Lyons were known at Court and mingled with the aristocracy, but like Arnold's family they also enjoyed the patronage of the Abbot of Keynsham who was a powerful figure thereabouts. The Blessed family lived in a simple fashion, but the farm was prosperous and they kept servants. The Abbot of Keynsham's latest interest at Fylton was more enlargement and improvement for the church. Back in the last century the chancel had been lengthened, and at about the start of the present century a large window had been installed at the eastern end. Now the Abbot had plans to widen the church by filling in the cruciform shape with a south aisle leading to a small chapel at the east end. This small chapel was intended exclusively for the use of the Lord of the Manor and church dignitaries, and young Sir Thomas was very keen to assist with this project. It meant quite a lot of structural work, for most of the southern wall was to be taken down and moved back to allow for the proposed south aisle, and the Abbot had some excellent stone-masons he could call upon for the intricate work, but some local heavy labour was needed in addition.

It was with this purpose in mind that Sir Thomas called on Arnold one chill December day in 1347. Arnold readily agreed to supply what assistance he could. Although he only had four labourers he could release a couple of them to help with the work at St Gregory's from time to time. He was happy enough to help the church and although he did not live in the village he and his wife Esther and their children attended church every Sunday when they enjoyed the pleasant drive from the edge of Fyllwood along the rough track beneath the hills on one side and past the old original Fylton village ruins on the other side.

On such a Sunday morning Arnold was driving to church with his family when one of the cart wheels became stuck in some soft mud. It had been raining heavily although the morn was now fair and bright. Cursing through his teeth Arnold jumped down from his seat, bidding Esther his wife to hold the reins while he searched for some roughage to put under the wheel. After about ten minutes he managed to get the cart wheel turning and free, and swung himself up to take over the reins again. They had trotted about twenty yards when Esther suddenly noticed that his Caerdragon medallion was missing. They drove back to the spot where they had been bogged down, but there was no trace of the medallion. The mud was very soft and Arnold poked at it frantically with a stick. Esther climbed down to help him but to no avail. It was hopeless and for all they knew they could have been pushing the medallion deeper into the quagmire. Arnold was desolate as they made their way to church. Esther, who was of an optimistic nature, suggested they might look again on the way back. This they did, but nothing yielded up from the mud except a few stones.

Arnold blamed himself. He had noticed of late that the leather cord on which the medallion had been strung was getting soft and thin in places, and he had decided that he must replace the cord fairly soon. In its history the medallion's cord had been replaced several times. Arnold remembered his father telling him of how his grandfather had fitted a strong new cord when on one occasion he had nearly lost the precious heirloom, and now he, Arnold, had lost it for ever through his own negligence. Till the day he died Arnold was to look at that spot on the track whenever he passed it, hoping to see a glint of gold. The knowledge that he had lost his family's most treasured possession, something that dated back at least to the time of the Norman occupation, filled him with deep grief. There was now no medallion to hand on to his eldest son Giles, and the legend that went with it, the legend of prosperity and good fortune, was no longer there to make his family special. Even their very name, Blessed, now seemed to be a mockery.

Arnold's only daughter Rosalind, who was thirteen years old, was very interested in the church buildings, and especially in the old tapestries in the church, some of them several hundred years old, it was rumoured. Indeed one of them was purported to have been stitched by the wife of Davold, the builder of Fyllwood Farm. Rosalind was a romantic by nature, like most young girls of her age, and whenever she went to church with the family, she loved to look around her at all the things associated with her family and Fylton. She would often linger behind after a church service while the family were gossiping with others in the church porch. One Sabbath morning Rosalind decided to explore the steep stone steps that led up to the tower. She had climbed halfway up when suddenly a disturbed bird fluttered about her face, causing her to lose her balance and to bounce and crash heavily to the bottom of the steps. She made no noise so it was some little time before the family missed her and eventually discovered her in a crumpled heap. She was unconscious and it took a few minutes for her to come round, after they had patted her wan cheeks and rubbed her cold hands. She whimpered and tried to stir but her father stopped her. He could see by the way she was lying that something was terribly wrong with her back and legs, and although she was very frightened she did not seem to be feeling much pain. The village apothecary Tom Swallow, a learned capable fellow, was summoned and he gave her a soothing potion. She was then gently lifted on to a litter to be borne home as carefully as possible.

Arnold's heart was sore. Rosalind would never walk again, her back was broken. Tom Swallow had summoned a knowledgeable friend who gave the verdict. She lay all day on her couch like a broken bird. Sometimes for a change her brothers and sisters would take her for a ride in the handcart that Arnold had carefully fashioned for her, but Rosalind was changed. No longer was she the bright eager young creature on the threshold of life. Arnold constantly had nightmares when he would dream of Rosalind as a little girl, golden curls dancing as she skipped prettily down the track from the farmhouse to greet him when he returned home across the fields. He felt in some way that he was to blame for this catastrophe, he felt it was all to do with the loss of the Caerdragon medallion.

It was true that in the years that followed, the farm at Fyllwood became less and less prosperous, for in 1348 a terrible pestilence swept through the land. The Black Death was to become a fatal illness for a large proportion of the population of England. Labour became scarce for the plague did not differentiate between the young or the old, the rich or the poor. Many young men were taken in their prime. As a result of this, labour became scarce and wages rose by about fifty percent, for nowadays the villeins who served under their lords were paid wages, unlike the serfs, bondmen and liegemen of a hundred and fifty years earlier. The wages had been quite frugal before the Black Death, but with its advent some labourers became freeholders, buying land quite cheaply from their lords, as the latter did not have sufficient men to work their large areas of land. Although Arnold's farm was not so extensive as Lyons Court he was no exception and he lost a couple of labourers to the plague. He simply could not afford to replace them with the wages that were now being paid. His eldest son Giles also fell victim to the pestilence, but surprisingly the rest of the family, including Rosalind, survived. These were sorry times indeed, and Fyllwood Farm gradually became very run down.

With all the deaths there was a need to bury more bodies, and Father Berengere, the present Abbot of Keynsham, gave instructions that a certain patch of church land slightly to the south of St Gregory's should be used for this purpose. The piece of land became known as Black Acre.

The pestilence had been profuse in Brigstowe. In this city they sequestered a particular patch of land belonging to the parish of St James to inter the countless plague-infected bodies. There were many churches to be found in the City of Brigstowe and St James was one of the most ancient and also most central. On the southern outskirts of the city near the track which led to Fylton stood the Priory of the Order of the Templars or the Poor Knights of Our Lord. This foundation had been there for nigh on two hundred years, since the time of the first Sir David de Lyon. The members of the Order, like the second Sir David, had originally been Crusaders, trained in war, but wounded or sick, and unlike Sir David without worldy goods. They had been given land on which to build their priories and to till and provide for themselves, and thus the Order had been born. This particular foundation had started off as marshy land originally owned by Robert of Caen, the builder of Brigstowe Castle. The members of the Order had painstakingly drained and worked the land called The Meads, later to be known as Templars' Meads. The Brothers Templar from this foundation had been very charitable in assisting the townsfolk of Brigstowe at the time of the plague. Their priory was overflowing with the sick and dying, and invariably many Brothers Templar had also succumbed to the deathly disease. In future years the once well-founded priory would never be the same and would eventually crumble and lessen.

Eight or nine miles to the south of Fylton the Knights Templar had also founded another priory on a high hill which they called Templars of Clouds, subsequently shortened by the village folk to Temple Cloud. This foundation served the many poor travellers and devout pilgrims who passed through its portals for rest and refreshment while on the road to Glastonbury, the Place of the Holy Thorn. Legend had it that Joseph of Arimathea himself had planted the Thorn for his nephew, the Christ Jesus, when long long ago he had visited the verdant hills of what was called the Summer Country. Many pilgrims also passed through Fylton these days and Brother Paul, the present village priest, was always happy to provide bed and board in the annexe at Lyons Court where he dwelt. Formerly village priests had lived in the church, but nowadays the Manor house provided their shelter.

When the pestilence had lessened and the countryside began to return to normality it was officially estimated by the wise ones of the realm that almost a third of the population of England had been wiped out. Things were certainly different at Fylton. The Potters had gone from Whyte Cross, their number diminished by the plague. The plans by the Abbot of Keynsham and Sir Thomas de Lyon for the extension and widening of the church had been temporarily abandoned, so great was the effect of the plague, and they would not live to see their plans eventually brought into beings. Fyllwood Farm had fallen into disrepair. Arnold Blessed died in 1350 of a constantly recurring painful stomach ulcer.

Tom Swallow the apothecary had shaken his head many times over Arnold. He had mixed the right potions, potions that had healed other folk with the same ailment, but it seemed that Arnold did not respond because he did not want to. He was an unhappy man, Tom had noticed, full of bitterness and sharp words, except with his crippled daughter Rosalind. Esther his wife and his other children had long since accepted the constantly despondent Arnold. Esther was a good wife, keeping a full larder and a clean house, but in spite of her practical support, her suggestions and efforts, the farm fell into even greater ruin after the plague. It was a fact that the plague had not helped much, but some other small farmers had survived. It was evident that Arnold had long since lost his taste for life. He had always been a rather quiet man, but ever since the loss of the medallion and Rosalind's terrible accident he had been a changed man, lost in himself and his troubles. It seemed as though he had become bound permanently in a self-fulfilling prophecy of ill-fortune. The only brightness in his life had been his "Rosie" as he called Rosalind.

Rosalind lived until she was twenty-three years old, and during the time between her accident and her death in 1357, seven years after her father's demise, she had become an adept needlewoman, inspired by the intricate stitching she had so often admired in the church tapestries. In the beginning she had found her accident to be a life-sapping tragedy, but gradually she had changed, and had become a more tranquil person, more accepting of everything and everyone, including her father. Esther called her "My little saint", and in an empathic way shared Rosalind's acceptance of her plight as Arnold never could. After Rosalind's death Esther moved out of Fyllwood Farm to a dwelling in Fylton village near the church. It had become impossible for her to manage the very run-down ancient farm that Fyllwood had become. Her remaining two sons were working at Lyons Court, for the old farm had not been self-supporting for years. Esther felt very sad about leaving the old homestead to decay, the walls crumbling and the roof developing bigger holes, but there was nothing she could do about it. The forest was slowly encroaching on the land too. For a while after Esther and her family left, the Brothers from Keynsham Abbey had endeavoured to work the fields, but labour had become so scarce that eventually circumstanaces dictated that their hands were needed elsewhere and nearer home.

In the years that followed, the original plans for the enlargement of St Gregory's were put into operation, and the work began in the 1380s and was completed by 1395. Sir Thomas was dead, but his son, another Sir Thomas, enthusiastically pursued the task his father had been unable to complete. St Gregory's was now much bigger with a new south porch as well as an additional south aisle. With these alterations it was no longer its original cruciform shape. The steps to the top of the tower where Rosalind Blessed's life had been changed so drastically were now enclosed within the building. At the end of the new south aisle where it formed a junction with the original south transept a private chapel had been built, specifically for the Lord of the Manor and his family. Sir Thomas and his family sat comfortably in this chapel every Sabbath, set apart from the village folk who listened to the service in the main body of the church. There were always plenty of clean rushes on the floor, and since the renovation some rough forms for seating had been placed. Hitherto people had stood for the services, but now Fylton was following the pattern of other wealthier churches by providing the luxury of seating. The Lord of the Manor's chapel was very ornate. A particularly skilled carpenter named Edwin Burcomb, a fellow from beyond the hills recommended by passing pilgrims to Brother Cedric the present incumbent, had been employed to carve the screen-work between the chapel and the chancel, and also the adjoining screen between the chapel and the former south transept. The delicate wooden tracery was a joy to behold, and indeed the fame of Edwin Burcomb had led him to undertake some similar fine screen-carving for other village churches in the region called the Summer Country.

For many years after St Gregory's was extended and rebuilt, the buildings at Fyllwood Farm fell into greater ruin. Several people had tried to reclaim the land and had plans for renewing the old farmhouse, but they had all failed. The place had certainly not been fit for human habitation for a very long time. Indeed the last people who had tried to save the land from the embracing tentacles of the forest had also used what was formerly the kitchen as a sty for their pigs. It seemed that Fyllwood Farm was doomed.

To the east of Fyllwood another farm had already been saved from former desolation. Whytecross House had been left to moulder for quite a few years, for the plague had taken most of the Potter family except for two young sons who were packed off to an aunt in Bath. Whytecross had had new occupants since 1378, when a young man called Christopher Chase had returned from war. He had seen service in France and also in Ireland, and he had originally joined the militia as a young man of seventeen. He was a Fylton lad, an orphan, for like many others most of his family had been wiped out in the great plague in 1348 when he was an infant. He had seen some of the world and foreign places, but throughout his travels his one desire had been to return home to the land.

He had seen opportunities at Whytecross which had become run-down, though nothing like as bad as Fyllwood had become. He had married a local lass, Molly Cousins and they had reared a family of three sons and two daughters. Christopher Chase died in 1421 at the age of seventy-three, and Whytecross had been left in the capable hands of his eldest son, also Christopher, who now had children of his own. Through his father's hard work and foresight Whytecross had become a thriving livelihood, and looked like remaining so while the Chase family were in occupation. The realm was gradually recovering from the scourge.

It took a good one hundred and fifty years for the population of England to become reinstated in numbers equivalent to those prior to the Black Death, and in 1508 a young man named Samuel Candler had plans for rebuilding Fyllwood Farm and reclaiming the land. Samuel had worked at the Manor house since he was a boy and the story of the saving of Whytecross Farm from its former desolation was well known to him. He cherished dreams of one day owning his own land and riding around it giving orders. He was ambitious and prepared to work hard to achieve his dream. Many Fylton folk shook their heads over Samuel's plans. The place had sunk into real disrepair and it was barren and isolated on the edge of the forest which had all but engulfed it. It would need complete rebuilding. Better to leave it to the forest, some said, but Samuel was bright with youth's optimism. He had a widowed mother and also three strong younger brothers who were willing to aid him in this heavy undertaking.

The de Lyons were no longer Lords of the Manor, for back in 1499 the family had been without heirs except for a daughter, Edith, who had married a country gentleman named Thomas Holbeach. The Holbeach family now administered the Fylton lands at Lyons Court, and Thomas Holbeach had his doubts when Samuel put his plans for Fyllwood to him, but he gave the fellow his blessing. If Samuel could bring the ancient farm back to life, if he could save the land from certain wilderness, then this was all to the good, so he gave Samuel stones from his stone-yard, and some timber, and let him borrow tools and implements from Lyons Court in return for a measured number of hours of Samuel's labour. His younger brothers worked full time at Lyons Court, but whenever they could they worked hard and long with Samuel on the ancient farm, and at the end of three years the place was just about habitable. His mother, who was still in early middle age, was delighted, and set about the furnishings with gusto. There was still quite a lot of the house to be renewed, but for the moment they were happy to live in a few rooms, and the fine old main hall that had been restored with great care. Samuel's next task was to start clearing the land.

Samuel had been in possession of Fyllwood Farm for quite a length of time when he had a mind to get wed. The farmstead had taken on a new life with its restoration now complete and the pastures neat and manageable; Samuel felt there was a need for children's laughter about the place. The maid who caught his fancy was Bertha Lea, a comely smiling girl from Charlton, a village a few miles to the east of Fylton, between Fylton and Keynsham. Samuel had caught view of Bertha several times when he had ridden across to Charlton for wool for his mother to weave. There were some fine sheep flocks on the Charlton Meads and the wool was of especially good quality for spinning. Bertha was a milk-maid, strong and capable as she trod the lanes comfortably with her yoke of full wooden milk pails. She was good-tempered too. What more could a man want? Bertha accepted Samuel's proposal of marriage readily for she knew she had a good catch. When Samuel wed, his brothers who had long since discontinued working at Lyons Court, stayed on at Fyllwood, for there was plenty of room, but sadly his mother died of a fever a month before his first child was born. They had all looked forward greatly to the birth, but the baby, a girl, was sickly and died when she was barely a week old. Bertha was a strong girl and within a year she was pregnant again. Samuel was overjoyed, especially when the child turned out to be a healthy bouncing boy whom they called Jack. Samuel had a son and heir now, and life was good.

One of his brothers had left the farm a year since, also to get married and to rent a smallholding of his own in Bishopswerde, a tiny hamlet just down the lane from Fyllwood. Another had enlisted in the militia and gone off to see the world, but Samuel's youngest brother, Rufus, stayed on. Samuel was easygoing; as long as his brother needed a home, Fyllwood would be there for him, though no doubt he would strike out on his own one day as the other brothers had. In the meantime he was glad of the help, although the farm was now doing so well he had taken on another couple of farmhands full time. Samuel's easy acceptance of the situation was to prove to be tragically miscalculated.

It was in the haymaking season when he came across them, in the clearing at the rear of the house with only the forest trees to bear witness to their treachery. Rufus and Bertha in the act of love. Samuel was a proud fellow and quick-tempered when principles were at stake. He dashed full tilt with rage at Rufus with the heavy wooden fork he had in his hands. 'You evil rat . . . despoiler of the holy sacraments . . . adulterer . . .'

Rufus was halfway to his feet trying to adjust his breeches when the fork caught him hard and wicked in the chest, pinning him against the ground. The prongs were very sharp and one had pierced right through his heart and he screamed in agony. The blood gushed out frothily for a half-minute before he died. Bertha had run to the house and was crouching in the doorway shaking and shocked when Samuel came for her. He thought he would throttle her. Then Baby Jack started crying in the kitchen behind her. That brought Samuel to his senses.

He made signs to her with his hands and choked out, 'Go inside woman, the child needs you.'

She went inside and pulled the baby from his cradle to quieten him. She was still very shaken, but she looked at Samuel defensively. 'You've killed him! You've murdered your own brother!'

Samuel's tone was hard, 'And with good reason too, the cunning toad!' He began to think then. How long had this deceit been going on? He asked her this aloud.

Bertha was a simple girl. In any circumstance she had no guile. 'Since we were wed,' she answered.

Samuel couldn't take this in. 'Since we were wed?' he asked unbelievingly.

'Yes.' She cast her eyes down to the well-scrubbed flagstones. These were still slightly damp from the labour she had been at when Rufus had come in unexpectedly and swept her out of the kitchen.

Samuel's forefinger was shaking as he pointed to the babe in her arms. 'Does this mean that he is not my son?'

She shrugged her shoulders. 'Could be, could be not.'

That enraged Samuel. 'You mean you don't know!'

She shrugged again. 'What does it matter. The blood's the same!'

In that one moment he saw Bertha for what she was, an ignorant farm girl, eager for the pleasure of the moment, with no higher principles or care for the result of her actions.

Samuel was calm now and without passion. He said coldly, 'Get out!'

She stood her ground. She felt he couldn't mean it. She was too good a wife, she ran the farmhouse too well. He couldn't do without her. She was very wrong.

'Get out and take the child. Go on woman . . .' he threw the infant's woollen shawl at her, 'Get out and never step inside these doors again. You've defiled our home and my good name. I want nothing more of you or the child. Get out . . . go on!' He moved menacingly nearer and she went as she was. Luckily the weather was warm and the day was young. He heard later that she'd gone back to kinsfolk at Charlton, had walked all the way there with the babe in her arms.

The troopers came for him two days later. He had buried his brother Rufus where he lay. At the trial the judge was lenient, for no decent man wants an adulterous wife, and the brother deserved his fate. Afterwards Samuel returned to Fyllwood Farm but his feelings were no longer centred on his ambitions. He sent his hired helpers away and lived alone as a hermit for the rest of his life, just scratching a living from his fields. He died at quite an early age, some said of malnutrition, others said of despair, for since that tragic day when his hopes and dreams had been so cruelly diminished he had lost his motivation. Fyllwood Farm fell into ruin once again.

In 1509 Henry the Eighth had come to the throne and his reign was to bring many far-reaching changes in the kingdom. The monarch wielded a great deal of power over the church through his cardinal, Wolsey, but his attitude to marriage and divorce and his quarrel with Rome finally ended with Henry demanding complete power over the church in England. Thus came about the dissolution of the monasteries, and on 23 January 1539 the Abbey of the Blessed Mary at Keynsham was no more, the Abbot stripped of his power.

Although the Manor at Fylton had been under the patronage of Keynsham Abbey it somehow survived the dissolution. The Holbeach family administered the Fylton lands at Lyons Court quite efficiently and the Church of St Gregory did not suffer too greatly for the loss of its mother abbey, for the Holbeachs were good Christians, true upholders of the faith, and they undertook to still provide for the upkeep of the church and its priest. Many terrible things had happened in other churches during this period but St Gregory's had not fared too badly. The only thing that disappeared from the church after the King's men had paid it a visit, shortly after the demise of Keynsham Abbey, was a fine coloured statue of the Virgin which had stood on a ledge over the inner entrance door from the south porch. There were nasty tales of the sacking of priceless church treasures, the melting down of medieval metalwork, pillaging and burning of libraries during the downfall of England's monasteries, but Fylton had never been a rich parish, so perhaps did not pose too great a threat to the new order envisaged by the monarch. The simple Holy Water stoup in the south porch was untouched, whereas many other churches had been deprived of their more ornate and expensive stoups.

The priest at St Gregory's, Brother Aldous, had continued his ministry according to his vows although he was now without an Abbot to direct his perseverance, and he had been told in no uncertain way by the King's men that he was now fully answerable to the Crown in his duties. Brother Aldous was a pious man who seemed to accept all happenings as the will of God, and so it was that the downfall of the monasteries, an event that was to change the course of English history in a remarkable way, caused only a few ripples in the everyday life of Fylton village, or Whytechurch, as many folk called it nowadays. The name had persisted stubbornly with some of the villagers, especially those of Saxon descent, and although the occasional pilgrim passing through might become confused that the village had two names, inhabitants lived with the disparity quite comfortably. At Lyons Court the Holbeach family did to a certain extent miss the co-operation and friendship of the Keynsham Abbot and Brothers, but Thomas Holbeach, son of Edith de Lyon and the first Thomas Holbeach was an independent man and welcomed the chance to manage the village his way, without the constant direction of a mother abbey. The fact that he was not an aristocrat was another point in his favour, for the monarch only felt threatened by the very powerful and the aristocratic. So the Crown was content to allow the village to be administered by the Holbeach family, happy that as good Christians they would be responsible for the stipend of its priest, albeit Brother Aldous was now answerable to King Henry, as the monarch stipulated all good Englishmen should be.

However, although Lyons Court and St Gregory's appeared to have survived the dissolution quite well, and on the face of it the Holbeachs and Brother Aldous appeared to be in full co-operation with the monarch, there were tales whispered between the village folk that lots of "happenings" were hidden from the general gaze. For instance why should a tunnel need to be dug between the church and Lyons Court? It was but a minute's journey across the fields; why should humans burrow like moles when they could stride the pastures? Unless they had something to hide! The rumour was, at one time, that Brother

Aldous and Thomas Holbeach between them managed to hide, and eventually help escape, priests and persons on the run from the King's men. Folk who had found disfavour with the Crown, for the King made many enemies when he loosed his men on the monasteries. Outwardly though the village seemed acquiescent enough to Henry's new dictates.

Secretly there were many funny happenings and comings and goings in the tunnel. Rumour also had it that there was a further tunnel leading from the church to The White Hart, an old alehouse to the east. Packhorses and travelling carts called regularly at The White Hart so strangers there were a common sight, as indeed they were at Lyons Court where pilgrims had always been, and were still, offered shelter in one wing of the house. Nobody spoke openly of these matters but folk whispered between trusted friends and in the privacy of their families. Thomas Holbeach was a respected Lord of the Manor, nobody would say otherwise, and he managed the village and its lands well. Also most of the village folk were in his employ or enjoyed his patronage. This was the age of new men, not necessarily aristocrats.

Another such man was John Smyth, a rich shipping merchant from the city of Bristowe, formerly called Brigstowe, the place to the north of Fylton or Whytechurch. In 1545 John Smyth purchased an estate at Ashton, a village to the west of Fylton-Whytechurch. John Smyth was a City Alderman, and it was not uncommon nowadays for officials from the city's administration to indulge in buying as much land as possible. With the fall of the monasteries and the sharing out of the many spoils, these city fathers gained a lot for their city, and also for themselves. John Smyth had sprung from humble beginnings; the son of a hooper, he had been apprenticed to a Bristowe merchant in his youth, worked hard, and had become a successful merchant himself.

Bristowe was now a thriving seaport, especially with the Spanish trade, and all manner of goods were brought to the city by ship. There were everyday commodities like wood and cotton and iron ore, but also goods to satisfy the luxurious tastes of the rich and the noble-born, things like French and Spanish wines, figs and sugar. The common folk at this time were mostly self-supporting, and tradesmen in the towns were employed almost exclusively in providing services for the wealthy and aristocratic; tradesmen such as carpenters and tanners and furniture makers. Although John Smyth purchased the estate at Ashton for nine hundred and twenty pounds, a goodly sum, he continued to live in Bristowe where his business was situated, in Corn Street, and from 1549 in Small Street. Both these streets lay under the western lee of Bristowe Castle and near to the river where his ship *The Trynyte Smyth* came regularly to harbour. The estate at Ashton included a manor house and a large amount of land, and later John Smyth added some more land bought from the Crown as a result of the dissolution of Bath Priory. His thirst for land increased and he purchased more acres in Keynsham and Wookey to the south, for in the years that followed the break-up of the monasteries, abbeys and priories and their power, there were many opportunities for land acquisition by merchant princes from seaports such as Bristowe.

John Smyth, like Thomas Holbeach, was a man of the new age and he became Mayor of Bristowe in 1547 and again in 1554. He did not travel much to Ashton Court, the name used for this big new estate he had acquired, but he sometimes entertained his merchant friends there. The drawback to living there on a regular basis was that the roads out of Bristowe to Ashton were not good, and the only bridge that spanned the river was the old wooden Bristowe Bridge. This entailed a long ride round the parish of Redclyffe where stood a magnificent church, and through the village of Bedmynster to Ashton. If the weather was bad then the tracks were even worse, and on his death John Smyth left money for improving the road from Bedmynster to Ashton.

John Smyth had two sons, Hugh and Matthew, and like the sons of many of the self-made rich they had proved troublesome to their father, in particular Hugh, who seemed to be the main instigator of the troubles they got into. As befitted the sons of gentlemen of means, Hugh and Matthew Smyth had been sent to Oxford, although they received no degrees and went later to the Inns of Court in London to become trained as lawyers. At Oxford University they had become very unpopular, getting into many scrapes and being continually berated by their tutor, Jeremiah Potter, a young academic in his twenties. Jeremiah Potter had put their trouble-making and difficulty in coping down to the fact that they were now mixing with the sons of aristocrats and gentry of long standing and found this beyond their powers to deal with, in spite of the wealth behind them. These same difficulties became more severe when they were at the Inns of Court for they were involved in several brawls, considered unseemly for young trainee barristers. On one occasion the altercation was serious and their father, John Smyth, had then to use his knowledge of people in high places, no less than Dr Owen, the King's physician – forty pounds were sent to buy his sons out of trouble. The social structure in the realm was changing radically, and it seemed that men like John Smyth and Thomas Holbeach were becoming the new wielders of power.

7

Winifred the Witch

In the year 1545 Sarah Sylvester was a pretty dark-haired maiden with eyes as blue as a June sky. She had known Fyllwood Forest since she had been able to walk, for she belonged to the forest folk, the forest folk descended from some of the many travelling people who had always moved through Fyllwood. Nowadays the nomads in the land were the gypsies, who had reached England in the last century. They were thought to have migrated through Egypt and north Africa, some of them travelling on to north–west Europe and eventually crossing the sea to England. They were dubbed gypsies because of the Egyptian connection, but wise men in places of learning believed they had originated in India. They were certainly dark-skinned in appearance and not at all like the former travelling people; indeed as a small child Sarah had been taught to fear and avoid the gypsies. She was a true child of the forest though, and she felt she knew every deer, squirrel, badger and song-bird within that great multitude of trees, as well as every track and clearing, every kind of tree, bush, flower and berry. All the creatures knew her and there was no scurrying away when young Sarah appeared; they would come to greet her or follow her and she would touch them kindly and talk to them. She loved the forest in all its seasons, from the bright greenery and bluebell carpets in spring and summer's wild roses and elder flowers, to the autumn's golden display and winter's starkness, when the robins who lived on the edge of the clearing where she dwelt with her parents were so tame they would greet her cheekily and fly to perch on her shoulders whenever she stepped outside. She always carried a few crumbs in her pockets to satisfy them.

It was in the forest one summer day that Sarah met the love of her life. She was nearly sixteen and ripe for love, as her mother said so scathingly afterwards. Jack Candler was twenty-two years of age and he came from Charlton village. He was about to join the army for the King's cause against France, and he had no parents or kinsmen. His mother who had died recently had told him often of his father who, she said, had died of a sudden malady when he, Jack, was but a babe. Jack was now as free as the wind and he had always fancied the life of a soldier. He had first come across Sarah while she was tending a young fawn that had hurt its leg. The mother doe was standing by watching Sarah's ministrations when Jack had come crashing clumsily through the forest startling everything in his pathway. The doe galloped off into the surrounding trees with fright, and the fawn had tried to follow its mother, but Sarah restrained it gently and it cried with pain. Sarah's blue eyes flashed angrily, 'Now look at what you've done, you noisy lout!'

Jack was taken aback, but amused. 'I had no way of knowing, wench, that you were an animal's nursemaid. Pray can I ask you to look at my poor blistered human fingers skinned to the bone with gathering wood for my humble fire?'

'Get off with you!' she retorted, not too unkindly. There was something about his cheekiness that was very appealing. He was a ruddy-faced lad with golden curls, tall and strong and dependable-looking.

'I'm sorry for sure,' he said, sensing her softening, and softening himself. 'Maybe I can help?'

'Just keep very still by my side and the mother will come back.'

He did just that, and presently the doe crept back to look expectantly at Sarah. She finished binding the baby animal's leg with healing leaves, and she tweaked its soft ear playfully, 'There you are then, little one, back to your mother!'

The doe came up to Sarah and nudged her sleeve affectionately, and then mother and babe trotted off into the forest again.

'Well, I'll be a frenchie!' exclaimed Jack stroking his chin thoughtfully, 'She even thanked you!'

'Of course she did. Some animals have fairer manners than folk!'

He ignored that. 'Are you from hereabouts?'

'Yes, I live in the forest.'

That explained it, thought Jack. They were a different breed, the forest folk. Even so he felt that Sarah was someone special, she seemed to have such a way with creatures. Jack was a no-nonsense, matter-of-fact fellow. He had killed many animals in the forest for his stew-pot and had never thought about them much before. He became fascinated with Sarah and waited for her and met her regularly in the next few days on her jaunts about the forest. It was inevitable that within a week they should fall in love. Sarah, through her contact with the creatures about her knew all about their mating habits, and so, instinctively, young and innocent that she was, did not feel it wrong to let Jack have his way with her. Jack was a full-grown headstrong man, and very much in love with Sarah, as she was with him, and so without question or guilt they daily made passionate love in the deepness of the forest.

On one such day, two weeks since their first meeting, they were sauntering back towards the clearing where Sarah lived when Jack cut through her joy with his news.

'I travel to Portsmouth in two days' time. I've enlisted with the military and they've now sent for me. I'm sorry but I was signed up for it before I met you . . .' his words trailed off lamely when he saw the blue eyes brimming with tears.

He endeavoured to reassure her. ' 'Twill not be long. P'raps one bout of duty and I'll make my fortune and come home and marry you. I swear by all I hold precious that you're the only one for me!'

She knew that he truly meant it, and nodded through her tears.

'Time will pass quickly, you'll see, and I'll be back for you!'

Her mother's sharp eyes had not missed the change in her daughter's manner over the last couple of weeks. Sarah, always a happy lass, had gone about her chores even lighter-hearted than usual with a small secret smile forever on her lips. She did not want to share the secret of her love with anyone for a little while but her mother became increasingly worried when in the next five or six weeks Sarah, who had never been ill in her life, became quite sick. When the nausea had persisted for three or four mornings Mother Sylvester knew without a doubt that Sarah was pregnant. She eventually prised the truth from the girl, and it was then that she muttered about her being 'ripe for love'. Sarah was not perturbed for she knew that Jack would eventually come home for her, and until then she was content to have the babe and wait. She told her mother so, in just those words. Her mother didn't know whether to believe Sarah or not, and it seemed that this Jack Candler had no living relatives with whom she could consult. She loved her daughter dearly, and her Sarah, her unique Sarah, was someone very special with her love and knowledge of the forest and its animals; she only hoped Jack Candler would feel the same way about Sarah when he got home.

Jack was never to get home. The ship he had set sail in, the *Mary Rose*, was lost off Portsmouth on 19 July. All on board perished within the hour of leaving, in sight of the land and the monarch who had bade them so proudly farewell. Henry the Eighth had become very engrossed in building up a navy of wooden ships and had access to plentiful supplies of timber from the large forest to the north of Portsmouth. The *Mary Rose* had been grossly overloaded and top-heavy with the many fighting men on board, and she had sunk swiftly. News of this tragedy did not trickle through to Fylton until a good four months after. News of events in other towns and places came through word of mouth from the many pilgrims who trav-

elled through Fylton on their journeys to and from Glastonbury. Many of these pilgrims rested up for several days at
Lyons Court in the annexe where dwelt the village priest.
Mother Sylvester had a woman friend she had confided in,
who did occasional laundry work at the Manor, and this
friend had been endeavouring for months to find out any
scrap of information she could glean about Master Jack
Candler. Poor Jack would never now make his fortune, he
had never even had the chance to get to grips with the
King's enemies. Poor Jack was in a watery grave, drowned,
and out of this life forever.

Mother Sylvester pondered on how to tell the news to
Sarah. Sarah, past the first few months of unease was very
fit again and looking forward eagerly to the birth of her
babe. Her mother eventually told her the news one crisp
October morning. Sarah was unbelieving of the truth to
begin with, but after a while reason took over, and then
acceptance, but not until she had wept her anguished eyes
dry. In these last few happy weeks before the news of Jack's
death she had frequently gone over in her mind her
eventual reunion with him and how she would tell him of
the babe . . . she would greet him first . . . better to let him
savour the joy of their meeting . . . and then she would tell
him of their child. She had pleasantly rehearsed again and
again the endearments she would use, and now, now . . .
there was nothing.

Her father who was a hard man had wanted to turn her
out. He was, after all, descended from the travelling folk
who cherished the chastity of their daughters. Mother Sylvester, though, was a strong character, cunning and practical in her thinking. She pointed out to her husband that
the babe would be an asset, especially if it was a boy. It
would be someone else to help them in their old age; for
Sarah was their only child. He had reluctantly agreed that
she was right.

Baby Jack was born at the end of the following March
when the snow was still lingering on the ground and the
robins were noisily fluttering around the clearing, appar-

ently missing Sarah. He was a fine baby with his father's golden curls and Sarah's sky-blue eyes,. The Sylvesters were proud and as they lived in such a remote spot only a few close friends knew that he was the child of Sarah. Most people took it that Baby Jack was a late baby of Mother Sylvester. The one thing that Sarah had been adamant about was that he must be called Jack; he would at least have that much of his father to be remembered by, and Sarah felt that when he was old enough she would tell him the whole story of his father and their love.

As his grandmother had forecast, the child Jack proved to be a blessing to the Sylvesters in their old age. He kept the small homestead going when they grew frail and old. Sarah was still a delightful woman to behold even in early middle age, but she had never looked at another man and all her love and energy had gone into rearing young Jack. She had taught her son to love the forest and its creatures as she did, and there was no young man more at peace with himself and his world than Jack Sylvester. He had grown into a handsome lad. His hair was still as bright and curly as the day he was born and he was broad and strong but with hands as gentle as a maiden when dealing with animals. He did not eat flesh, and while his grandparents frowned and clacked when he was old enough to state his case firmly for not doing so, and with the authority of one who now ran the homestead, his mother was on his side. The small-holding was turned over to more vegetables and they kept two cows for milking and a few hens for eggs. Jack was a good manager and what the smallholding could not supply he would barter for at market with his produce. They lived comfortably enough in their forest retreat and Jack drove them regularly to the Church of St Gregory every Sunday. It was an outing for the old folk and a chance for his mother to have a gossip. Also a chance for him to run his eye over the village girls, for Jack was of a mind to take a wife. His mother was not unaware of this, and she realized that human nature would take its course. She only hoped he would seek out a suitable maid.

Mary Potter stopped one Sabbath to cross herself with holy water in the south porch of St Gregory's. As the stoup was still there this habit lingered with people although the new form of church worship was doing away with all these kind of practices. When she lifted her eyes from the stoup they met those of a young man standing in the inner doorway. His eyes were very blue and they held hers for a moment and then a half-smile hovered around his lips as she scuttled past him into the church. Jack had been waiting for his mother who was delayed outside trying to adjust his grandmother's bonnet against the cold March wind. The old lady had become very irritable of late and it took much patience to deal with her. After the service while his mother was still fussing with old Mrs Sylvester he sought out the girl he had met momentarily in the porch. Jack was a personable young man not given to shyness and he approached Mary Potter confidently. He had not seen her before, she was obviously new to Fylton and he was very attracted to her vivid red hair.

'I wish you well this day,' he said inclining his head slightly, 'I am Jack Sylvester of this parish. May I ask the pleasure of your name, for I know you are not from these parts?'

'My name is Mary Potter and I dwell in Bath although I believe that my family came from these parts a long time ago. I hope to find out more about this during my stay.'

She was kind but cool, and Jack was even more intrigued when he discovered she was staying at Lyons Court. Why had she not sat with the Holbeaches in their private chapel as was the wont of guests of the Manor house? He was to discover later that Mary Potter had quite a mind of her own. She had declined the privilege of sitting in the private chapel as she wanted to meet and mix with the village folk. She was a highly-educated young lady, an almost unheard of happening in Jack's limited circle of acquaintances. She had come to Fylton at the invitation of the Holbeachs to sort out their family papers as she had a knowledge of such things. Jack was very intrigued that such an attractive lass should bother herself with musty old papers and the like. She stayed at Lyons Court for nigh on six weeks and every Sunday Jack sought her out, and each time he felt a little more attracted to her. The Sunday before she was due to return to Bath he asked if he could take her for a walk that evening and to his joy she pleasantly agreed. His mother had watched all this preamble with some pleasure, and some doubt, for she did not want her Jack to be made to feel inferior with such an educated girl, and yet the girl was very pleasant and presentable. She need not have worried, for as Jack and Mary walked together that pleasant spring evening Jack with his native intelligence felt on very equal terms with Mary, and she the same with him. She was not pretentious or hoity-toity and was genuinely interested in Jack and his forest-lore.

When Mary came to Fylton again, but two weeks after they had taken their evening walk, Jack's mother knew that Mary was more than a little interested in her son. The friendship blossomed into a courtship, and it seemed that although Mary was a girl with academic pursuits she appreciated the wonderful freshness that Jack brought into her life with his love of the forest and its creatures. For a girl who had been reared in an atmosphere of manuscripts and learning, her horizon had suddenly broadened with this handsome gentle young man. Her mother had died when she was but a small child, and her father, who had been a tutor at the University of Oxford had brought her up alone and educated her himself. Jeremiah Potter had passed on his knowledge to his daughter who had been a bright and willing pupil with an exceptional interest in history.

When they had known each other a little while Mary asked Jack to ride to Bath to meet her father. Old Mother Sylvester, his grandmother, was quick with her tongue as always, 'You be careful what you're letting yourself in for lad. She's not going to make you a good wife with all her book nonsense. You need a maid strong and wholesome to help you work this homestead and bear your children!'

Sarah Sylvester quietened her mother impatiently, partly

in an attempt to banish some of the lingering doubts she felt about the relationship. 'Silence, mother. If he's of a mind to meet her kin then so be it.'

She wanted Jack's happiness more than anything in the world, and he seemed to know his own mind. The relationship was serious if Mary wanted Jack to meet her father.

Jack for his part dressed himself up like a young fighting-cock, for this was an important meeting for him. He wore a green doublet of fine wool, a fanciful purchase a day or so ago in Bristowe market, obviously the former possession of some gentleman who had fallen on hard times. The doublet was buttoned down the front and had matching breeches with tagged laces. Over this he wore his best scarlet home-spun cloak. His everyday riding boots were polished with loving care, and a black broad-brimmed hat sat upon his bright curls. Sarah's heart was full of pride as he galloped off on his faithful brown mare. He looked a dashing enough fellow for the most fussy young lass.

Jack had never visited Bath before and he was excited at the prospect of seeing a new place, its dwellings and people. Mary's father's abode impressed him greatly. He had never had close dealings with an academic before, apart from the local priest, and he was full of wonderment with the books he saw, and objects from other countries, also the many finely drawn maps, some of local places. He had not known such things existed.

Jeremiah Potter was in turn intrigued by Jack. Jack Sylvester was certainly no ordinary country bumpkin, a thing he had half-feared when Mary had talked about him so enthusiastically and asked if she could invite him to their abode. The boy had an innate intellect and a keen will to learn about everything, and above all he was his own man. That was plain to see. Jeremiah was about fifty, dressed in academic fashion, black velvet gown and white ruff, his fading red hair styled in a scholarly tonsure, short and neat. One could see where Mary had inherited her red mane, thought Jack when he was first introduced.

On this occasion Mary had a lot to talk about concerning

her recent sojourn at Lyons Court and the records she had perused there. She had discovered many manuscripts appertaining to the de Lyons family, and there had been mention of one Will Potter, a man from the Crusades and the original owner of Whytecross House. Jack could not help but be interested for he knew Whytecross and the Chase family who lived there quite well. It transpired also that Mary's father knew a little of their ancestral kin. It was a story that had been handed down in the Potter family very carefully from generation to generation, and it appeared to match the information that Mary had found. The Potter family story was that one of their forebears had travelled on one of the Crusades back in the twelfth century as liegeman to the son of one of the de Lyons, and on his return he had married the Lord of the Manor's daughter. Beyond that Jeremiah knew nothing more of that particular story.

Mary now had a fresh challenge. She felt she must seek out some further manuscripts. Perhaps the church at Fylton might yield some more information, for she had previously only looked closely at the papers lodged in the Holbeach household, and also it was a chance to see Jack again. The Revd Simon Perkis gave her permission readily for he was glad of someone to take an interest in sorting through the many manuscripts that were to be found in St Gregory's. He was too busy with his flock to do it himself, for nowadays a village priest took on far more duties than his predecessors, including the rudimentary education of the village children.

Mary's speculation proved to be fruitful. The very ancient faded writing of Lady Jane de Lyon came to light among the church scrolls, of which there were many, secured in an old oak chest that had been pushed into the north transept. Mary had been untying the scrolls, all of which were finely rolled and secured with leather laces, endeavouring to get them into some kind of order, when the name Potter leapt at her. She forgot her original methodical intent and set about reading the three-and-a-half-centuries-old writings of Lady Jane. It was all there, the complete story of Will and

Eleanor and the building of Whytecross, the original disapproval of Sir David, Lady Jane's husband, the story of Will's
shared interest with her in the church records – Mary
relished that bit – and there was even mention of Will's red
hair and what her daughter Eleanor wore on her wedding
day. There were also details of her son, David the Crusader's
wedding, and stories of all her children. Lady Jane, with her
own interest in family and records, had indeed bequeathed
a rich record of her times for her descendant Mary Potter's
sixteenth-century eyes. It was also a wonderful find in view
of the fact that Lady Jane in her instinctive wisdom had
deposited her writings in St Gregory's Church, which was
well, for the original Lyons Court had burned down in
1275. Mary felt that a lot of Fylton's history must have gone
with it although Sir Ralph, the builder of the present Lyons
Court, had, in his loneliness, written a few records of what
he had been told of his forebears. It was from these writings
that Mary had gleaned the original story of a Potter at
Whytecross, but nothing like the detailed stories written by
Lady Jane, stories that had been locked away for centuries
in the Church of St Gregory. Mary had no doubt at all now
that Will Potter the first owner of Whytecross was her
ancestor.

Jack was as excited as Mary about her find. He only
wished he could find out more about his forebears, but that
was not to be, and it was just as well. His mother had told
him of his father, the loss of the *Mary Rose*, and of their true
love, and it mattered not a jot to him that he had been
born out of wedlock. He wished however that he could have
known something of his roots, but that secret had been well
kept, and the hermit of Fyllwood Farm who had murdered
his own brother would never be connected with Jack Sylvester. He did not even bear the same name.

There was now a new family at Fyllwood Farm by the
name of Hall. Benjamin Hall had worked hard and long to
save the farm once again from the searching arms of the
forest, for after the death of Samuel Candler the place had
been empty and neglected once more for a long time. It

had become part of the many acres of land bought up by the Smyths of Ashton Court, and Ben Hall was a good tenant.

Jack Sylvester and Mary Potter were married one spring morning in 1564 about a year after they had first met. He brought her back proudly to his home in the forest. Mary brought with her the volumes and papers she had so much love for, and did not feel at all out of place. They matched their love and concern for each other so well that their home became a very happy place, and the family they bore was a constant joy to them. The older Sylvesters, Sarah's parents, had both passed away by the time Jack and Mary's eldest child, Crispin, was five years old. He had been born in 1565. They had a daughter, Eleanor, named for Mary's ancestor, and their third child, Silas, was but a babe. Sarah Sylvester was a happy grandmother and a much-loved mother-in-law to Mary. All her former fears about Mary's suitability and Jack's happiness had long since flown. Mary was a wonderful mother, eager to learn about everything from the older woman, and Sarah helped greatly with the rearing of her grandchildren.

In 1574 word reached Fylton that Queen Elizabeth herself was to visit Bristowe, and the Sylvester family planned to go to town for the day to see the Monarch and to join in the celebrations. Jack prepared the family cart with plenty of soft cushions for Mary, his mother, and their children, six of them now, Crispin, Eleanor, Silas, Winifred, Rebecca and baby Cornelius. The women packed a large box of victuals and they set off early through the forest for it was a goodly journey with a family. As the horses plodded the ancient tracks the squirrels were capering in the trees and a few of them scampering tamely before the cart. One baby squirrel even dropped on to the cart, to the great delight of the children, and their father stopped the cart and quietly dismounted with the tiny creature for it to find its mother again. They came to a stream where there were a few baby foxes playing around. They didn't run away but stayed bright-eyed to watch the family cross the rough wooden bridge, and Jack made a few noises of greeting to them, which the children tried to imitate, to everyone's amusement. Their grandmother, Sarah, smiled happily; the creatures of the forest knew her family well. When they came to the banks of the river they turned towards Bristowe and followed the rough road beside it. It was full tide and a few merchant ships were making their way up to the town. They were all in high spirits as they clattered over Bristowe Bridge.

The city was in festal mood, with the usually dirty streets cleaned and sanded for the occasion. There were many citizens as well as visitors like themselves from the surrounding villages and hamlets, awaiting the Queen's arrival. When she did arrive she was resplendent as she rode through the city gates on a white horse with her retinue and a whole procession of others snaking slowly through the central streets. The many churches in Bristowe City rang out a welcome, and pie-sellers and other traders did magnificent business. The Queen eventually entered into the Great House by St Augustine's Quay, where, it was rumoured, she was to be entertained for a whole week. Many city officials were there to greet her, including one Hugh Smyth, J.P. and landowner, of Ashton Court.

Eleanor was more than delighted at seeing the Queen. Apart from the wonderfully rich velvet dress, the snow-white ruff, the elegant shoes and flashing jewels that Queen Elizabeth was wearing, Eleanor was very impressed with the fact that the Queen had red hair! Eleanor had inherited the Potters' red locks, but her older brother Crispin had his father's yellow curls. Eleanor's hair was of a very bright red, brighter even than her mother's and she had long been teased about the colour of her hair by some of the other children at the village priest's weekly school, but now, see here, the Queen of England herself was blessed with red curls!

As they drove home out of Bristowe after a day to be long remembered, Mary pointed out to her children the Church of St Mary's at Redclyffe. It had a tall truncated tower for the top of the spire had crashed to earth in a thunderstorm over a century before. The children were full of awe for they had never seen such a great building before. 'Taller than the trees in our forest!' pronounced young Crispin. The Queen herself was to wax more eloquent. 'The fairest, goodliest and most famous parish church in England' was Elizabeth's verdict when she was taken to inspect its beauty. In fact Queen Elizabeth was so impressed with the beautiful church that some years later she granted back the church lands, which had previously been confiscated by the Crown, for the sole reason that the rents should be retained for the upkeep of the church to retain its beauty in good repair.

Jack and Mary Sylvester's brood proved to be an unusual and talented family, as one would expect, and they were well-respected by the Fylton/Whytechurch village folk. The name Fylton was still used but more and more folk were calling the village Whytechurch. While their grandmother had helped practically in rearing them, Mary had educated all her children to a high standard, and they had additional instruction from the village priest, Revd Simon Perkis, for it was now a decree in the land that children should be taught their letters. Crispin was to attend the University at Oxford, his grandfather's old seat of learning, but Jeremiah Potter was not to live to see it; he had died of a chest malady three years since.

It was Crispin's ambition to become a priest and take Holy Orders and Revd Perkis had assisted greatly in his tutoring the last few months before he set off for Oxford, coming to the Sylvester home to school the boy most days. Fortunately Jack and Mary were able to finance the boy in this venture with some money that Jeremiah had left, for they would never have managed it with the income they got from the homestead. Mary had also inherited the fine house in Bath and as they loved their own home so much there was never any question of them going to live there. Instead Mary had sequestered what furniture, books and treasures she desired and the rest of the stuff she gave to her father's younger brother Isaac who also lived in Bath. He had a family of eight children, including twins, so was always glad of anything extra. Jeremiah's house fetched a goodly price and this money enabled Jack and Mary to build on some extra rooms to their dwelling, and also to invest in some sheep for wool, more cows for milk and dairy products to market. They built a barn and rented more land, and they still had some money left for a nest-egg. When finished their home looked very attractive, it was no longer a simple smallholding, but a farm.

In 1581 there was great excitement in the Sylvester family when they packed young Crispin off to Oxford. He was but seventeen years old and he had at least seven years of study ahead of him, so there was not a little sadness on Mary's part to see her first-born fly the nest. His father rode first with him to Bristowe and from there Crispin was to board the rough carriage that was to take him to Oxford. Sending a son to Oxford was an expensive business, for the scholar's tuition fees must be paid for in addition to his lodging and his books and sundries such as candles. The journey too was expensive, and Mary had packed a good assortment of food for her son in his stout home-made wooden travelling box. He also had quite a tidy sum of money in his pouch, well-hidden under his long travelling-cloak, for in addition to all the other expenses, when he reached Oxford there would be the cost of buying a scholar's gown and other academic necessities.

Revd Perkis had instructed Crispin with diligence on the waywardness of town life, of brothels and stewhouses, and crooked men with dice who would tempt a young stripling from the country. Crispin, despite his youth, was an astute young man, his desire set upon academic pursuits, and Mary felt sure he would stay safe from harm. Her father had often told her that the colleges had very strong stipulations and curfews about who was allowed into their halls of residence; rules mainly for the protection of the students although there were always unruly fellows to break the rules. Mary also remembered the stories of the Smyth brothers from Bristowe, at Oxford under the tutorship of Jeremiah

117

Potter. Because their father had been a wealthy Bristowe merchant they had felt they could throw their weight around not a little, and because they were not lacking in money they employed poorer students to do menial tasks for them. These poorer students were known as 'battelers' and Mary hoped greatly that they had provided Crispin with enough money to pay his way, albeit frugally, without having to resort to 'battelling' for other richer scholars.

The next of the young Sylvesters to leave home was Silas, their third child. Silas had long nurtured a passion to go to sea and serve the Queen. When he was fifteen years old, John Holbeach at Lyons Court, knowing of the lad's desire through Revd Perkis, invited Silas to Lyons Court to meet one of the Queen's Navy Board Officers who happened to be a guest there. The Navy Board had been established in 1546 and had been developed from the office of the Keeper of the King's Ships, an establishment which had been in force for two hundred years. More and more it was felt by the monarch's advisers that, being an island race, the kingdom was dependent upon a strong navy to defend its shores. Silas was a forward-speaking lad, not inclined to bashfulness as some boys of his age might have been. The Queen's Officer was impressed with the red-haired boy's confident manner and his polite but enthusiastic questions about the Queen's navy. The lad knew how to conduct himself too; he had been properly raised as well as being good with his letters and educated well beyond normal standards. There and then the Queen's man told young Silas he could go to sea to train as a junior ships' officer an upper yardsman, if that was what he really wanted. Arrangements would be made and he would be sent for in due course.

Silas returned home from Lyons Court elated, and his grandmother Sarah became very thoughtful, for she could only think of the *Mary Rose* and the loss of her lover. She had never been to the sea and the nearest thing she had seen to it was the river that went through Bristowe and the ships sailing up it from the sea. The thought of her grandson sailing away on a wooden ship to face goodness knows what perils was disturbing, but Sarah kept her own council, the lad was young, craving for adventure, a red-blooded young man anxious to serve his Queen and country. One half of Sarah was proud, very proud. Silas was to become an officer with the Queen's Commission, and that was something to be really pleased about, so outwardly she congratulated young Silas with the rest of the family. Within three months he was off to Plymouth to join his first ship, and the family once more waved farewell to one of its sons.

Eleanor envied Silas after a fashion; to be able to set off on a new venture. Being a boy he could have more freedom to go his own way, and she knew she would miss him sorely. Of all the Sylvester children Eleanor and Silas had been the closest to each other.

A little while after Silas had gone Eleanor began to take an interest in other young lads outside of the family, and in particular young Timothy Hall, the eldest son at Fyllwood Farm. It began with chattering together after church, and then they began walking out and courting seriously. Mary Sylvester was very pleased when Timothy Hall asked Jack if he could wed his daughter. They were ideally suited, for Timothy was a thoughtful intelligent fellow, solid and dependable, a perfect partner for Eleanor.

Old Sarah never lived to see the marriage of Timothy and Eleanor. She had long suffered with her chest and she passed away peacefully one summer morning as the dawn was breaking, much loved and mourned by her family. Jack and Mary ensured that she had a good service said for her, and as the procession that carried her body wound its way to the edge of the forest to cross over the pastures to St Gregory's, all the animals and birds in the forest were strangely silent and it seemed as if they knew that a friend had passed this life.

Sarah's forest lore had been passed on not only to Jack but to her grandchildren. Cornelius the youngest was the one who seemed to appreciate not only the wonder but the power of the herbage that abounded in Fyllwood, and he was full-minded to become an apothecary and a healer as soon as he was grown enough. When he was twelve years old Jack and Mary apprenticed him to the village apothecary.

For the rest of the family, Rebecca had long had her eye on Robin Chase, the second son at Whytecross. Mary was secretly a trifle disappointed it was not the eldest son Rebecca had set her cap at, for that would have meant a Potter returning to the original Potter home, but it was not to be. Mary stifled her dreams and wished them well with all her heart when they eventually married, for Robin was a likely lad and had been well set up by his father in a small farm at Dundry on the hills to the west of Fylton.

Winifred, Jack and Mary's second daughter, had always been different from the rest of the Sylvester brood, even in colouring. Whereas all the others were either golden- or red-haired, Winifred's hair could only be called mousey, or an indefinite dun. She was even-dispositioned enough and appeared to love her family, but somehow Mary always felt that this daughter of hers was different in some way. Winifred always seemed to be holding back something of herself, aloof and apart from the general jollity that reigned in the Sylvester household. Mary loved all her children equally but felt disquietude with Winifred at times, something she could not quite explain. Mary and Jack were close creatures and they had often discussed this, for Jack felt the same. He had long ago told Mary the story of his birth and the lack of knowledge of his roots; perhaps young Winifred was a throwback from part of his former kin, for blood would out. Poor Jack and Mary, with their many years of wedded happiness their instincts and worries were to be found correct.

Winifred was found out after at least three of the village lads had bragged about their relationships with her; a nudge in the ribs, a coarse whispering, a raucous chuckle, and the knowledge was passed on that Winifred Sylvester was a willing wench. When the rumours reached the ears of Jack and Mary they were very upset and at first couldn't believe the stories. They taxed Winifred with the rumours and she admitted they were true. The part that made Mary so sad was that she showed no shame. How could a daughter of theirs behave like this? Why couldn't she get herself a decent young lad and get wed like her sisters? They put such questions to her and the vehemence in her reply shocked them.

'Wed? Wed? Never! I want my life without a master to cook for and bear children for. Wed, why should I? I love being free like the animals!'

'You wouldn't be free if you had a babe wrong side of the sheets, my lass, and that is very likely to happen if you carry on acting like a trollop!' said Jack angrily and a little defensively, aware of his own coming into the world, albeit in different circumstances.

Winifred had laughed cynically at them then. 'I'm no fool, I know what potions to take to keep free of babes, a little bit of ground charm-wort and a pinch of nasturtium seeds, that does the trick, I swear by it!'

Mary was astonished at the arrogance of Winifred's attitude, Jack even more so. Winifred was in full swing now, it was as if the part of the girl that had been hiding away from them all these years was showing itself fully now that she had been found out.

'I do lovers' potions too!' she boasted archly, 'How do you think Rebecca captured Robin Chase?'

'That's enough.' Mary was really angry, but Winifred was not to be stifled now.

'I'm far more skilful with the herbs and roots than Cornelius, I'll have you know. He only does remedies. Anyone can do those.'

Jack was curious, 'How do you mean?'

'I put spells on folk for their troubles and maladies as well as give them potions!'

There was a terrible silence, and Mary's usual composure left her. How long had this been going on? They had been utterly blind to it, utterly blind. Outwardly she said, 'But that's witchcraft, daughter, that's evil!'

Winifred laughed harshly, 'No one can prove anything,'

Mary became really upset. 'Winifred, I beseech you, forget all this nonsense. They'll have you for the ducking-stool that's for sure, and think of the disgrace, your brothers, your sisters, have you thought of them? Crispin who is to be a priest, Silas with the Queen's Commission, your sisters married into good families, Cornelius and his talents with herbs will be misjudged, branded with you! Just think of the harm they will feel when the gossip gets really going. You are to go to the Revd Perkis at once and confess and ask for forgiveness and penitence!'

Winifred laughed again, 'The Revd Perkis, HIM!' her nostrils flared, 'Holy man he may be, but I won't have anyone telling me what I should do, how I should live my life. Indeed if I'm an embarrassment to my kinsfolk then I'll uproot and go and live in another part of the forest!'

'Go then!' said Jack, firmly but sadly, 'for I'll not harbour anyone under my roof carrying on as you've behaved, daughter. 'Twas bad enough that you behaved indecently, but I'll not be party to a soul that relishes wickedness as well as wantonness, even though it be my own flesh. 'Tis evil!'

Mary's heart was breaking at this but she gave no utterance.

Winifred tossed her mousey mop haughtily and drew her shawl closer to her shoulders. Her dark eyes flashed, 'Then I'll go right now, father, if it so please you.'

'But where will you go, lass . . .' Mary moaned half to herself, 'Where will you go without a roof?'

'I shall manage. I have a rough shelter on Avon Leigh.'

This was a stretch of the forest to the west where the cliffs of the great gorge rose above the river Avon matching the soaring rocks on the opposite side of the river where Cliff Town stood.

The girl's deceit was even more complete than Jack and Mary had imagined. She actually had a retreat where she could fly from them! How long had she had this hermit's cell, this witch's den, how long had she been deceiving them all? Had they been too preoccupied with their other children to notice Winifred getting more and more wayward? It was true that she did go off on her own quite a lot. How much did her sisters know?

Winifred went and it was a sad day.

When next Jack saw his daughter Rebecca he taxed her with the question of the love potion. Rebecca burst into laughter, ''Twas just a girlish prank, father. I didn't really believe in it. It was just Winifred being so serious, as you know she is, I just went along with it for fun!'

Rebecca's laughter stopped however when Jack told her of their recent confrontation with Winifred. Her eyes grew round, first with surprise, and then horror, 'Oh father, you don't mean you really think she is a witch ... and she has this hideout in the forest? The crafty cat ... you say she refused to go to the Reverend for penance? I warned her about being too friendly with the village lads, but I never guessed the extent of it . . .' She had a sudden thought, 'Oh my soul, supposing the Chase family get to hear of this! I shall never be able to hold my head up with them again ... a witch in the family, and a whorish witch at that . . .' There, she had said it. She had said the word, the description that nobody else had dared to say!

Winifred had left the homestead of her childhood the day of the terrible argument with her parents. Mary had pleaded tearfully with her daughter to think again and repent and to go to St Gregory's for confession and good counsel with the Revd Simon Perkis, but Winifred would not hear of it. 'I shall live my life as I intend it to be,' was all she would say.

She had left before sundown, and Mary, being a good Christian mother gave her a couple of good laying hens in a crate and a pack of food from the larder. The last she saw of Winifred was the girl walking swiftly down the track into the forest, the hens clucking and flapping noisily in their temporary prison. One consolation for Mary was that Winifred was a hardy girl. She had never suffered great sicknesss as a child and she was strong in body. Jack did not watch her departure, he was as heartsick as his wife, and throughout the rest of his life he was never to come to terms with the fact that one of his spawning should have turned out so bad despite the love that surrounded her.

The truth was that Winifred was not really evil. In later more enlightened centuries she would have been called a white witch. Naturally there were whispers in the village after she left home and Revd Perkis came of his own volition to see Jack and Mary. He offered what comfort he could, and they said a prayer with him for the wayward soul, but the heart pain was still there within them both. There was worse to come. They never knew the whole story, nor did they desire to know too much because of the pain, keeping themselves apart from the hurt of it as much as they could. A few years after she had walked away from home, Winifred had been apprehended in the casting of some kind of spell on an old man in the village, a spell to rid him of rheumatism, but he had died suddenly, probably of a heart condition, or just old age. Winifred was blamed and they had dragged her to the village pond and the ducking-stool at the back of Lyons Court, for the Manor house had been used as a court-house for many years, as its name belied. She had never recovered from the ducking, and folk said that meant that she truly was guilty of being a witch. She was buried in the ground outside the church with not a single prayer said publicly over her, but Mary was told the spot by a friendly verger man, and she often placed flowers from the forest over the place where wicked Winifred was interred, although she never told Jack of this.

Cornelius had witnessed the whole event from start to finish, standing well back at the edge of the crowd. He knew he would never forget that day as long as he drew breath, the sight of his sister bound fast to the ducking-stool, like an angry cat, and after the first ducking her eyes flashing, her hair heavy with pond water. She lost her spirit after the fourth ducking and later with the sixth she was dead, her head rolling lifeless on her breast against the homespun blue of her soggy robe. Could these really be the village folk of Fylton he thought he knew so well, people who were usually placid and amenable to their neighbours, now whipped up to a frenzy with crowd fever? To Cornelius it was the ignorant drive for revenge against the unknown, which to him was not the unknown, but the misunderstood.

Cornelius was a deep thinker like many of the young educated men of his day; the spirit of enlightenment was spreading through the realm, very slowly, but in a real fashion. Cornelius earnestly wished he had shown more interest in his sister, for there was no doubt she had been clever with herbs and potions. Her big mistake had been to use them in conjunction with verbal threats, promises or insults, whether it be love potions or brews to cure bad tempers, or mixtures to administer to scold wives. Cornelius knew without a doubt that the love potions mixed by his sister were a mixture of constituents that made people feel good, stimulants with the added promise that a desired person of the opposite sex would begin to look at them with interest. This was simply a psychological ploy, a placebo, for when a person felt good they sparkled, especially when they really believed that their charm would work, as indeed it sometimes did. If it didn't Winifred would blame the mixture; she had made it too weak, or the ratio of the elements had not been balanced correctly.

Cornelius also knew that the cures for bad tempers were no more than strong purgatives, and Winifred's line of chat here was that the emptying of the bowels emptied bad temper also. Then there were the mixtures Winifred had brewed for husbands to slip into the drinks of their scold wives, obtained from her by more than one of the men who had jeered at her and put her to her end.

Cornelius knew that this potion had a temporary paralyzing effect on the jaw muscles. It was sad that these very men who had used her cleverness had also mocked her to her death. Also at her end were a couple of the village lads who had bragged about her favours to them. Cornelius could not help but think of the scriptures where Jesus had said "Let he who is without sin cast the first stone" to the men who were about to stone a prostitute. If only he himself had had the courage to say this to the fickle folk of Fylton/ Whytechurch village . . . and yet it would have been to no avail. The crowd were intent only upon carrying out what they thought was justice.

Young Cornelius was a good apothecary and was serving his apprenticeship well; some troublemakers were talking yet about his skill with herbs matching his sister's same interest. However his back was broad and he had the logic of education to withstand such taunts. The ducking of Winifred the Witch was a nine-day wonder, and after a while the village people found something else to gossip about.

8

The Midwife's Mistake

When word arrived at Whytechurch in 1588 that the Spanish Armada was about to make for England's shores there was much busyness and great preparation to light a beacon on the Dundry hills above the village. The spot chosen was a tump called Maes Knoll, an ancient place surrounded by myths and legends that went back into the mists of time, and a landmark well-known to all around. With the news that the Armada was sailing for England came the edict that beacons should be lit in as many high places as possible in order to warn the population of the impending danger of invasion. Most of the people of Whytechurch, like many in the realm, did not believe that the Spaniards could really be successful in an invasion of England. The navy was strong and plentiful with good ships and good men, Henry the Eighth had seen to that, and good Queen Bess, God bless her, would never lose England while she had strong men like Francis Drake to command her fleet and fight her battles. Only a few folk whispered pessimistic warnings such as 'You know the Spaniards have HUGE ships, three times the size of ours, great galleons that will mow down our little vessels in no time!'

Mary Sylvester heard some of these negative rumours and worried silently. She knew that when the haughty Spanish eventually came up the Channel, Silas, who was now a lieutenant, would be there with his shipmates waiting to defend their homeland. Silas was in her thoughts and prayers constantly at this time, and indeed all other mothers with sons at sea were in the same sway. Jack didn't say much but Mary knew he was fretting too. Jack was not a warlike person, never had been, yet at the same time he felt immensely proud of Silas, for was not the lad willing to defend his country and die if necessary against the aggressors? In silent harmony Jack and Mary made their way to St Gregory's and lit a candle for their son and said a prayer with the Reverend Clement Dauncey, the new incumbent, for his safe return.

When word did come that the Spaniards had been sighted and Drake had set sail to intercept them, practically all the inhabitants of Whytechurch village climbed up to the tump to witness the torching of the beacon. Even the Holbeaches rode up on their horses. Great cords of wood cut from Fyllwood had been placed ready, and the huge bonfire which stood as high as three men was soon well ablaze, sending out the message to all that the battle was imminent. Down to the south, many miles into the summer land they could see another great beacon flaring brightly. It was on the hills above the cathedral town of Wells, declaring the news to that local population. The village children were wild with excitement, dancing around the flames with childish chants, carefree in their ignorance of the meaning of this beacon. Eventually most people traipsed back down the hills again led by the Reverend Dauncey, and they were all making for one place with one accord, the church. A few men, labourers from Lyons Court, stayed behind to tend the beacon, for it had been decided to keep it flaring for a day and a night.

In St Gregory's a very moving service was held, and prayers for swift deliverance from the enemy were said. Mary shed several tears as she knelt and Jack was there as always to hold her hand in comfort. Eleanor and Timothy were there with their children and the Halls, and Rebecca and Robin and their children were with the Chases. Cornelius was on the other side of Jack, open and philosophical as usual, and Mary knew that Crispin, now an Oxford don, would be in his college chapel at this time. Only Winifred lay cold and dead in the earth but a few yards away. Was

128

this to be the same fate for Silas too? To lie cold and drowned at the bottom of the sea, as his grandfather before him?

Mary stirred herself and dried her eyes and attempted to rid herself of these mournful thoughts. She must take a hold of herself for she had supper to prepare when they got home. The Holbeaches were in their private chapel and after the Reverend Dauncey had given the blessing and they were all leaving, John Holbeach came through the screen and towards Jack and Mary.

'I trust we shall have good news of Silas quite soon. If he's under Drake's command he's in good hands. They'll whip the breeches off the Spaniards!'

Mary smiled acknowlegement of his greeting and moved on, and Jack said, 'Tell me sir, I would not know readily, living in the forest as I do, are there any more sons of Whytechurch out there in this great battle?'

'Oh yes indeed,' Holbeach scratched his chin, 'Let me see ... there's Pip the son of my head forester, Tom Blessed, and Sammy Gale, son of the alehouse keeper. They are both Whytchurch lads born and bred, and both serving with the Fleet, although what ships they are on I could not tell you right now.'

'Silas is on *White Angel*,' Jack volunteered proudly.

'Is he indeed?' Holbeach slapped his thigh. 'A fine lad you have there, and he can take care of himself too, I'll wager, when it comes to a fight! Never fear, Silas will be fine. Wish I was there myself. I'd run a sword through a few Spaniards' guts!'

Jack touched his cap and turned away. He caught up with Mary and Cornelius. 'Mr Holbeach tells me there are a couple more lads from hereabouts with the Fleet.'

Mary said with interest, 'I wondered if there were. Did you see that man in the dark blue doublet with his wife? They lit a candle. A forester I believe he is, leastways I think I've seen him about the forest.'

'That's it,' said Jack 'His name's Blessed and he's head forester at Lyons Court, and there's another lad by the name of Gale, son of the alehouse keeper, he's out there too!'

'Well then we're not alone in our supplications,' said Mary, and with lighter heart stepped into the cart to drive home for supper.

When the news came of Drake's great victory over the Armada there was wild rejoicing. They rang the set of bell chimes kept in the church for special occasions; they rang them long and loud, several men taking turns with the hammers until they grew tired and every head in Whytechurch was re-echoing their joyful sound long after the ringing had stopped. The children ran around excitedly and the dogs joined in with barking, picking up the atmosphere of relief and excitement. The young maidens put garlands in their hair and the village lads blew their reed pipes for them to dance. All pilgrims and beggars were showered with ale and pies and cheeses, and even the gypsies came out from Fyllwood to join in the celebrations. The Sylvesters joined in, but anxiously, for they wanted yet to hear that Silas was safe, as indeed the Blesseds were waiting for news of their son Pip. Mary had sought out the Blesseds and exchanged news with them at the start of the festivities. The alehouse keeper and his wife were too busy to be approached, but no doubt they were thinking of their son too, for although there had been a great victory some of the English ships had been sunk.

Silas strode through the front door a week after, tall and gallant but looking very thin and older. Mary and Jack were ecstatic. He unbuckled his sword and embraced them both long and wholeheartedly.

'Oh my Jesus! Oh my Jesus I thank thee!' was all that Mary could say.

'I was given some free time after the victory,' said Silas, 'so all I wanted to do was come home to the forest.'

'Well well,' said Jack, 'Was it bad, my son?'

Silas looked at his father quickly, guardedly, and Jack knew in that moment that he would be told only what his son wanted him to hear.

130

'We really rousted the Spaniards!' Silas answered, 'They were like squatting hens on the nest! Too big and cumbersome to move quickly, and we darted all around them, in and out, and we gave them hell! Drake is an expert at that sort of game and knew what he was about – they never stood a chance against us!'

When Silas was fed and rested Mary said, 'Have you heard of a fellow Pip Blessed? He comes from Whytechurch and his father is head forester at Lyons Court.'

'No, I can't say that I have, although the name is familiar. He's not on my ship. Does he hold the Queen's Commission?' Silas spoke with the authority born of training, although he was still only a junior officer.

Mary thought for a while wiping her hands on her apron. 'I couldn't be sure, but shouldn't think so.'

Pip Blessed was fit and well. He arrived home two days after Silas and the Sylvesters made his acquaintance in church the following Sunday. Pip was a strong square blond young man, older than Silas, very easygoing and likeable. He did not hold the Queen's Commission but he was a petty officer in command of common seamen. Many girlish heads were turned in church that morning for both Silas and Pip.

Word came that Sam Gale had been wounded and lost at sea, and the alehouse closed for three whole days with the poor parents' grief. Revd Dauncey held an extra service of thanksgiving and remembrance, and John Holbeach did not retire to his private chapel, but sat instead with the village people and gave a speech in tribute to all the brave defenders of the realm. Mary would never forget that morning, the pride and gratitude mingled with sadness for the Gales and other families who had lost loved ones. It was after this that she felt at last she could live again with some semblance of well-being after the terrible business of poor misguided Winifred. She considered this philosophically and it seemed to her that all life was like this; the dark and light patches, the bad and the good, all to be lived through and dealt with.

131

Before Silas returned to his ship she felt strong enough to talk to him about Winifred. She and Jack had not said much about it to each other, or other people, but she felt now that she could talk about Winifred dispassionately. Silas knew of course what had happened although he had been away at the time. Like Cornelius he viewed the whole episode as unfortunate, and felt that Winifred was foolish rather than wicked. Mary appreciated his wisdom, but then she realized that this young man, her son, held the Queen's Commission, was a leader of men, and had seen death at close quarters in battle. In his tough-minded way he saw things in different proportion to his parents, and while he was fond of his sister it seemed to him that Winifred had really brought events upon herself, shameful as it was to have a sister dubbed a witch and sentenced to the ducking-stool. He was Silas, he was his own man and he could hold his head high. He was more concerned for his parents who had obviously taken the matter very much to heart, and he said as much. Mary smiled to herself; he was not so wise after all. His youth could not deal with some feelings, he would be a parent himself some day, God willing, and then he would truly know how it felt. Young Silas might be experienced in death and battle but he still had a lot to learn about life!

Cornelius Sylvester, dealing with herbs and plants also knew quite a lot about trees. Since he was a child he had loved and admired the beautiful cedar of Lebanon which graced the ground before the north door of St Gregory's. Of late he had been perplexed about the state of his favourite tree. It was very old, he knew that. It was huge and spreading but it was also dying. He hated to see this and he knew exactly what he was going to do. He carefully selected a few healthy seed pieces for propagation, and at the right time he tried cultivating them in a sheltered covered spot alongside his precious plants and herbs. To his great delight they sprouted strongly, gathering momentum with each month that passed. Eventually other folk, including the priest, noticed that the old church tree was dying. The branches were brittle with some kind of disease, a fact that made them unsafe to those who walked beneath, and several people had experienced narrow escapes when large lumbering branches had come crashing down to earth unexpectedly. The danger had also been recognized months ago with the sister cedars situated in the Manor house grounds. They had all been chopped down and used as firewood the previous winter. Revd Dauncey regretfully agreed with everyone that the church tree must go. It was then that Cornelius told them of his seedlings, so carefully nurtured and protected.

The old tree was felled and dispatched without ado, and one of the seedlings was planted by some local farm workers in the same spot under the watchful eye of Cornelius. They carefully ensured that there was not a trace of the disease-ridden root or surrounding soil left to hamper the progress of the new young cedar. They fulfilled their task well, for the tree, from the very start, continued to flourish and spread. At this time Cornelius offered the remainder of his young cedar plants to John Holbeach at Lyons Court to replace the loss of his cedar trees, but the Lord of the Manor declined, albeit graciously. Eventually Cornelius gave the plants to some passing monks on their way to Glaston-bury, men who had seen and known what beautiful trees these young plants could become.

Mary became very friendly with the mother of Pip Blessed after their sons had returned to their ships. Her name was Margaret and she and her forester husband, Tom Blessed, lived in the heart of Whytechurch village quite near to the church. Margaret was about the same age as Mary and most of her children were full-grown and married or had left home. Margaret was an open-minded woman and cared not for the prattle of other more ignorant women who hinted that she was befriending a woman who had borne a witch. She liked Mary, she admired her intellect, and the friend-ship was returned. They grew into the habit of taking time with each other occasionally, for Tom Blessed was out most of the day carrying out his duties for Lyons Court, and Jack

Sylvester always had something to do on the farm. Mary relished a womanly chat with Margaret in the Blessed's snug cottage, although sometimes Margaret did call at the farm when she found it her business to visit the forest, usually with a message for Tom. Mary enjoyed her visits to the village; apart from Margaret's company it gave her a chance to hear the local news and learn about some of the village people. During the years of bringing up her brood she had not had time for much else, and her interest in the church, its history, and Lyons Court was renewed. The present Lord of the Manor, John Holbeach, was the son of Thomas Holbeach who had first invited Mary all those years ago to sort out the family papers. Margaret Blessed also shared an interest in the past history of Whytechurch, so they had lots to talk about.

John Holbeach had not married a local girl. Barbara, his wife, was the daughter of John Coxwell, Gentleman, of Albington in the County of Gloucester to the north of Bristolle. The eligible local maidens had sighed with frustration at this match and Barbara had never been fully accepted in the village. Tom Blessed, working as he did for the estate, knew all the comings and goings of the Holbeach family, heard all the gossip, and relayed it to his spouse, who in turn relayed it to Mary Sylvester. Mary heard all the stories of the escapades of young Nathaniel Holbeach, heir to Lyons Court, and both women would sit and shake their heads together at the follies of the young.

'Of course,' Margaret said one day, 'If it hadn't been for bad luck a couple of centuries ago during the plague, our family, the Blesseds, would still be at Fyllwood Farm.'

'How can that be?' queried her friend, 'I thought the Halls had always been at Fyllwood.'

'Oh no no!' clucked Margaret. 'I've seen some papers relating to such matters in the church.'

Margaret, living near the church, often took a few flowers from her garden patch to brighten the building and cheer up the rather solemn Revd Dauncey. 'He really likes a bit of company sometimes, for the only other company he's got in that building are his dead predecessors under the north transept!' she had said one day when she met Mary as she was coming down the church path. It was the custom at Whytechurch to bury their dead priests in that part of the church. It was on one of Margaret's visits that Revd Dauncey put it to her that there were some documents in the church, probably written by a former priest, referring to some previous Blesseds. In former years it had been the custom of some priests to write down accounts of local happenings. Margaret could only read a little so had not been able to fathom out the real gist of the papers. When she told Mary of these papers Mary offered to help.

Together they paid Revd Dauncey a visit and what Margaret had said seemed to be true. The priest had unearthed some papers that Mary had not seen before, or maybe the impact of the information had not been so relevant years ago before she had met Margaret and her family. It was true – the Blesseds had left Fyllwood Farm and come to Whytechurch village at the time of the Great Plague. It was what followed this that truly intrigued Mary. The account of the farm at Fyllwood lapsing into dereliction, and then the arrival of young Samuel Candler who had shown such enthusiasm for the property and married a maid named Bertha from Charlton, and had a baby son Jack in 1523 . . . thereafter the scribe who had so painstakingly set down the details seemed to have gone beserk; the only words written after this were in large hideous scrawl – ADULTERESS . . . MURDERER! and there the tale ended. Mary became very thoughtful. Could it be? Oh no! Best not to think – Jack's mother Sarah had often talked of her lover Jack who had drowned with the *Mary Rose*. His dead mother's name had been Bertha, and she had come from Charlton, or Queen Charlton as it was now generally known. Mary knew this for sure, for when Sarah was talking family she had often said that if her son Jack had been a girl she would have named the child Bertha, for her dead lover's mother. He had often talked about his mother in their short sweet relationship.

Mary told herself over and over again that it was best not

to think – how could one guess at the story behind those two bold words, Adulteress, Murderer, that had leapt at her from the old script? Was this the explanation to her dear Jack's past, his lack of knowledge of some of his antecedents?

Margaret had not noticed anything, had not even scanned below mention of the Blesseds, being interested only in that name . . . best not to think. Best not to think. Margaret had gone on her way and Mary was standing musing by the stream below the church watching the otters at play. The otters had a holt further upstream in the meadows beyond St. Gregory's, and often of late Mary had stood silently by the lush tall grasses of the bank to watch the mother otter and her cubs at play and learning to dive and swim and fish. She became completely fascinated with the attractive little whiskered creatures and their capers. They appeared to be comparatively clumsy and cumbersome on land, but in the sparkling clear waters of the stream the proof of their agility was unquestionable and delightful to watch. Swift as an arrow the mother otter dived and curved to catch small fish to demonstrate and teach her skill to her young. The loud persistent call of a rook returned Mary to reality. Best not to think. Best not to tell. She made up her mind; her beloved Jack would never be told of her suspicions that his grandfather had been a murderer.

She made her way thoughtfully through the forest and home. Eleanor was there on a visit with her children, bright-eyed, rosy-cheeked and excited. All was well with the world, for whatever dark secrets Fyllwood Farm had previously known they were now dead forever. The proof of this was in the innocent faces of Mary's grandchildren and the happy countenance of Eleanor. Eleanor and Tim were very happy together and the farm was flourishing, and would continue to flourish even when old Ben Hall had gone and Tim had taken over. Best not to think, best not to tell!

Revd Dauncey died two years after the routing of the

Armada and a new younger priest arrived in his place. He swept through the village of Whytechurch like the proverbial new broom. He was young, ambitious, disliked clutter, and barely suffered tradition, so when he came across all the very old dusty manuscripts that were taking up space in his church he decided to make a bonfire of them. His excuse was that now that proper records were being kept under the decree of Queen Elizabeth, which stipulated formal registration of all the happenings in the realm's parishes such as baptisms, marriages and burials, there was no need to keep what he considered to be superfluous documents. In his bureaucratic fashion he did not even think about the historical value of the ancient writings pertaining to Whytechurch and its inhabitants, undertaken casually by former priests as forms of information or as journals. Posterity would be shocked, but Mary was pleased. Margaret bemoaned the fact that any connection her family might have had in the past with Fyllwood Farm was not on record any more, but Mary, beside her relief, was philosophical. It was meant to be. When young Pip Blessed came home for a few weeks at Christmas 1590, she could not help but say to her friend, 'Your Pip is a fine young fellow, of much greater worth than all those burnt documents! Mary, you can be proud of such a son.'

Indeed, although they could not know it, young Pip Blessed with his square stocky blond figure and merry features could have been the brother of his ancestor Davold, so strong was the Saxon blood in him. Young Pip was courting and he had come home to tell his parents of his joy and of his proposed wife-to-be, a maiden from Plymouth. Her name was Nancy Foulds. Most of her male kinfolk were sailors so she understood well the implications of being a sailor's wife. Her parents were dead but she lived with an elderly maiden aunt. Nancy was a wholesome girl, and not long after Pip had returned to Plymouth to wed her and after a few joyous days together had returned to sea, Nancy knew that she was pregnant.

Aunt Foulds, who was really quite fond of her niece in a

stiff unbending way, snorted when she heard Nancy's news. 'If it's a boy mark my words he'll go to sea!' Nancy laughed cosily in her happy expectation, and she did not mind at all. She had four brothers at sea and no sisters. If it was a boy and he went to sea then so be it, that was a long time yet. Pip, when he heard the happy news on one of his brief visits home, said 'If it's a little lad I'd like him called Francis after our great hero of the Armada. 'Tis a fine name that. I'm serious, lass!'

Nancy promised Pip this would be so. However when her time came she had not just one child but two – twin boys. They were big bonny babes for she had looked after herself well, but she had a very bad time with the birth which had been difficult. Aunt Foulds, being a maiden lady and not knowing much about such things, had consulted Nancy's brothers' wives about a suitable woman to attend to the birth. They were all very tied up with their own children – between them Aunt Foulds had been made a great-aunt twenty-one times – and they were not of great help, but she did gather some information about a midwife on the outskirts of the town, Mother Gurney, who would not only undertake to deliver babes but would look after the mothers in her own home for a week or so afterwards, if she was well paid to do so.

This arrangement suited Aunt Foulds very well. In her timid waspish way she had secretly dreaded the upheaval of birth in her own immaculate spinster's abode, so she jumped at the chance of Nancy giving birth at Mother Gurney's, allowing her a couple of weeks to prepare herself for a different routine. The extra expense did not bother her for she knew Pip would repay whatever it had cost when he next came home; what she did not know was that Mother Gurney was an incurable alcoholic. Maybe she had enjoyed a good reputation once, but poor young Nancy certainly suffered pain and neglect in Mother Gurney's establishment. In her weakness she longed for the peace and orderlinesss of Aunt Foulds, but resigned herself to the fact that she would be home in a couple of weeks.

Nancy never went home. She died of septicaemia ten days after her boys were born. She had named them Francis and Frederick. Mother Gurney drowned her conscience with some more drink and threw up her hands and wept with genuine sorrow when confronted with Aunt Foulds. 'The poor lass never had a chance from the beginning – a dreadful travail it was for her – two days trying to bring the young 'uns made her so weak, and she lost so much blood!'

What she did not admit was that she had not attended to Nancy as she should have. The sheets were never changed and Nancy had more than once had to beg her for a sponge to wash her troubled body while Mother Gurney sat in the kitchen with her jug.

There was another woman, a jocular motherly woman called Jessie Border staying at Mother Gurney's. She had also had a son on the same day as the twins were born. It was her eighth child so she was experienced in the birth process, and she had given poor young Nancy lots of encouragement. Jessie only stayed for a couple of days after the birth. 'My man can't afford me to be here any longer, and I want to get back to my childer anyway,' she had said. So she left with her infant son who looked remarkably like Nancy's Francis. Nancy's twin boys were so different to look at that it was hard to believe they were brothers. Francis was very fair and round-faced but Frederick's face was thin and pinched and he looked darker in colouring, although he did not have so much hair as Francis. Nancy had mentioned this several times to Mother Gurney, who always replied to the effect that they were not identical twins. 'Came from two different seeds if you can understand. I've delivered dozens of pairs like that – there are two kinds of twins you know!' she had said on one occasion. Nancy was still puzzled and not happy about it. It was true that she could not remember much about the boys when they were born as she had been in so much pain. She tentatively asked Jessie Border about it the day Jessie went home.

'Bless you, Nancy girl, all babies look the same to begin with, you'll find that out. They change too with their colouring. I had a babe once, I think it was the fifth . . . no it was the fourth . . . was born with jet black hair, but it all came off and he turned out to be very fair. Don't worry about it. In three months' time your boys will be as alike as any two peas in a pod!'

This heartened Nancy a little. Jessie should know after all – and Jessie would know her own baby, wouldn't she? But Jessie's baby did look remarkably like her own Francis.

What Nancy didn't know was that a few hours after her twin boys Francis and Frederick were born Mother Gurney had gone into a particularly deep alcoholic stupor. The effort of delivering three babies in one day and particularly the difficulty with Nancy's long labour had led her to seek her usual solace in the jug. She had been rudely awakened from her alcoholic haze by the cries of two of the babes, one of the twins and Jessie's babe. Without lighting a candle she had eventuallly picked them up one in each arm to soothe them off to sleep again, and promptly once more gone to sleep herself in her big old chair. Her senses were so dead that she did not stir when the other twin had started crying. Jessie Border awoke, and unable to go to sleep again had staggered to the crying infant in the dark. She thought it was her child because she could just make out Mother Gurney snoring away in the gloom with the other two tucked against her ample breast. Jessie had eventually lulled her baby off to sleep, or the baby she thought was hers. She had taken him to her own bed and that was how the mistake had evolved. When Mother Gurney eventually awoke she put the two babies she was nursing down together and eventually found Jessie Border fast asleep with the other babe. It was a terrible and far-reaching mistake, a combination of alcoholic stupor on Mother Gurney's part, casual acceptance on the part of Jessie Border, and sheer unawareness in the case of poor young Nancy Blessed.

Even Aunt Foulds remarked on the difference in the two babies, and Mother Gurney used the same excuse as she had with Nancy. ' 'Tis amazing,' she added, 'folk think

140

there's only one kind of twins, but those babes, I'd swear on my life, are from two separate seeds, so they can't be identical can they?'

Mother Gurney had never spoken a truer word! Aunt Foulds in her ignorance of all things matrimonial could say nothing to that and passed on the same excuse to Pip when he came home, and wondered about the boys, even in his grief.

It was eventualy decided by Pip, when the babies were a year old, to take them home to his mother Margaret at Whytechurch to rear. The care of the boys had been unsatisfatory and had not been getting any better. Aunt Foulds hadn't been able to cope, and one of Nancy's brother's wives had taken them for a while. She had then passed them to another brother's wife to share the load. It was when the third brother's wife was about to take a turn that Pip stepped in and made the decision on one of his trips back to Plymouth. He organized a journey to Whyte-church and Francis and Frederick were at last safely and permanently installed with their grandparents Margaret and Tom, who had talked the matter over at length and decided that this was the only solution to their son's dilemma, much to his everlasting relief.

Margaret and Tom did not have an easy time rearing their motherless grandsons. Apart from the usual boyish quarrels and tiffs there seemed to be real underlying dislike between them, usually fostered by Frederick's unbending and sullen manner. Francis was merry and amiable while Frederick was quiet and cunning, and only pleasant when he was getting his own way. Francis was also very much like his father in looks, and folk remarked on it. Tom often said that perhaps this was why Frederick was so hostile, perhaps in his immature way he felt he did not belong because he looked different. Jessie Border's predictions to poor dead Nancy that the two lads would grow more alike could never be true. They were very unalike – Francis was flaxen-haired, chubby and square-built, with bright blue eyes, whereas Frederick was thinner and very dark, with eyes like black coals. Margaret often remarked that he must have taken after someone in the Foulds family. Tom, with his kindly heart, would go out of his way to give the young rebellious Frederick a little extra attention. He loved both of his grandsons dearly and really enjoyed having children around the house again. When Francis was occupied with other things he would sometimes take Frederick with him into the forest and attempt to interest the boy in all the wonders of Fyllwood, but Frederick would stay as cold and aloof as ever. He was not a responsive child. Francis on the other hand was full of questions and eagerness whatever his surroundings.

It was no surprise, then, that when the twins were just turned sixteen years of age Frederick announced that he was leaving home. Francis was not very concerned about this. As they had grown older they had not bothered to quarrel so much and they had grown much more apart. Both Tom and Margaret tried hard to speak deeply to Frederick before his impending departure. Tom felt a failure although he had genuinely loved and tried hard with the boy, and Margaret felt guilty, but, good people that they were, they were not to know that Frederick just didn't care for them. He had shown a few flickers of response sometimes when Pip had come home between spells of duty – maybe if Pip had been home when Frederick made his decision to leave he could have persuaded the boy to think otherwise, but it was not to be. Frederick took off and said he was making for Plymouth, and that was as much as Tom and Margaret could tell Pip the next time he came ashore.

'Maybe he's wanting to join the navy,' Pip said hopefully, and he made exhaustive enquiries on his return to Plymouth, but it seemed that Frederick had not enlisted to go to sea. He had just disappeared.

Time passed and Nathaniel Holbeach eventually inherited Lyons Court. Francis was employed there, like his grandfather before him, as a forester. Pip had died of yellow fever in the Far East, and Francis had no desire to follow his father into the navy. He loved the forest and country

142

life, and thought very rarely of his lost brother Frederick these days.

When Frederick had arrived in Plymouth it did cross his mind to enlist in the navy, but he then thought better of it. His mother, he had often been told, had been a Plymouth lass, so he felt it might be a place where he could look up a few relatives if the world was too hard on him in his travels. After a few enquiries he gave up bothering about relatives. The Foulds family, his mother's brothers and their wives and offspring were just not interested in his welfare, and being proud and independent he shrank from any further contact with them. He found himself a job with a man named Martin Prout, who owned a ships' chandler's warehouse in the Barbican, and soon fixed himself up with lodgings nearby. Work was all that Frederick had in his life and Martin Prout mistook his single-mindedness for diligence. He had no son, only one haughty daughter named Matilda. She was eighteen years old and gave herself airs and graces far beyond her station. She too mistook Frederick's inwardness for submissiveness, and she really enjoyed popping into the warehouse and behaving in the high and mighty fashion she felt befitted the merchant's daughter – something that Frederick couldn't be bothered to respond to. Mentally he had her labelled as a silly cat!

A decade on, when Frederick was twenty-six, Martin Prout summoned him to his private office at the end of the warehouse. 'I'm going to talk straight to you lad. Have you ever thought of getting wed?'

Frederick did his best to disguise his surprise, and before he could answer Martin Prout continued, 'You could do worse than marry my Matilda, you know! She may be a bit high-spirited, but nothing wrong with that if you're in business. My wife died early on in my marriage and I never bothered with another, and it was a great disappointment I never had a son to follow on with the business, but you have worked as hard as any son of mine would have – to put it square to you, I'll leave you the businesss jointly with my Matilda if you'll wed her. I shall die a happy man then to be sure. You'll make a grand team. I know she's two years older than you but that's to the good, she's past the age for being flighty – not that many men have looked her way I can tell you. She's got an acid tongue, but you and she, you get on don't you? I've watched you – you seem to understand the lass!'

'More than right,' thought Frederick cynically, but his scheming brain was afire with Martin Prout's suggestion. To think the business could be his! He knew he could deal with the silly cat.

Six months from the day that her father had approached Frederick he wed Matilda. Frederick had never had any romantic notions about women; the thought of marriage had barely crossed his mind until Martin Prout had prompted it. He dealt with his marriage as with everything else, keeping to himself his innermost thoughts always. Matilda, he surmised, had even more stupidity in her than he had previously thought. He had taken for granted his marital duties, but on their wedding night she had been obscenely coquettish. This had appeared quite bizarre to Frederick who understood quite well what was expected of him without all her silly games. As usual he did not complain. He was happy to know that he would have the business. He was well and truly made. He could suffer Matilda and her ways.

Eighteen months later she bore him a son. They called him Martin after many sly suggestions from his father-in-law and goadings from his wife. Martin Prout died a happy man three years later, secure in the knowledge that his grandson, his namesake, was there eventually to carry on the business. Just after her father's death Matilda produced another offspring, a girl whom they named Betsy, and the sanguine Frederick softened a little in his ways as baby Betsy grew into a very pretty little girl, with a beguiling manner that would melt any heart. His son Martin he had always ruled with discipline, as he ruled Matilda, but Betsy had somehow managed to seek out a warm corner in his being, and he found a special solace in her innocent chatter.

144

Meantime the business was thriving. Frederick came into contact with many men of the sea, but one fine day in August 1622 he had a most unusual experience. A ship's master came through the door of his warehouse to order some tackle, and Frederick, busy with some barrels looked up and stopped dead in his tracks. The fellow was the spitting image of his estranged brother Francis. He felt it must be Francis and was about to speak when the fellow spoke up.

'I'm Captain Border of *The Woodpecker.* Just docked yesterday from The Indies. I have a list here of my requirements. No great hurry, but I do need exactly what is written here – no fobbing off with other things, you understand. I have it from hearsay that you run an efficient trade.'

'Oh yes!' Frederick was obsequious at the thought of business, but still puzzled. Could Francis have run away to sea and changed his name?'

'Oh yes, Captain Border, it shall receive my direct attention.' The list looked long and there was profit to be made.

Captain Border sensed the other man's diffidence despite Frederick's verbal assurances. He looked at Frederick intently, his blue eyes keen and penetrating. 'You are sure, man?'

'Oh yes, I can deal with it.' Frederick was no fool. 'You must excuse me sir, but you caught me unawares,' he explained. 'You look so much like my brother Francis Blessed, although I haven't seen him for nigh on fifteen years; the likeness is so amazing!'

Captain Border relaxed then. 'That's as may be. 'Tis said we all have a double somewhere in the world.'

Frederick became relaxed himself then. It was definitely not Francis. It could not be. He put the matter from his mind and concentrated on Captain Border's list. 'I'll do this for you sir, exactly as listed, within a week.'

'Fine.' Without further ado Captain Border was off striding down the narrow streets of The Barbican again.

That summer of 1622 when Frederick was thirty-one had been very profitable. He was well-established, a respectable tradesman in the local community, a family man with two children and another on the way. He felt more settled and contented than he had ever been in spite of his loveless marriage. His business and his children were his main concern although for decency's sake he had always treated Matilda with the respect due to a wife.

For another fifteen years he continued in this way, and then it happened. When young Martin was nearing eighteen he made it quite clear to his parents that he wanted no part of the business. He wanted to join the militia. He was a quiet solemn youth but with very firm ideas on his own future. He had a keen brain too and was interested in politics; he did not fancy being in commerce. For all of his young life his father had browbeaten him and disciplined him, and shown more favour to Betsy and his young brother Roger who loved helping in the warehouse. His mother was no help, taking his father's side in everything. She pleaded and cajoled and wrung her hands but to no avail, young Martin wanted nothing to do with the business his parents felt he was meant for. He joined the local militia whose activities at that time were mostly concerned with catching smugglers around the surrounding coasts. He also learned about the law and made the acquaintance of magistrates and politicians. After a while his mother and father grew used to the idea. Roger, their younger son, would be more than able to take on the business when the time came. It was Martin's loss.

Martin Blessed enjoyed the military life. In 1642 he was twenty-four years old and when the troubles arose in England and a civil war was threatened he knew exactly which side he was going to fight with. Cromwell and his new ideas appealed to him greatly, for he had always been a rebel, and thought along radical lines. He felt no loyalty towards Charles the monarch and his thoughts were that the country needed new men in charge and less ritual in the church. Martin absented himself from the militia and donned the regalia of the Roundheads. Most of his comrades in the militia were Royalists so he waited for the opportunity and just ran off one day from his quarters and travelled to join Colonel Nathaniel Fiennes, a stalwart of Oliver Cromwell's 'New Model Army' who was massing his men. With his military background he was welcomed with open arms and soon commissioned. Thus began a remarkable period in his young life.

9

Cavaliers and Roundheads

While Frederick Blessed had been making his way in Plymouth and rearing his family, Francis Blessed had been doing the same in Whytechurch. He was a very able fellow and had progressed from being just a forester on the Lyons Court estate to being land agent in charge of the whole manor. He had married Beatrice Hall, daughter of Eleanor and Tim Hall of Fyllwood Farm, the grand-daughter of his grandmother's closest friend Mary Sylvester. His grandparents and Mary Sylvester were all now dead. Francis and Beatrice had a well-built roomy house just to the south of the village, and had reared four sons, Matthew, Mark, Luke and John. When the clouds of civil war gathered they all professed their position as being staunch Royalists like the rest of Whytechurch village, and like Bristolle to the north of them this part of the country was ready to defend its King. The Royalist garrison at Bristolle had been firmly established there since 1643 when Cromwell's men had been defeated.

For a little time after the war became a certainty, nothing much seemed to happen to disturb their peaceful village life and things remained unchanged. Whytechurch folk did now and again hear of the terrible goings-on in other parts of the realm, but that was all. Then one bright Sunday morning when they were all at church it happened. The prayers were coming to an end when there was a loud urgent knocking on the south door of the church. Tom Whippie the verger opened the door cautiously, all eyes turned, minds dragged from their heavenward thoughts, to see such a sight. There stood young Michael Lansdowne, a local shepherd's boy, supporting a badly wounded soldier, a King's man by the look of the feather in his cap. He was bleeding profusely from a gash in the forehead and one arm was hanging limply at his side. Beside them were two other Cavaliers supporting each other, wretched and filthy and wounded.

'Quick,' said young Michael, 'Cromwell's men are on their way . . . they're after them . . . quick give them sanctuary, sir!'

Revd John Brooke, the present incumbent, was already at the door assisting them. 'Come in my brothers, we will tend you. Michael, shut the door!'

'Hasten now!' said Tom Whippie. He pushed the bolts and hurried to secure the other door. Then they were safe.

'God bless you all,' said one of them weakly, 'They're not far behind.'

'Yes, yes,' Revd John was giving them drinks of water and looking at their injuries while young Michael was trying to explain how he had chanced upon them in Old Acre field while helping his father with the sheep. 'We were looking for a lost ewe and found them in the ditch just as the Roundheads were riding down the Dundry slopes.'

Apparently there were only four or five Roundheads on their horses, probably a patrol, his father had said. His father had bade young Michael get them to the sanctuary of the church while he waited to deviate Cromwell's men with useless information. Michael had crawled round with them through the ditches until they had come within reach of St Gregory's and they had made the last hundred yards or so across open ground. A distant shout of triumph had warned them that their pursuers had espied them.

A further loud banging on the south door told everyone that the pursuers were now there. An imperious Roundhead voice called out, 'Come out, you quaking cowards, come out and face us – we know you're in there!'

Some of the women in the body of the church shivered with fear but Revd John spoke up then strong and true.

'These men are wounded, they are in my care. In Christ's name they have sought sanctuary and healing. Go away!'

That seemed to rile Cromwell's men.

'We demand that they come out!'

'We demand you deliver them to us!'

'We shall fight for them, although we have no fight with you, priest!'

It was Revd John's finest hour then. 'Then you WILL have to fight me to get them!'

There was a silence, then, 'If you do not deliver them we shall be forced to use our muskets!'

The priest was silent then. He thought for a while and then turned to his flock. 'Quickly, everyone to the east end of the church!' There was a lot of terror. Wives clung to husbands and tearful children clutched at their mothers' skirts, but nobody really panicked and they all moved to the east end as they had been bidden, with Tom Whippie calmly arranging them against the stout stonework out of harm's way.

Just as they were all safe the Roundheads shouted again. 'We are still waiting. Send out those men!'

Revd John called out in a stong clear voice, 'Do as you will!' The south door was strong and would take a lot of shifting.

The sound of muskets aimed at the door suddenly echoed around the church. The Roundheads were not going to accept defeat easily. They fired again but the priest felt it was just bravado on their part. The sound of the muskets was frightening, but the door stood firm as he knew it would, although it was peppered with holes. The sturdy wood and the strong bolts had proved too much for Cromwell's men. After what seemed to be a long time they clattered around the outside of the church to the north door but realized that this door was just as strong and after a few more loud curses accompanied by some shouted threats they finally rode away on their horses, and all in the church breathed freely again.

Francis and Beatrice Blessed had been huddled at the

east end of the church with the others, and Beatrice shuddered at the thought of what might have happened if Cromwell's men had gained entrance to the church. She sent up a prayer for her eldest son Matthew serving with the garrison in Bristolle. Matthew was no soldier but he had been recruited with many others when Nathaniel Holbeach had been approached by Sir Thomas Smyth who owned many Whytechurch acres. Sir Thomas was a stout Royalist who had supported Prince Rupert and his men when they had taken Bristolle Castle from Cromwell's men in 1643. In Bristolle they were now expecting the enemy to retaliate soon, for Bristolle was an important city.

Revd John interrupted Beatrice's troubled thoughts. 'It is in my mind that these injured men need rest and sustenance, more than I can provide. Do you think that your sister Dorothy at Fyllwood could accommodate them? It would be safer there than in the village.'

Beatrice brightened at this suggestion. Here was something positive to do. Dorothy would help, she knew. Dorothy was a strong character, fearless in her beliefs. Since the death of the older menfolk in her family she had run Fyllwood Farm with tireless efficiency. Beatrice looked down at her best leather shoes and straightened the creases in her plum-coloured home-spun dress. 'I feel sure Dorothy will look after them. Francis and I will take them in the cart after noon – but first we will feed them.'

That evening the three soldiers were safely under the roof of Fyllwood Farm, well-fed and their wounds attended to, but that was not the end of the story. One afternoon two days after the church incident there was a loud knocking on the main door of Fyllwood Farm. Dorothy Hall, her young brother and a couple of servants in their kitchen exchanged meaningful glances for they had heard distant cannon fire all morning. Then a voice called out that they would come to no harm. It was the King's men and they had come hotfoot from the Castle at Bristolle. It had been taken at last by Cromwell. There were five of them and they were hungry, and some wounded. They were also surprised to see another three comrades already there. Dorothy bade them enter, and the officer in charge was both pleased and grateful, but she pointed out that she was taking a great risk letting even more Royalists under her roof.

'Cromwell's New Model Army would have me out of this place before I could blink an eye if they found you!' she said straightly. 'They seem to be gaining control around here, but,' she added not unkindly, 'you can stay until your stomachs have been appeased and the wounds are healing.'

The next day Fyllwood received a visit from some of Cromwell's men, but not before they had been espied by one of the servants who had been put on special watch. Hastily Dorothy ushered the King's men, both fit and wounded, out of the back of the farm across to the cover of the forest. Then she armed herself with the bar from the kitchen spit and stood ready and resourceful. When they came they searched the house thoroughly and then turned their attentions to her maid. They tried hard to get the girl to talk, to say if she had seen any of the King's men, but Dorothy's servants were loyal. Dorothy ordered the men to let the girl alone, and the officer-in-charge shrugged his shoulders and said, 'I'm warning you, Mistress, if we find any of the King's men hereabouts we shall seize your farm and put it up for auction!'

Dorothy knew well that this was no idle threat. It was a fact that this had happened in other places where the Royalists taking refuge had been discovered by Cromwell's men. She stood her ground. 'You frighten me not!' was all she said, hoping desperately that the fugitives were well into the forest by now.

'I'm a reasonable man,' continued the officer. 'I have orders to search all the farms around here for followers of the Crown. You'd best be speaking the truth, Mistress Hall!' He turned to his sergeant, 'We'll start looking through the forest now. I've a feeling there may be some hiding out there!'

As it transpired Cromwell's men found nothing in Whytechurch or Fyllwood Forest. All the King's men were under safe cover. They had cut quickly through the forest and over the hills to the south where there were plenty of Royalists to hide them. Local word had it that Lyons Court had hidden more than a few Royalists in the tunnel that was said to run between the house and the church, and indeed there was talk that a further tunnel extended to the alehouse. Wherever the Roundheads searched they left empty-handed; of prisoners that was, for they plundered plenty of food and goods.

When the news was confirmed that Cromwell's troops had taken Bristolle Castle Beatrice became really worried, but Francis consoled her staunchly, 'Have no fear for our lad, wife. He'll fight with honour if needs be, although he's no soldier. He's got a good cool head on him!'

When Matthew finally did come home a week or so later it was a great happiness to see him, but also a surprise that he brought this other fellow with him. This was how the story was told to Francis and Beatrice Blessed.

In the year of Our Lord 1645 on the tenth day of September at 7 o'clock in the morning, Martin Blessed, the son of Frederick Blessed, ships' chandler of Plymouth, was dripping with sweat when he finally managed to get over Bristolle Castle walls. He was with General Fairfax's parliamentary forces, and the fighting was more sporadic now. The resistance seemed to be less. Indeed there had not been too much resistance and Prince Rupert's men were falling back drastically. Martin had been on the move for many hours and he had left his men under the control of one of the sergeants, for he had suddenly felt the call of nature. Being an ex-militia man he knew the layout of castles and fortifications, so he looked for a garderobe along the wall nearest to him. Eventually he spied what he was looking for. He strode forward and pushed open the door, to surprise a fellow already using the facility. What was more the man was a Royalist!

'Ha ha, caught him with his breeches down!' he thought gleefully, but being the trained soldier that he was he said haughtily 'So this is the measure of Prince Rupert's men – hiding in the garderobes, miserable cowards!'

At that the fellow stood up sharply, adjusting his clothing, half-embarrassed, but as haughty as Martin.

'Hiding? Indeed no, sir. As the fighting had quietened a little I was seeking relief for my bodily functions – but now you are here stand fast!' He drew a sword swiftly from behind him. 'Stand fast, do you hear? No man calls Matthew Blessed a coward!'

Martin's jaw dropped then. For the moment he had completely put aside his reason for coming to the garderobe. 'Blessed? Do you say your name is Blessed, man?'

The other young man stared him straight in the eyes. He was stockily built with a shock of flaxen hair. 'Yes, my name is Matthew Blessed from the parish of Whytechurch to the south of this good city!'

Martin was still intrigued. This fellow must be a relation of some sort, for his father's people he knew had been Whytechurch bred. He laughed then and said, 'Put away your sword, Matthew Blessed. I am here for the same reason as thee. I am Martin Blessed from the city of Plymouth, and I think we might be kin.'

It was Matthew's turn to be surprised then. He relaxed and put away his sword. 'Plymouth d'you say? My father's mother was from there – I think we may be cousins!'

From this strange meeting in the garderobe there was to evolve an unusual friendship.

The castle was eventually taken by Cromwell's men at 8 o'clock that morning, when the Royalist garrison were separated and eventually surrendered to Fairfax's troops. As they had capitulated and were outnumbered, Fairfax allowed the men of the King's nephew to march out of the city and back to Oxford, a Royalist stronghold. It was bitter defeat for the Royalists, for they had held Bristolle for two years, since the 26th day of July in 1643 when they had at that time overpowered the enemy with ease – mostly two thousand untrained volunteers raised by Colonel Nathaniel Fiennes of Cromwell's New Model Army. King Charles had even come from Oxford to congratulate the defenders of Bristolle personally. Now two years later the tide had turned and Cromwell once again held the city.

Matthew, when he learned that Prince Rupert's men were to make for Oxford, decided to stay in Bristolle and eventually make his way home to Whytechurch to family, home and work, when it was possible to do this unnoticed. He felt he had done his duty to the Crown and the local authorities, and he was not really inspired to march to Oxford to fight again. There were many yeomen like him whose feelings were the same. In the meantime he continued to meet Martin discreetly to exchange snippets of family gossip and information. By now they had worked out that they were first cousins, the sons of the twin brothers Francis and Frederick Blessed. Nobody questioned Matthew's identity for he appeared to be a friend and relative of Captain Martin Blessed. The Roundheads had no proper check on those outside their own army, and indeed no longer cared greatly. They were in possession of the castle and that was all that really mattered to them. After a while when Cromwell's men had established a routine the cousins had been able to slip away to Whytechurch, Martin on pretext of family business, Matthew to disappear altogether.

So it was that the cousins turned up in Whytechurch to the joy and confusion of Francis and Beatrice. It was obvious that the two young men had become good friends, but Matthew's parents were at quite a loss to know how to treat Martin. He was a commissioned officer in Cromwell's army, and yet he was a blood relative. In the end they just accepted the friendship and told nobody outside the family of the Cromwell connection, for if it had become known that they were entertaining a Roundhead officer their standing in the local community would have been shattered. Indeed there were some hotheads in the village who would stop at nothing if they got their hands on one of the anti-Royalists, for there were sons and husbands who had been killed for the Royalist cause, although the actual village of Whytechurch had been comparatively lucky during the conflict. Apart from the fracas at the church when the Roundheads had attempted to blast open the door, and the confrontation at Fyllwood Farm where Dorothy Hall had given the enemy short shrift, there had been no terrible happenings such as those that occurred at Betteminster just to the south of Bristolle. The church of St John had been burned to the ground during Fairfax's advance. It had been used as a stable for Prince Rupert's horses, and not only the church but also a large part of Betteminster had been burned. During 1645 Bristolle was in the throes of another plague outbreak and many staunch Royalists believed that this was in no small way responsible for the defeat in September. Whytechurch had also suffered from the plague, and as had happened three centuries before, the corpses were buried deep in the field to the south of the church known as Black Acre. Matthew had found a few familiar faces missing when he returned.

Surprisingly enough Martin found himself enjoying village life, and he escaped from his duties whenever he could to spend time with his newly-discovered kinfolk. About a year after he had met Matthew, Martin went back home to Plymouth for a while to his family. Even at that time he was gradually disassociating himself from his rebel friends and was looking for a way to ease out of any further commitments to the parliamentarians. Back in Plymouth his mother and father seemed to be managing quite well, grooming his younger brother Roger for the time they would hand the business over to him. As far as they were concerned Frederick and Matilda made Martin welcome enough, but they had grown used to being without him; only his sister Betsy seemed to understand him. Betsy had grown into a beautiful young woman, guarded anxiously by a doting Frederick from all the hopeful young men who happened her way. It stirred Frederick's interest a little when he heard the strange story of Martin's meeting with Matthew, and also of his meeting with the family at Whytechurch.

Francis on the other hand had been really pleased to

have news of Frederick after young Martin had landed on his doorstep; to know at last what had happened to his long-lost brother. He had urged young Martin to ask his father to visit them in Whytechurch, but this Frederick firmly refused to do. He told himself, and others, that he felt his business which was flourishing could not be left, but really it was Frederick's insular personality that baulked against any further intimate contact with his Whytechurch kinsfolk. He had burned his boats the day he left home as a stubborn inexperienced sixteen-year-old, and he could not see fit to go back now, although he was puffed with pride that he had made such a success of his life and was glad for Francis to know that.

Betsy, however, was a different case. She longed to travel up-country to see these unknown kinsfolk at Whytechurch, for she had grown tired of her mother's relatives who always seemed to be bickering between themselves. Her father indulged Betsy in most things, but when she had mentioned her wish to visit Whytechurch he was adamant in his refusal. Subsequent events were to change his mind.

There was a certain young fellow named James Luccombe who had become particularly persistent in his attempts to further his acquaintance with Betsy. He was a personable young pup and not the first young man that Betsy had shown interest in. She openly defied her father and began meeting her 'Jamesie' as she called him, secretly: after all she was twenty years old and bored with being treated like a child. Frederick was puce with rage when he chanced upon them unexpectedly one day, kissing and cuddling in the orchard at the back of the messuage they now lived in on the outskirts of Plymouth, away from the business and the smells of the Barbican. Frederick's excuse was that Betsy was not ready yet for a romantic attachment, although deep within himself he knew that he was wrong. Many girls of her age were already married with families, her mother pointed out. Matilda huffed and snorted at Frederick for she really wanted to get Betsy married off. She was deeply jealous of her husband's devotion to their daughter and she was still hoping some day to have Frederick's full attentions. Then Matilda had what she thought was a brilliant idea.

'Why not pack Betsy off to Whytechurch for a while?' It would cool the girl's ardour and put an end to her seeing young Luccombe!

Frederick reluctantly had to agree, and one bright morning in 1646 Betsy, rosy-cheeked and excited, was packed off to Whytechurch in the company of her brother Matthew.

Since that day she had only returned to Plymouth once; that was to inform her parents that she was to marry young Tom Whippie of Lower Green Farm, son of the verger who had helped to hold Cromwell's men at bay outside St Gregory's. The news of Betsy's intentions had left them shattered. Indeed Matilda said it was the start of Frederick's colic and illness that eventually was to lead to his demise. He was right not to have wanted Betsy to go to Whytechurch, she pointed out smugly. He had been right all along and Betsy was 'a bad wicked girl to have been flouting her charms at the Whytechurch lads!'

Matilda had conveniently forgotten that the girl's visit had originally been at her suggestion, mainly because of her jealousy over Frederick's over-protectiveness. When Frederick had pointed out that the suggested visit had been Matilda's idea she had answered defensively, 'But what else could we do!' Frederick had no answer for that.

'After all we've done for you! It won't last you see, you ungrateful wench!' were her parting words to Betsy.

In spite of her mother's forebodings Betsy and Tom Whippie were very happy. The girl had found a new freedom in being married and away from the ever-watchful eyes at home. It was also nice to have her brother Martin near at hand, for he was still spending a lot of time in Whytechurch, and he had caused no interference to her plans. The Whippies were a nice family and took instantly to the pretty girl. The newly-weds made their home with the older folk at Lower Green Farm, where young Tom would eventually take over.

The Whippies had always called the eldest son Thomas

158

and the family abounded with Thomases. In 1648 Betsy presented them with another baby Thomas. Although she was invited Matilda never did make the journey to see her first grandchild. She was quite happy to stay in Plymouth bossing young Roger about the business until the day she died.

As time passed Martin resigned his commission with the parliamentarians. Prior to the execution of Charles I in 1649 he had considered entering the political world and becoming a Member of Parliament, but the execution of the monarch killed his idealism. It was as if he had awoken sharply to a different state of consciousness. He suddenly felt older and wiser, no longer the enthusiastic boy who had thrown in his lot with Cromwell's New Model Army. He felt that executing the King had been far too radical, and it was no way to solve the country's problems. For a little while he dithered around doing an odd job here and there helping farmers, but the time came when he felt he must make a firm decision about what he was doing with his life. He had a little money put by, he would go into business as a shop-owner in the village of Whytechurch. The village at this time had a population of around two hundred, and he had frequently seen the need for a shop that would sell all the commodities that folk usually made the trek into Bristolle for; things that were readily available there, Bristolle being a seaport like Plymouth. In addition to general victuals he would go for the more fanciful things like cocoa beans and foreign spices, sweetmeats and perhaps the odd twist of tobacco. Whytechurch had never been rich but there were steady incomes being earned there from the increasing flocks of sheep that thrived in that part of the country. West country wool was the finest and very much in demand.

In 1649 when he was thirty-one years of age Martin opened his shop and it seemed that his ideas were proved right. The village folk flocked to make their special pur-chases locally, saving the ride into Bristolle, and Martin had a good head for prices when he was bargaining for stock in the dockside warehouses. If his father, recently dead from the colic, had lived to see it he would have been grudgingly proud but puzzled, for after many adventures and changes of heart Martin had gone into business like his father before him, but of course Martin had done it in his own way and in his own good time. He did not begrudge his younger brother Roger the thriving business in Plymouth, for he was quite content with his own efforts and the life he had created for himself.

In 1651 on one of his frequent trips into Bristolle he was greatly interested to note a newly erected handsome statue depicting Neptune King of the Sea, on the road close to Temple Gate, the site of the old Knights Templar Monastery. It seemed to him to be a very apt piece of work for this seafaring city. He enjoyed his jaunts to the docks and when business was over he would stop for a drink at one of the many alehouses and rub shoulders with sailors and merchants and all manner of men. On this day the talk was of the Neptune statue, and Martin learned that it had been donated by a plumber of the parish of Temple to decorate a fountain which evolved from a subterranean spring flowing down into the city called Temple Pipe. There were several such sources in the city flowing down from the surrounding hills.

Of the cousins Matthew was the first to marry. He had fallen in love quite suddenly with one of the daughters of the newly-arrived alehouse keeper in Whytechurch, Jacob Potter. Her name was Catherine, a striking-looking damsel with dark red hair. In conversation with her father Matthew learned that the family had come from Bath and that a relative of theirs had lived in Whytechurch many years ago. They were married at St Gregory's and as Catherine was his eldest daughter Jacob Potter was determined to make the wedding and the festivities that followed really splendid.

The church was packed and it seemed as if the whole village had turned out to wish them well as they emerged from the north porch. They made a handsome couple, Catherine with her bright hair and creamy skin set off by a wedding gown of rich cream damask, embroidered at the

160

neckline with pure silk thread, and Matthew with his flaxen hair and merry blue eyes looked very resplendent in dark red breeches of the finest wool with jacket to match over his fine lawn shirt with lace jabot. His white silken hose and black large buckled shoes set this off to perfection. It was a very happy day and Martin, dear friend that he was, made sure that the wedding feast at the inn was provided with many extra delicacies. After this Martin quite understandably did not see quite so much of his cousin, and a year later he too became married, to Elizabeth, the daughter of a farmer from the neighbouring village of Norton Malreward. He had been instantly attracted to her when she had first come to the shop to make some purchases. She proved to be quite an asset in the shop but sadly as the years passed there were no children, whereas Matthew and Catherine seemed to produce a child every year.

In 1654 Cromwell ordered the destruction of Bristolle Castle and by 1655 most of it had been pulled down. The majority of people thought it was a wholly wanton act, especially the folk of the city who were justly proud of the mighty fortification which had stood for hundreds of years, but this was the way of the parliamentarians. They had no great reverence for tradition, for establishment, in the church as well as in the kingdom generally. There was a lot of debris from the destruction and later many houses and other buildings were to be built on the original foundations which were still strong; also many of the actual stones saved from the destruction were destined to be used to build houses and shops in the surrounding area. There were quite a few people who were pleased when Cromwell died on the 3rd of September 1658, and as the years came and went, the political turmoil ceased and a King, Charles II, son of the unfortunate beheaded Charles I, was once more on the throne. The good folk of Whytechurch forgot all about politics and returned to thinking mainly about their land, their crops and their sheep.

The Wool Acts of 1666 and 1678 enforced very strict rules about coffins and burials. Corpses had to be buried in shrouds or shifts made of pure wool only, not even to be blended with flax or hemp or sillk. Also it was stipulated that coffins should not be lined or faced with any material other than pure wool. Affidavits had to be sworn before witnesses by relatives of deceased persons that these rules had been adhered to, and heavy penalties were ordered if the rules were broken. This was a wonderful time for the west country sheep farmers. Not only was their fine wool purchased in plenty by the living, it was also compulsory for the dead to go to their Maker clothed and protected in wool!

In 1685 Charles II died and was succeeded by his brother James II who was a staunch Catholic. James had plans to make the country Catholic once again, but there was a lot of opposition to James and his ideas, and the Duke of Monmouth led a rebellion against the Crown and was joined by many west country followers. Folk shook their heads and asked each other sadly would there ever be peace and contentment again? There was a bloody battle at Sedgemoor outside Bridgwater in Somerset, quite a few miles to the south of Whytechurch, and Monmouth was defeated and eventually beheaded. The new King came down very hard against the rebels who had joined Monmouth's cause and promptly appointed Judge Jeffreys, a cruel sadistic man, to conduct the case against the rebels at the Assizes. In the west country over three hundred men were hung and left to rot where they died, on local hills and prominent places, as a lesson to others. Just to the south of Whytechurch where a big hill swept down towards Glastonbury and the Pilgrims' Way was one such shocking place, and thereafter the lane along the top of this hill was called Gibbet Lane. Folk would cross themselves as they passed the spot and Matthew Blessed's grandchildren were not allowed near the place. Approximately another eight hundred rebels were punished by being shipped across to the West Indies as slaves for the plantations that were thriving there as a result of investments by merchants and shipowners. Rumour abounded that many of these men had died on voyage due to ill-treatment and starvation, and countless families grieved for their sons and husbands not knowing if they were alive or dead. James II was eventually deposed and fled the country. In 1688 he was succeeded by William of Orange, a grandson of Charles I who had married Mary, daughter of James II. The cousins were invited to England and declared joint sovereigns in 1689.

Whytecross Farm at this time was thriving. A family by the name of Lukins had long since replaced the Chases, and the old house had been repaired and rebuilt in so many places that the former owners would not have recognized it. The road to Bristolle which passed by its gates had also been altered and widened from the original country track.

Some of the gypsies and travelling people who had for centuries travelled through Fyllwood Forest were now settled in camps in suitable clearings, and were not a burden on the parish, for at this time near the turn of the century the church was taking more and more responsibility for the running of the community. The gypsies troubled nobody and the local farmers found their presence very useful when extra labour was needed for haymaking and the like, for although the Romanies were in many ways a proud people, a race apart, they were not above earning a penny or two when the chance happened. Like all communities there were those of their number who were not so honest, and occasionally a farmer would find a chicken missing, but although some folk continually blamed the gypsies, a missing chicken could also have been the work of a fox, and if it was a Romany who was responsible then the general concensus was that some people would always steal whatever their race or background. Losing chickens was an occupational hazard.

Some of the gypsies reared their own poultry but mostly they enjoyed a plump wood pigeon. The wood pigeons were prolific in Whytechurch and Fyllwood. Unafraid and adventurous in spite of being continually hunted, it never took the pigeons long to find food, as many a farm labourer had learned to his cost when sitting with his midday bread and

163

cheese and cider, maybe against a haystack or a hedgerow. A moment of unawareness, a temporary dozing off with the help of strong Somerset cider, and the wood pigeons would seize their chance and swoop. Rabbits were in abundance as were hares. There was always meat on the table for Whytechurch families no matter how poor they were. The well-off ate prime cuts of beef and lamb most of the time, but the ordinary Whytechurch folk were never at a loss to produce a good rabbit stew, a jugged hare, and some folk kept a pig or two, so if you were lucky there were flitches of bacon as well.

10

The Whytchurch Foundling

Lyon's Court had passed out of the possession of the Holbeaches in 1688, for in the last century there had been gradual changes in the realm regarding ownership of land, and the Lords of the Manor did not now wield so much awesome power over the community as in former times. There were more farmers and smallholders now, although most of the Whytchurch farmers were renting tenants of the Smyths of Ashton Court, who had owned quite a large proportion of Whytchurch land since the 1570s, including Fyllwood Farm, and the Halls were still at Fyllwood. In 1730 Sir John Smyth of Ashton Court had an extensive survey made of his farms and properties in Whytchurch. The Smyths were also the patrons of the church, together with their relations the Gore-Langtons of Newton Park in Bath, and between them they paid £200 per annum for the perpetual curacy. This was the normal practice since the demise of the monasteries and abbeys, for the crop of new landowners in the country, of which the Smyths were typical, had replaced them in the exercise of power and responsibility.

At this time in 1730 the landlord of the White Hart was Benjamin James; the Lukins had gone from Whyte Cross, and a well-known family by the name of Goodhind were now in possession there. Although Lyons Court was no longer their home, the Holbeach family lived in Whytchurch for quite a while after. Lyons Court at this time was not primarily a farm, although some of the fields surrounding it were rented by locals. The old house still stood in all its glory, firm in foundation and strong still in structure in spite of its age. The builders employed by Ralph de Lyon four centuries ago had made a thorough job. The house now functioned mostly as an administrative centre. Previously it had only been put to use as a court in a spasmodic fashion, but with the steady increase of population and more frequent movement of people between villages, calling for communication and transport, the court became busier. One contributory factor to the increased movement of folk between villages was the fact that when people engaged servants it had become increasingly popular to chose them from outside the village. The reason for this was fairly obvious. Private family matters would not be locally discussed by servants who came from another district.

The church had a fine set of bells, and the last one had been cast in 1770. For quite a long time before this the upkeep of the church had deteriorated, for as mentioned earlier the Smyths and their relatives only provided the curacy, or living. In 1787 the newly-appointed curate at the church was Revd John Collinson, F.A.S., an academic highly interested in antiquities; so much was his interest that his parishioners did not see very much of him. Being under the patronage of the Smyths he also had connections with Ashton Parish Church in the precincts of Ashton Court. Some folk would go so far as to say that Revd Collinson's parish was the whole of the county of Somerset, for in the year 1791 he published a work entitled *The History and Antiquities of Somerset.* In the pursuit of writing this massive work, he travelled extensively throughout the county; eventually his health suffered and he died at an early age; more than one who knew him said it was overwork. He was officially curate of Whytchurch for six years until 1793, but whatever folk said about him they had to admit that, through his interest in antiquities, he had contributed a lot to the local history of Somerset and of Whytchurch. However during his curacy at Whytchurch Collinson had neglected the church registers and the tedious task of updating them was left to his successor. To this day the accuracy of the records of this period is questioned.

In 1791, the year that Collinson published his great work, the Whytchurch churchwardens held a vestry meeting to discuss what they were to do about the ruinous state of the church. There was not much money available so they decided to sell one of the bells. They found a purchaser in the original maker, Thomas Bilbie, clockmaker and bell-founder of Chew Stoke, a village away to the south on the road to Wells. They sold the bell back to Bilbie for ten pounds. With the aid of this money they contrived to patch up the church as much as they could and engaged a man from Bristolle called Robert Pobjoy to do this work, but the old building needed a lot to be done to keep it in good shape and there never was enough money. Over the next fifty years the church was to let most of the bells go to the church in the neighbouring village of Queen Charlton, as the woodwork in the belfry was badly deteriorated making it dangerous, and there were fears that the bell frames would not sustain the weight of the bells. In the end there was only one bell left, the last and newest one cast in 1770.

At this time the Whippie family still worked several farms at Whytchurch. The Whippies had always been regular churchgoers and in 1794 they were faced with a difficult problem. Robert Whippie, one of the younger sons, and his wife Mary were tenants of a smallholding which had fallen upon hard times. At this time the church employed an official overseer to the poor, and anyone in the parish who faced financial problems could ask for help from the church. In this case Robert and Mary were unlucky, for although the majority of Whytchurch folk worshipped at St Gregory's there were a handful of dissenters who preferred nonconformist worship in the chapel which had been established in the village. Mary Whippie was one of this minority. The Overseer was firmly of the opinion that the church could not settle the debts or pay the rent of any dissenter. Furthermore one of the signatures of the parish vestry members supporting the Overseer's decision to order the removal of Robert and Mary to the Poorhouse was that of Richard Whippie, another member of the family. The Whippies were a large family and would soon find another cousin, a staunch churchgoer, to run the smallholding. Nobody in the village seemed to feel that Richard had been uncharitable to Robert and his wife. The church was the established place to worship, everyone paid their poor rates, and nobody wanted their money squandered on dissenters. So Robert and Mary went to the Poorhouse.

In 1787 when Sally Waxon, maid at the White Hart, finally realized she was pregnant she was not in a great state of panic, although it would not be true to say she did not feel a trifle anxious at the state she found herself in. In fact the knowledge had come to her gradually, creeping into her awareness stealthily, remorselessly. The persistent nausea, not only in the mornings, the unusual revulsion to eating eggs which she normally loved, the strange feeling that she no longer knew how her body functioned; her physical being was in chaos. Yet she could not remember when she first felt that this was so, and in an equally strange fashion she felt that she must have known subconsciously for quite a while that she was with child. Ironic that just one glorious encounter with Stephen Blessed had led to this. Even in her perplexity the thought of that one heady evening in Long Acre field filled her with remembered joy and warmth. The question was, what was she to do? She loved Stephen, always had, but he was already wed with a child on the way, and in any case she felt a certain amount of guilt about the whole thing, for had she not led him on, that fateful night? It was true that in the past he had always treated her with a little more than plain courtesy and she had known instinctively that he returned the attraction she felt for him, but fate and families had decided otherwise. Stephen, great-great-grandson of Matthew Blessed, had married quite young; his parents were well-positioned, with no shortage of money, and had wanted to get him settled with a "suitable girl". The suitable girl turned out to be the daughter of one of his father's friends, a pretty lass, and

Stephen, being an easy-going lad had seemed to be well pleased. Sally knew that his parents would not have looked kindly upon a marriage between herself and their son, for she was just a simple servant girl at the White Hart. That was how she had first met him when he used to come in with the local lads to sup ale and swap tales.

Her downfall had been that summer evening when it was her night off, and she happened upon Stephen quite by chance returning from the hills with his dogs. They had chatted quite naturally for a while and then boldly she had mentioned her surprise at his marriage. At the time of his wedding she had thought she would never recover from the surprise when she had heard the news. She had, in her girlish heart, cherished dreams of Stephen being the man in her life, and here he was being married off without even a chance to look around properly. Because of this she was full of mixed feelings when he'd said to her that fateful evening, 'My marriage is no good. I'll stick with her, but I wish I'd waited . . . oh how I wish I'd waited, Sal!' The despair in his eyes had prompted more boldness on her part.

'I always thought that you and I would be right together!'

'I know, I know . . . oh Sal, I'm so lonely!'

The intensity of it had got to both of them. He had suddenly embraced her for they were well hidden by the trees. The dogs ran off home, bored at not walking with their master, and Stephen and Sally had sunk to the long grass consumed with sadness and love. Afterwards she had been ashamed, and Stephen had been very apologetic.

'Let us try to forget it. It'll never happen again. I am a married man, after all!'

No mention of his loneliness now. If Sally had been older and more experienced she would have realized that Stephen was just a foolish young man, and she was not the great love of his life as she would have liked to be. Instead she took all the blame on her young shoulders; she had been stupid and very forward, and she had committed adultery. The shame of it, the horror of it! If anyone found out she was carrying a bastard child she could be sent to a house of correction once the child was born, or worse still it was within the power of the authorities that she could be publicly whipped.

What should she do? Who could she turn to? The ugly thought of abortion slanted darkly across her mind more than once, like an evil shadow, but each time she hastily dismissed it with disgust and loathing. These thoughts conjured up visions of dirty old dwellings and merciless old hags, from memories of conversations she had occasionally heard taking place between older women when they thought the young were out of earshot.

What was she to do? There was the babe to think about. What sort of future would this love-child have? She was adamant in her own mind that she would not involve Stephen Blessed. Eventually the solution came to her. Her home was in Wells, the small cathedral city south of Whytchurch. She would have to go and tell her mother – a terrible thought, but it had to be done. She knew that after the initial censure her mother would eventually stand by her, although she did not intend to burden her mother with the child. She would bear the infant and then she would come back to Whytchurch and leave the babe as a foundling at the Poorhouse; foundlings had been left there before. She knew this was the only way she could enlist the help of her mother, for Widow Waxon was a proud woman and had always held her head high in the community at Wells. She could not burden her mother with an illegitimate grandchild.

So it was that Sally told her employers at the White Hart that her mother had been taken seriously ill suddenly and would need to be looked after for a few months. She was four months pregnant at this time and barely showing. Her employers clucked their concern, told her to take her time with her mother, and she was always welcome back to her job if things improved, for Sally was a good worker and well liked.

Her mother, as expected, was full of condemnation when

170

Sally arrived home with her problem unexpectedly one Saturday night, but after a couple of days and the first shock she agreed to Sally's plan of action, realizing that this was the best way to deal with the situation. Poor Sally, she was not prepared for the mixture of love and agony she was to feel when the baby was eventually born. He was a beautiful child, chubby and fair-haired like his father, and Sally felt her heart would break at the thought of parting with him, but it was the only way. You could not hide a babe for ever, it had been hard enough hiding herself during the waiting months, but luckily her mother's cottage was quite isolated on the smallholding that kept her going, and they had managed quite well; her mother didn't have many visitors, mostly tradespeople, and Sally kept well out of sight knowing how local tongues might wag. She only went out into the adjoining fields for air under cover of darkness. The birth was not difficult, for Sally was young and strong and her mother knew what to do.

The day came when Sally decided to return to Whytchurch, to leave her child to be found on the doorstep of the Poorhouse. He was but five weeks old. She planned it very carefully, taking with her an extra warm blanket and catching the late coach to Bristolle. The journey was uneventful; there was only one other passenger, a farmer who slept for most of the journey, not at all interested in a young woman and her infant. As she alighted from the coach she took a quick look up and down the road but fortunately there was no one about and it was dark. The Poorhouse was a gaunt grey stone building built on church ground to the east of the church. It was under the control of the parish's Overseer to the Poor, and Sally knew that her baby boy would be cared for until he was old enough to be sent out to earn a living. Foundlings were usually sent out to service or as farm labourers. She gritted her teeth and looked up and down the road again in the glimmer of moonlight but it was still deserted. Now was the time. She gave her son one last fierce hug and shoved his basket into the doorway of the Poorhouse. She hoped he would be

171

found soon for she didn't want him to spend all night on the doorstep although he was well wrapped. It was spring-time and the nights could still be treacherous. As it was a Saturday night she was hoping that some of the late revel-lers from the White Hart would pass that way and see the basket with its precious bundle. He was a good babe and didn't cry much; perhaps when he got hungry someone would hear him.

She sped across to the White Hart and her heart was afire with love for her son and remorse at having to cast him away. She paused for a moment or so to gather her thoughts before she went into the inn. When she appeared, Mistress Molly the landlord's wife saw her instantly.

'Sally, you poor dear girl come in! How are things with you? Is your mother better? 'Tis lovely to see you back – I expect you caught the late coach. You must have a drink and a bite to eat after your journey!'

Sally could only nod assent to all these questions as Mistress Molly led her through to the warm kitchen. They were good people, the innkeepers, and she hated the lies she had told them and the lies she was about to tell them.

The next morning in the White Hart there was much talk of a baby boy, a foundling who had been discovered crying on the doorstep of the Poorhouse in the early hours of Sunday morning. Sally was relieved. Her son hadn't spent the whole night outside. There was a certain amount of talk and speculation for a while, and various village girls were mentioned, but on the whole the male customers at the White Hart were not over-talkative on the subject, for there were some in their number who had enjoyed certain liaisons with one or two of the girls mentioned. The parish auth-orities eventually named the child Sunday Whytchurch. All local foundlings were given the name Whytchurch, and they dubbed him Sunday for the simple reason that Sunday was the day on which he was found.

In 1798 some new Poorhouses were built next to the old one and at this time the child known as Sunday Whytchurch had grown into a fine strong lad, and was now a farm-boy for the Colstons at Whytecross Court. The Colstons were relatives of Edward Colston, the famous philanthropist from Bristolle. This same Edward Colston had founded an excellent school in Bristolle in 1707 on the site of the great house on the quay which had belonged to Sir John Young and where Queen Elizabeth had stayed centuries ago on her visit to the city. All the Colston sons attended this school. Whytecross Court Farm had been entirely rebuilt in 1786 after the last occupiers had left and given up farming. All this while Sally kept an eye on the child that was hers whenever she could without arousing suspicion. Sundays were a joy to her because she was always certain of seeing him in church. Maybe one day she would reveal herself to him as his mother, but whenever the thought occurred she dismissed it, pleasurable as it was. It would not do. The boy would be sure to want to know about his father, and she could not lie about that. The truth would cause a lot of strife. Better to watch the lad from afar and know that he was all right; he was a fine lad, everybody said so, and her heart was filled with both pride and deep sadness for the son she could not own. Back in 1793, on February 1st when her son was nearing five years old, France had declared war. Sally told herself that it would all be over by the time he was full-grown, but she was to be proved wrong.

In due course Sally's mother died and left her the smallholding in Wells. She really had to decide then what to do with her life, but she knew that there was only one answer. She left her job at the White Hart to go home to Wells. Her employers were sorry to lose her. They never had been able to understand why such a pretty lass had not married, but the plain truth was that Sally, after her bitter mistake, had never encouraged suitors, although many admiring glances had been thrown her way. So she packed her bags, said her farewells, and made her lonely trip back to the family home. She felt quite satisfied about Sunday, or Sunny as everyone now called him. Satisfied but resigned. He was getting on well at Whytecross Court, a hard-working cheerful boy, and the Colstons apppeared to be very pleased with him.

As for Stephen Blessed, Sunny's natural father, he had settled down to make his marriage a success and his wife had borne him three children, a son and two daughters, strong healthy offspring and all very much alike. They were all like their mother who was raven-haired and slightly built. The Blesseds were quite well-off, owning and managing a few moderate properties around Whytchurch. In 1799 nobody was surprised when the Smyths eventually purchased Lyons Court for they were still by far the biggest land owners in the district. Since the era of the Holbeaches Lyons Court had undergone several changes of ownership.

In the years that followed Sunny Whytchurch went off to the wars with a handful of other Whytchurch lads. Some were killed fighting the French on foreign soil, like young Tom Whippie from Lower Green Farm, and great was the mourning in that family when the sad news arrived. The Whippies had two farms in Whytchurch and more land on the edge of Keynsham. Young Tom had been the apple of his father's eye, and his hope for the future. All this was now destroyed. There was no other son to inherit, only three younger sisters. Of his kin there was only one other Whippie to continue the male line, for in latter years there had been a preponderance of female children born into the family.

Jimmy Blessed, Stephen's only son, had felt the call of the sea like so many lads before him and joined the navy. When the news of Nelson's splendid victory at Trafalgar on 21 October 1805 stirred the whole kingdom to rejoice, there was a triumphant ringing of church bells throughout the land, and the villagers of Whytchurch celebrated as joyously as any in the nation. The Blesseds looked forward anxiously to the safe return of their son from the wars, as indeed had Tom and Margaret Blessed, Stephen's ancestors, prayed for the safe return of Pip well over two hundred years previously, and like all others before them they went with their neighbours to church to pray as well as to celebrate.

It was October and the weather was seasonal. The merry-

174

making lasted for two days, with the roasting of several pigs and oxen in Old Acre field which was lying fallow at that time. There was plenty of ale for all provided by the two village ale houses, and the men got tipsy, the women gossiped and the children chirped with excitement.

There was great rejoicing when Jimmy Blessed came home from the sea, and his father Stephen was rightly proud of him, but although they celebrated this great victory many were still aware that there were families in the village who had menfolk away with the army.

'I swear by all the saints in Heaven this village has served the country well whenever the need has arisen,' Stephen said as he sat comfortably at his hearth with his wife. He remembered fondly the tales his grandfather had told him of his great-great-grandfather Matthew Blessed, who had been with the Royalist garrison at Bristolle Castle, and the unusual turn of events in the meeting of Martin who turned out to be his unknown cousin from Plymouth.

Stephen's wife, sitting in the inglenook with him toasting her toes, agreed. 'It's been a great time, but more's the pity that Nelson himself didn't see the celebrating of it!'

Stephen hugged her fondly. In spite of his early reckless behaviour, or because of it, he had made a good marriage.

'Aye, and there's young Tom gone from Lower Green,' he said thoughtfully, 'I must take a stroll to see them. It can't have been any consolation to them to see everyone pleasuring so much.'

He did not add that he also intended to visit the Colstons to find out how young Sunny Whytchurch was faring, for he now knew that the boy was his son, and he felt a certain reponsibility towards the lad.

The discovery that Sunny Whytchurch was his son had come about in a most unusual manner. Stephen now enjoyed an excellent position as estate manager at Lyons Court where the Smyths were in possession. In the course of his duties he had occasion to visit Wells down to the south. He had been sauntering through the main market square tinkering with the idea of taking a trinket of some

175

sort back for his wife when he had spotted a woman whose face looked somewhat familiar. She in turn had stared back at him, and then the truth dawned upon them both simultaneously.

'Sally!'

'Stephen!'

There had been a brief period of embarrassed silence, for after their short mistaken romantic interlude all those years ago they had hardly spoken one word to each other, apart from a polite time of day. Whenever Stephen had been in the White Hart she had kept her distance as much as possible, and so words now did not come easily to either of them. Stephen recovered first. He was a mature man now and the youthful foolishness of yesterday had long been put away.

'I'd quite forgotten you lived here, Sally. How are things with you?'

'Quite fair, thank you. How are things in Whytchurch village? Are many of the lads gone to war?' She was thinking of Sunny, for the war with the French was at its height at that time.

'Yes . . . yes, my lad Jimmy's gone, and Tommy Whippie and the Lukins lad . . . oh and young Sunny Whytchurch, you know the boy from the Poorhouse that the Colstons took on.'

At this Sally started. 'Oh my, oh my . . . the poor boy, have you heard how he's faring, is he . . . is he in the thick of it?' She was plainly anxious.

Stephen had stared at her intently then. She looked older, gaunter, but she was still a good-looking woman. He was puzzled as to why she should single out the Whytchurch foundling to fret about to such an extent when so many lads had gone to war. What was he to her? Then with a flash of instinct the truth had come to him. Sally realized then that she had betrayed her secret when she saw the look in his eyes.

'So many young men have been killed . . .' the words trailed off helplessly. She was trying to act normally.

176

Stephen's curiosity was aroused now, and he had to pursue what he was thinking. He came straight to the point. 'What does Sunny Whytchurch mean to you?'

She could not evade the question. 'He's my son,' she said weakly.

Stephen kept on. 'You mean OUR son?'

She nodded silently.

There was a further silence and then Stephen said, not unkindly, 'Why did you not tell me?'

'How could I? You had a new wife, a babe on the way. You said yourself it was all a mistake!'

He rubbed his chin thoughtfully. 'What a young fool I was, and I've escaped all the guilt, all the shame, while you had to hide your motherly feelings and part with the babe. I never even guessed . . .' Suddenly he felt very heavy-hearted, the pleasure of the day had gone.

Sally said 'No matter now. I've survived, and I'm quite happy, indeed I'm proud that the lad has gone to fight for England!'

'But Sal,' he used the old endearment now, 'we cannot leave it like this. I want to make amends. If the boy survives the war and makes it home I want to make amends for the miserable sinner that I was, and you a virgin girl . . .' he broke off, filled with the immensity of the situation. Around them stall-holders were calling their wares, people were jostling, but neither of them took heed. 'I want to make amends,' he repeated.

'How can you? Your wife will be distressed, your children will be embarrassed! How can you?'

'I don't know, Sal, but I'll find a way with honour, without my wife and Jimmy and the girls knowing. I can't hurt them, and she's been good and true and the making of me.'

Sally nodded wisely, she was fully recovered now. 'Tread carefully Stephen Blessed, tread carefully. The boy has done all right for himself up to now without any help from you or me. The Colstons value him greatly I've heard.'

'Leave it to me, Sal. I feel I've done great harm in the past. You've been denied the joy of rearing your own child through my stupidity, and that is a hard thing to bear, but if young Sunny survives I'll watch out for him, I promise'.

What could she say?. The secret was still safe, and in a way she was relieved. Sunny had someone else to watch out for him now, albeit from afar.

After a little while Stephen had politely taken his leave, and they had gone their separate ways, Sally back to her smallholding and Stephen back to Whytchurch and his wife, a much subdued man.

After Trafalgar and the safe return of his son Jimmy, Stephen Blessed found himself one cold day in early November making his way to Whytecross to pass the time of day with the Colstons. He had already called on the Whippies at Lower Green Farm, a place hung with sorrow, and he shivered as he wrapped his heavy cloak around his sturdy shoulders. Since his meeting with Sally some time before he had made a point of chatting more to the Colstons, realizing that this was the only discreet way he could find out about Sunny Whytchurch. On this day he did have some real business to discuss with the Colstons so they were half-expecting him. Annie Colston welcomed him into the warm kitchen and gave him a dish of warm broth, bidding him to warm his bones by the fire. In the course of conversation they were discussing Jimmy and his homecoming and quite naturally the subject of the foundling Whytchurch came up. The Colstons had heard nothing of him and went on to say that when his soldiering was over there would always be a place for him at Whytecross as he was such a promising lad and a good worker to have around the place

'But,' said Annie, ' 'Tis a long hard war for the army, and we've heard nothing of the lad, but I'm sure he'll send word when he's finished his soldiering. Whenever that is we shall be pleased to welcome him back.'

It was indeed a long hard war and Sunny came marching home eventually in the spring of 1816. Stephen came across him quite unexpectedly one morning. He had walked down the hills from Dundry, and from the slopes the old church made a pleasant sight in the May sunshine. The weathered grey tower nestled in a comfortable fashion beneath the pale blue sky amid the greenery of the surrounding fields lush with buttercups and cowslips. The stream that ran below the church swirled merrily over the stones, heavy with the welter of spring rain from the Dundry hills, and the apple trees in the smallholdings opposite the church were in their annual array of pink blossom, fluffy and ethereal. As Stephen came abreast to the lane beside the church he spied Sunny leading a horse to the forge. The young man looked broader, blonder and very weatherbeaten. Stephen wondered how he had never guessed about the boy before because he was every inch a Blessed. In fact he looked more like Stephen than his legal children, who took after their mother.

He caught up with Sunny. 'Good morn to you young fellow,' he said, 'Welcome back from the wars!'

Sunny swung around cheerfully. 'Good morn, sir, to you. Yes, we taught Old Bonaparte a few lessons!'

They went on to discuss Wellington's victory at Waterloo the year before, and after a few pleasantries they went their separate ways.

Stephen became very thoughtful as he walked along. With what he had in mind how was he going to approach the boy? It would be difficult, he would have to take his time. For the next week or so whenever he met Sunny he stayed with surface talk about the village and the weather, for he had it in his mind to make a friend of the young fellow before he did anything further. Sunny was not surprised at his attention. Stephen had noticed that a lot of the older men in the village stopped to chat with Sunny now, some to recount past deeds and campaigns, others with a certain amount of respect for the young foundling who had been to war. The younger men had always accepted Sunny with the uncomplicated ways of youth. Many of the villagers bought him a jug of ale in the White Hart, and one evening four months after Sunny's return Stephen Blessed did the same. The opportunity presented itself as he had known it would. Quietly and without too much preamble he told Sunny that he was his father, and the manner of his birth. He felt he knew the boy well enough by now for the avoidance of any sort of scene, and he was right. Sunny of course was dumbstruck at the news, but he was self-disciplined and self-assured enough to hide the wild emotions tugging at him. He looked at Stephen with new eyes. And what of his mother, who and where was she? As if reading his thoughts Stephen told him of the chance meeting with Sally some years ago.

'I must go to her!' said Sunny. If there had been any thought of reproach that she had abandoned him he now cast it away. He well knew what village communities were like, and how Sally would have suffered, and he would have still been brought up in the Poorhouse even if she had admitted her lapse to the world! The marriage of Stephen would have foundered as well. Yes, she was right to do what she did.

Stephen said, 'I will try and make it up to you, boy. I cannot live contented until I have made some amends. I cannot hurt my family but I will do everything in my power to bring happiness to you and your mother.'

Sunny nodded thoughtfully. 'I'm glad you told me, sir. It took some telling, but I'm glad I know at last where my roots are.' As a little boy he had dreamed of a long-lost mother coming to claim him; he had dreamed of belonging.

Stephen said, 'I'm right proud of you ... son ...' He added quietly, 'Never fear I shall not call you that very often,' for he had noticed Sunny's cautious reaction to the term. 'I'm right proud of you,' he repeated, 'for all the hardship and wondering you must have had, for all that you've turned out a good'un!'

Sunny thought then of Stephen's legal son Jimmy, and how proud the Blessed family were of him from the stories he had heard. Good gracious! The thought struck him suddenly, he not only had a mother and father, he had a half-brother and half-sisters as well! That fact, however, would have to remain a secret forever for the sake of all concerned.

On a Saturday late in Septmber 1816 Stephen Blessed, estate manager for Lyons Court, and Sunny Whytchurch dressed in his Sunday best, both happened to board the same coach bound for Wells. It was Sunny's day off and he had announced his intention of going to the town to look around the market.

'More likely to go looking for a wench!' Annie Colston had said teasingly, but Sunny had smiled his usual pleasant smile and kept his own counsel saying goodbye politely. He was never to divulge the secret of his parentage. He was such a stable personality it was enough to know that his parents, whatever they had done, however foolish they had been, cared about him, and what was more he had other people around him who cared, such as Annie Colston, who had been like a mother to him since he had first been apprenticed to the farm at the tender age of eleven years.

Now that he was going to see his real mother he was feeling both curiosity and gentleness. From what Stephen had told him, and he could remember vaguely, the rather quiet barmaid at the White Hart was the same one who had seemed so fond of children and had always taken little toys and sweetmeats to the children at the Poorhouse at Christmas. Poor woman, how she must have suffered!

Stephen was quiet throughout the journey. Sunny thought they would never get there. When they alighted from the coach they looked a very odd couple, the prosperous estate manager dressed with elegance and style, fancy waistcoat, high boots of the best leather, and the farm labourer in his homespun jacket and breeches, his thick hobnailed boots, albeit it was his Sunday best.

Stephen enquired of a passing stranger the whereabouts of Mistress Waxon's abode, and they were directed a little way out of town to Sally's smallholding. Sally was taken entirely unawares. She was throwing feed to the chickens at the back of the cottage when she heard the tap on the front door. When she opened it she didn't know what to say. They all just stared and then young Sunny spoke up.

'I know the whole story. I've come to make your acquaintance, Mother.'

The word was like a blessing. She took a swift intake of breath, 'You're back safe from the war, praise God! I had heard nothing for so long I was afraid you were dead! Praise God!'

Sunny nodded and shifted his feet. Stephen was quiet.

'Come in both of you, come in!'

They followed her through to a spotless room. An old collie dog asleep by the hearth opened one eye and then went back to sleep again.

'Would you care for some cider?'

They both nodded and mumbled assent and she busied herself fetching the mugs.

Stephen spoke then. 'I wanted to do the right thing, Sal. I wanted to bring the two of you together.'

She nodded and smiled faintly. It was obvious that she was still a little shocked, but very pleased. 'Upon my soul I never thought I'd see this day!'

This seemed to break the ice and they all started talking at once.

Stephen said, 'It was only right that I told the lad and brought him to you.'

Sunny said, 'I'm very happy to be here – I always used to dream of meeting my mother.' It was obvious he was deeply moved.

Sally, deeply moved also, said, 'I hope you don't hold it against me, boy – it was the only thing I could do. It tore my heart out to part with you.'

He reached for her hand then and patted it gently. 'It must have been awful for you, but 'twould have been worse if you'd owned up to me, and I would have gone to the Poorhouse just the same. Don't worry, Mother, your secret is safe with me.'

Stephen noticed that Sunny was using the term Mother quite naturally, but Sunny had never once called him

Father. Best that he didn't maybe. It could easily slip out if they were together in Whytchurch company. What a fine lad he had turned out to be, wise beyond his years. Maybe that was the war, but the lad did have something special about him.

So it was that Sally Waxon became a contented woman with the acknowledgement of her son. Stephen Blessed had truly made amends as promised. She was to be made even happier a few months later, for Sunny decided to move to Wells to live with his mother. Sally told people that the son of an old friend from Whytchurch was going to come and help her with the smallholding, and he told the Colstons that he had a chance to take over a smallholding in Wells, which of course was entirely true. When they talked about it between themselves the Colstons decided he was probably drawn to Wells by a young lady, for they had offered Sunny his own piece of land if he stayed at Whytchurch. This was also true, for after the initial meeting with his mother he went to see her regularly and during these travels he made the acquaintance of a very comely maiden while browsing around the market stalls. Her name was Charlotte and she helped her parents run a small haberdashery business. Sunny was nigh on thirty years old and more than ready to settle down. In due course he married Charlotte and she went to live on the smallholding with Sunny and his mother. Sunny had great plans for the land and in time he acquired more. Charlotte was a great help and they produced four bonny children, two girls and two boys. In her mature years Sally Waxon felt she must be the happiest woman on earth. She had missed Sunny's childhood but she felt greatly compensated with the joy of having her grand children around the place.

Stephen Blessed eventually retired from his post with the Smyths and Jimmy took his place as estate manager. In his old age Stephen too became a contented man, happy to sit and dream, and from time to time he would get news of the other family down the road in Wells. The priest at St Gregory's who was friendly with Stephen travelled to Wells

183

from time to time to meet with other clerics and came back with snippets of news. On one occasion he mentioned that he'd met a pleasant fellow called Whytchurch who ran a small farm on the outskirts of Wells. His curiosity had been aroused at the name and he'd thought 'Surely one of our foundlings?' He was proved to be correct. Stephen had said cautiously that he knew of the fellow when he was a young lad just back from the war, and thereafter whenever there was any news of the Whytchurch family Stephen eventually came to hear of it.

Later in the century the Halls were still at Fyllwood Farm. One of the sons was destined to rent Lyons Court later in his life. The Colstons continued to thrive at Whytecross. Whytchurch now had a tollgate situated on the main highway leading to Bristolle to the north and Wells to the south. This meant that all travellers now had to pay to travel the highway. An official way warden was appointed under the jurisdiction of the Parish Council and it was his duty to ensure that the tolls were properly collected, and that the roads in the parish were kept in a proper condition. For this purpose there were two highway labourers. In the late nineteenth century Whytchurch was quite a self-sufficient village, but still very much under the influence of the church. Only men of a certain standing were chosen for the task of way-warden, and they were usually selected from farmers or traders. The village now had a variety of shops and craftsmen plying their trades. There were carpenters, butchers, boot-makers, and of course the blacksmith. The other alehouse now situated next to the White Hart was called the Black Lion, the name no doubt taken from the crest belonging to Lyons Court, two black lions rampant facing each other. Most important of all was the grocer's or victualler's shop, still standing where the original Whytchurch grocer, Martin Blessed, had conducted his business.

11

Sarah Whippie the Philanthropist

In the first part of the nineteenth century a great revolution had started to take place in England. The age of industrialization was arriving and all over the country factories were being built and agricultural workers were being lured to the towns and cities to work in these establishments. Steam railways, another innovation, were beginning to network the land, and it was a time of great excitement with so many modern miracles of engineering and ingenuity taking place.

Whitchurch, although only a few miles away from the rapidly expanding city of Bristol, remained comparatively unaffected by these great changes. There were still plenty of young men working on the land, although a few had drifted off to the city to learn new skills and work in factories.

Sarah Whippie's ideas and desires for a proper education for the village children had been germinating for quite a while. There were three daily schools in the village but only for the sons and daughters of those who could afford to pay. There was also one boarding school where children of the privileged from the wider community came, situated in Whitchurch House, a fair-sized building just down the road from the two village inns. The only schools available to the children of ordinary working folk were the Sunday schools.

Sarah had been well educated and a willing and very able pupil herself. Her father was John Whippie, long since passed on from this life. Her family home was at Chestnut Court, Bishopsworth, (formerly called Bishopswerde, and at one time Bishport), and her father was a cousin of the

Whippies who were former tenants of Lower Green Farm at Whitchurch. John Whippie had employed a private governess for Sarah to instruct her in the basics of reading, writing and arithmetic, and later, when she was older, the curate of St Gregory's at Whitchurch had been only too happy to teach her classics, history and literature, for Sarah had an abiding and lively interest in everything under the sun. John Whippie's family were regular churchgoers at St Gregory's, for Bishopsworth had no church of its own at this time, and its inhabitants were to be seen regularly on a Sunday morning traversing the pretty leafy lane that led past Fyllwood Farm to Whitchurch.

It disturbed Sarah to see the bright-eyed quick-witted children of Whitchurch not being given the privilege of knowing other than the fact that the boys, when they were old enough at twelve, eleven, or even ten years old, would be hired as farm labourers, and the girls packed off to service further afield. Sarah had been so keen for the local children to learn reading and writing that she spent a lot of time teaching at the Sunday school at the church of St Gregory. She had previously sought permission of the parish for a local carpenter to fashion some large boards to form a gallery, partitioning off part of the church on the south side exclusively for her young charges. Her first duty, she felt, was to teach the children to read and understand the Holy Bible. The Sunday school was a great success and well attended, but even this was not enough for Sarah. She felt there should be a properly established daily school to give a much broader education to the farmworkers' children. At her time of life, for she was well past her middle years, she was well provided for financially; she had plenty to spare to carry out her plans. The curate, Revd Markham Mills, and the parish were in full agreement with Sarah's ideas for a new day-school for the working-class children of Whitchurch. Thus it was that in the year 1837 on the 29th May, Sarah's birthday as it happened, the foundation stone for the village school was laid.

The parish had chosen a site close to the church, to the

right of the main gateway, and a sizeable one-roomed building was envisaged, with adjacent scullery and necessary out-buildings. It was to be built of good local stone, and further enhanced with a tablet above the entrance to inform people that Miss Sarah Whippie founded the school in 1837. It was quite an occasion for the village. The local Bristol newspaper printed a glowing report of the proceedings:

The Revd Markham Mills, curate of the parish, headed a procession of children and a band, as he was commissioned to lay the stone. As they approached the spot a salute was fired and cannon continued firing during the ceremony. After a short and appropriate speech the clergyman distributed cakes to the children. An excellent dinner was prepared at the White Hart and the following toasts were proposed and drank as soon as the cloth was removed – The King and Royal Family, Miss Sarah Whippie, Sir John Smyth and Col. Gore-Langton who have given the ground for the School Room, the Rev. Markham Mills. The band attended and played appropriate airs after each toast, in fact the oldest inhabitant of Whitchurch cannot recollect a more jovial and pleasant and happy day.

The writer of the newspaper report did not give the name of the "oldest inhabitant", but it might be suspected that this person was Sarah's very elderly aunt, from her mother's side, a very proper old lady who perhaps had asked to keep her name out of the paper for fear that folk would think she had been bragging too much about her favourite niece.

The school was erected quite swiftly during those summer months of 1837, because a further Bristol newspaper item dated 2 September 1837 recorded the completion and opening of the school:

Our readers no doubt recollect our mentioning, a few months since, the circumstance of the laying the foundation stone of a Protestant Schoolroom, in the parish of Whitchurch, near this city. We have now the pleasure to announce its completion, being a neat and appropriate building in the Tudor style, from the design of Mr. Rumley, architect. The opening took place on Thursday last, the 3lst ult., when various banners and flags were displayed, independent of those carried; they were suspended from the church tower to the new schoolroom, indicating the union which existed between the two edifices. A most impressive sermon was preached by the Revd Israel Lewis, from the 17th verse of the 4th chapter of the general Epistle of St James, and a handsome collection was afterwards made.

The Revd Israel Lewis is known, from records kept at this time, to have been the vicar of Long Ashton, also under the patronage of the Smyth family, and quite a few years before had been described in the Smyth family letters as 'The honest Welshman Vicar of Long Ashton'. He hailed originally from Carmarthen.

The paper's report continued 'The children of the school sang a hymn printed for the occasion, and repeated the 10th chapter of St Matthew, after which they were entertained with wine and cake given by Miss Whippie the founder of the school, and afterwards enjoyed their tea and cake in the new Schoolroom.' (The writer does not say what type of 'wine', but no doubt it was a type of nettle cordial, or perhaps ginger, which women used to brew at the time.) The enthusiasm of the writer shows again when the children were said to have afterwards enjoyed their 'tea' and cake in the schoolroom. Whether 'tea' meant a meal or a beverage it cannot be surmised, but the 'wine' was obviously a special treat! The report continues:

The Whitchurch choir attended and an excellent dinner was provided at the White Hart. After the cloth was removed the following, amidst various toasts, were pro-

188

posed, accompanied with appropriate airs and songs – Church and Queen, Miss Whippie, The Revd I. Lewis, The Revd Markham Mills, etc. The party broke up at an early hour, having passed the day in perfect harmony.

A very interesting point about these two newspaper reports was the mention of the King (William IV) in the first article, and the Queen (Victoria) in the second, for in that brief space of time during the building of the Whitchurch schoolroom, England had lost its King and a new eighteen-year-old Queen Victoria now held the throne.

Sarah Whippie died five years later, a happy woman. She had fulfilled her destiny. Many were sad at her passing, for her influence and philanthropy had extended well beyond her home village; she had also been a very keen benefactress to the Bristol Royal Infirmary, a charitable establishment in the heart of Bristol, where the sick and the poor found hope and succour. She had been the last of the Whippies, for in latter years the male line of her family had died out.

Some years later in 1848 an account was written of Miss Whippie's Whitchurch school, by a gentleman, a bachelor, one Joseph Leech of Abbots Leigh, a place situated on the edge of what was once the huge Fyllwood Forest. So many trees had been chopped down, so much land cleared, that there were now unconnected patches of woodland, some of them still quite sizeable, dotted around where once the mighty forest had reigned. The woodland that existed around Abbots Leigh was now called Leigh Woods, and it still extended down to the banks of the river where all those centuries ago Llewellyn had given Davold the golden medallion, and where, in a later century, young Ralph de Lyon had fallen in love with his adored Rachel.

Joseph Leech made it his business to visit the local churches to make notes of interest for a book he was writing called *The Church-goer*. While visiting the church he noticed the school with the tablet over the door recording the fact that Sarah Whippie had founded the school. He was interested, and was invited inside. He wrote:

A troop of little boys and girls headed by the Curate were issuing out of the Schoolroom as I entered and I noticed their chubby, comfortable little faces. I could not help saying as each made her curtsy, or pulled his forelock, let no one reproach elderly maidenhood or venerable celibacy on the part of either sex again; see what the spinster Sarah Whippie has done, and what she probably would never have performed had she died a Mistress Smith or a Mistress Brown and left a number of little commonplace Smiths or Browns!

One of these little children with 'chubby comfortable faces' happened to be Tad Whitchurch. Tad was short for Theobald. His grandfather, Sunny Whytchurch, had kept a small farm just outside of Wells where the cathedral stood, and Tad's father, the younger of Sunny's two sons, had come to Whitchurch to work, to begin with only temporarily helping out with the harvest, met a young lass, got married and settled down permanently in Whitchurch. Now and again Tad's father had wondered about his name being the same as the village where he now lived, and even if he had heard various knowing remarks about his name from some of the older inhabitants it would not have bothered him over-much, he was far too busy with his farming job, caring for a wife and rearing a young family to think too much about such things.

The world at this time was becoming a very exciting place. There was the new young Queen on the throne, a lady who showed the promise and determination of that former great Queen, Elizabeth.

In Bristol the Great Western Railway had been established, and folk who could afford the fare actually travelled between towns on this new invention, enjoying the scenery of the countryside in far greater comfort than previously in horse-drawn carriages over bumpy rutted roads. It was all

190

the rage, and the rich and prestigious flocked to the new platforms and stations that were being built all over the west of England, to try out this new form of transport, and gloat to their friends about the new experience. One such stopping place had been established in Bristol at a place called Temple Meads, on the site of the old meadows where the Knights Templar had once established their hospice and monastery.

Tad's uncle, his mother's brother, Charlie Tinker, had gone to Bristol to work on the railway, and when he visited he had so much to tell Tad's family about all the new things that were happening in the city; the boy was agog with the wonder of it all. He became very excited when Uncle Charlie promised to take the whole family to see the wonderful new suspension bridge being built at Clifton, formerly the Cliff Town of Saxon days. The man who designed this bridge was the same man who had been building railways, railway bridges, and all manner of other engineering marvels in the region. Even the new station at Temple Meads was his brainchild. He had also invented other more mundane things, like plumbing attachments, such was his versatility. He was a genius named Isambard Kingdom Brunel. There had long been a need to throw a bridge across the great Avon Gorge where old Llewellyn and Gudrum and Engel had fished eight centuries previously. The whole idea had been sponsored by a competition for designers and engineers, and Brunel had entered and gained the honour. The bridge had been started in 1836 and by 1840 the main piers had been completed, but sadly the work for the main structure of the bridge had stopped through lack of money. Undeterred, the establishment in charge of the bridge had started ferrying travellers across in a basket slung from a cable. It was safe enough, but not for the faint-hearted. Uncle Charlie had been across in the basket, and Tad was fervently hoping that his parents would allow him to go across if possible.

Tad was very alive to all these wonders, and could not wait for the day of the trip to come. The modern industrial world of the mid-nineteenth century was fast replacing the agricultural world, the only world that his parents and forebears had known. The trip to Clifton did not leave him disappointed. The whole family went on a Sunday after morning church. They had waited for a fine day, and everyone was in high spirits as they packed up two sturdy old farm carts with provisions for the journey. Tad's mother and aunts had cooked and baked the day before, for Grandfather Tinker with his country eye had forecast fine weather, and he was rarely wrong. There was a fine cold topside of beef, sliced, a succulent home-cured ham also sliced, newly-baked apple pies, fresh cream, home-made bread and scones liberally buttered, and fresh fruit, all to be well washed down with plenty of ale and home-made nettle wine for the children. There was great excitement when they eventually reached the Downs of Clifton and saw the magnificent piers of the bridge looming up before them. Uncle Charlie, who knew all about the bridge, explained to them that the piers had been altered from Brunel's original planned design. He had originally intended to give the bridge an Egyptian look with sphinxes adorning the piers, but then for some reason had changed his mind. Looking at the bridge with even his inexperienced eyes Tad felt that this had probably been the right decision, the present piers were so high, so graceful, no amount of further adornment could have possibly improved it. His next wondering thought was how were they going to build the actual bridge? He said as much to Uncle Charlie who was sure to know.

'Well, lad, you can see they already have a strong cable across with the passenger basket. They start off with sending a single cable over, and they then start adding material to send across, working from either side, until it all gets joined up.'

It was a simple explanation and it sufficed for Tad. It also made him think a little deeper. 'Well then, to do that, Uncle Charlie, they'd have to be sure they got it all exactly right. They'd have to be good at their sums!'

192

'That's it boy!' his uncle nodded thoughtfully. This child's imagination was working!

Tad's mother, an uncomplicated pleasant soul, tut-tutted, 'Now don't go filling the lad's head with so much, Charlie. He's fanciful enough as it is!'

His uncle laughed and he and Tad looked at each other with a new understanding, and Tad knew instinctively in that moment that he would not be riding across in the basket that day, but he was not too bothered, he had seen the bridge.

In the months that followed Charlie visited the family several times and always Tad would seek to have a chat with him to glean knowledge of the railways and all the wonderful things that were happening in the industrial world. Charlie told him more of the genius of Brunel and of the wonderful steam-driven ships he had designed, especially the *Great Britain*, the very first screw-driven ocean-going steamship which had been launched in 1843 in Bristol. This had been a very auspicious occasion when Prince Albert, husband of Queen Victoria, had travelled down from London to perform the launching ceremony.

One fine afternoon when Charlie was not working he took Tad into Bristol to see the busy port, and Hill's shipyard where he had several acquaintances, to see some wonderful great ships being built. For a farmboy from a simple background the size of the yards, the immensity of the shipbuilding and the skills of the workmen was astounding. It was this visit perhaps that influenced him most of all in his growing decision to become an engineer.

This shipyard had started off in a modest way but at this point in time was booming with business. The Hills employed a lot of workers, and quite a few of their own family, sons, cousins, uncles, were involved in the shipbuilding. At this time great engineering projects had their risks for the work force. Indeed one workman, a shipwright, had fallen from the top of the framework supporting a great half-constructed vessel in the dockyard and had been killed instantly. Great was the mourning and consternation, for

193

he had been a family man and left a widow and young children.

Tad, being a deep thinker, later pondered on these matters. It seemed to him that every age in history had its dangers as well as its discoveries and enlightenments, for did not the hunters of old face many dangers when scavenging for food? He was quite oblivious of it of course, but he was very near to the truth in his ponderings, for many centuries before, even before this tale began, had not an ancestor of his, Gudrum's father, been killed by a boar while hunting in Fyllwood Forest?

The world beyond Whitchurch was fast changing and Tad very much wanted to be part of it. As he grew he became more determined, and it was no boyhood whim that attracted him to becoming some kind of engineer. He was quite steadfast in his decision and his parents had become accustomed to the fact that this was what he wanted to do. They decided they would not stand in his way although they shook their heads at the way the world was changing so quickly; they had long accepted that Tad was a strong-willed lad and would go his own way. His brothers and sisters were untouched by it all, content to stay in the farming community that had always been enough for their parents. On a few occasions their Uncle Charlie had taken them, with Tad, to see the new railway station and the noisy powerful steam trains he worked on. They had been interested but always eager to go back home to the country life, unlike Tad whose eyes always sparkled with excitement on such trips.

In this changing world the need had arisen in Bristol for a new drainage system and more copious water supplies were needed to deal with the many industries that had sprung up throughout the city. Years before a waterworks company had been formed, but the flow of clean water was quite irregular, and in 1844 a Royal Commission on Public Health had described Bristol as the third unhealthiest city in the kingdom. In the summer of 1849 there had been a terrible outbreak of disease connected to dirty water and

194

between June and October of that year there had been 15,000 cases of sickness. Of these cases, 778 were confirmed as cholera and 444 people died of the sickness. It was then that the civic authorities had decided to set up a Board of Health, and large sums of money had been spent on a sewage system and storm-water drains to sweep everything away into the Avon. Streets became properly paved, doubtful unclean lodging-houses were closed, bakeries were given strict hygiene regulations, and the same rules were applied to slaughterhouses. As a result of all these changes the death rate from such diseases went down quite drastically.

In Whitchurch there were no real problems with the water. There were ample wells, the spring water was pure enough, and the country folk had shuddered and felt happier with their lives when they had heard of all these awful diseases in the city. By the time he was fifteen years old Tad knew exactly what he wanted to do. He wanted to become a water engineer. He had seen the wonderful engineering feat of the Clifton Bridge, the Great Western Railway and the great seagoing vessels being built in Hill's shipyard. He was also a realistic young fellow and knew that his simple education had not been sufficient to enable him to carry out great engineering feats, but he had found out that young men were needed as water engineers by the waterworks company, and they would be trained by the company. He was eager for new knowledge, to meet new people and the company was a comparatively new industry and something worthwhile. Tad had always read widely, everything and anything in print from the moment he had learned his letters at the village school. His interest in water supplies and the engineering associated with it had been greatly stimulated by a book on ancient Rome, lent to him by the curate, who was interested in the lad's enthusiasm for knowledge.

In this book Tad had been greatly surprised and impressed to read that the Romans, all those centuries ago, had prized their water engineers very highly. In ancient Rome water engineers were seen to be higher in status than

195

physicians and healers. In the Rome of the Caesars clean supplies of water for drinking and bathing had been absolutely essential. The fact that impressed Tad the most was that although the Romans had conquered and occupied the British Isles for three hundred years, Romans with all this knowledge of piping clean water, no vestige of their skill in this had really stayed within the population. It was true that there were the famous Roman baths and relics and antiquities at Bath, but no person had really allowed the fact of their expertise with pipes and drainage to have any real impact, until this century. It was true too that there had been pipes and conduits in Bristol with fresh water from the Dundry hills, but these systems had happened sporadically. No need had really arisen, no spur had been needed, until the terrible summer of 1849 when there had been all those deaths in the city of Bristol. Tad had been nine years old at the time and he well remembered the talk of it.

So it was that young Tad Whitchurch left the family home for the neighbouring city of Bristol, to be trained by the waterworks company in the complexities of water engineering. The company found suitable accommodation for the young trainees, who worked long hours and needed good food and board, and Tad found himself housed in a spick and span terraced house in the district of St Philips, near the Temple Meads Railway station. Tad was pleased about this because Uncle Charlie worked in the station for the Great Western Railway Company, a company that had been established by Act of Parliament in August 1835. The actual station had been built between this time and 1846. Tad could sometimes pop over to see Charlie briefly whenever the occasion presented itself, although he and the other trainees were kept hard at it for most of the time by a portly gentleman called Mr Brown. Mr Brown was a typical man in charge, always attired in the usual garb of a person of importance, top hat and tails, full of himself, with a loud mouth and, officious manner, but kindly enough.

In due course, by the time he was twenty-one, Tad

became a skilled water engineer and much valued by the company. Most people in the company had recognized from the start his keenness and interest in the job. When he went home to Whitchurch, sometimes on a Sunday, he was surprised to see some of the lads he'd attended school with already married with children, working on the land and quite happily expecting to do so for the rest of their lives. His brothers too had gone in for a smallholding, although later they were to try their luck at shopkeeping in a village a few miles away. Tad had been saddened by the death of Brunel in 1859 and equally by the fact that the bridge at Clifton was as yet unfinished, the work still held up for lack of funds, although the plans were still available. By 1864 though, when Tad was twenty-four, the bridge was finally completed, a wonderful engineering feat for all to see, spanning the gorge, dominant and graceful.

Around this time things were happening in the church at Whitchurch village. For quite a few years previously the place had fallen into sad disrepair, but a new curate, Revd Lewis Coyle, had set his heart on giving the whole place a new look. It was reputed that this earnest young man sometimes went short of food to purchase various materials, so keen was he to set the church right. An ornate new stone pulpit was installed; this was his ultimate pride and joy. New tiles on the floor, new fancy tiles, very much of the Victorian age, were put in place behind the altar, new pews with screens, and new wooden stalls for the choir. Many people believed that this young man of the cloth starved himself of good food, became ill and died an early death in the course of saving money to carry out these extensive changes to the church. This was the hearsay at the time at the Black Lion Inn where Martha Allen was the landlady, but how true the stories were will never be known. At the White Hart next door one of the Colston family, James, was the landlord, and the tittle-tattle there about the curate's untimely passing was the same. Eventually a stained glass window representing Christ as the Good Shepherd was installed by a grateful congregation, replacing the window at the east end of the church, with the following inscription: 'To the glory of God and in memory of Lewis Henry Coyle B.A. during six years curate of this parish, who died April 2nd 1862 aged 35 years.'

About the same time another beautiful stained glass window was installed on the north wall, donated by a member of the Colston family in memory of his wife. The inscription was 'This window was erected in memory of Mary, the wife of John Day Colston who died September 14th 1860. Glory be to God.'

In Victorian times it had become quite fashionable for those who could afford it to donate such visible memorials to their churches. Churchgoing for the Victorians seemed to have been a firm social ritual, apart from any other spiritual tendencies people might possess. There was a social conscience also, about the poor. The evidence for this showed itself in the carving of a simple message, 'Remember the poore' on one of the stones to the right of the inner north door, to be plainly seen as people came away from their worship. This was supplemented by a tall sturdy wooden alms box placed beneath the message.

The actual name of Whitchurch village church changed between 1840 and 1861. Since Norman times it had been the church of St Gregory, but during this period it had been renamed the church of St Nicholas. This was the third name given to the church, for the original tiny Saxon building had been dedicated to the female saint, St Whyte.

During the latter part of the nineteenth century the non-conformist church in the village, Zion Chapel, had increased its congregation greatly from the mere handful of dissenters that had existed when Robert and Mary Whippie had been banished to the poor house back in 1794. In 1867 a brand new chapel was opened, built and paid for by an unknown benefactor. Gradually the parish authorities and the village had come to accept the fact that not everyone wanted to worship at St Nicholas.

These were stirring times for the whole district. The revolution to industry was accelerating, and Bristol, which had long been a seaport of high standing, had some magnificent docks built in 1877 to the far west of the city at Avonmouth, the mouth of the river, to accommodate the larger ships and the ever-increasing trade which was overtaking the country. The first Bristol docks had been built between 1220 and 1245. People were on the move more, and many companies which had originated farther north in the country, and in the midlands, came to Bristol to seek business and to deal with the demands that were arising for all types of manufactured goods. One such company was Thomas Richards and Sons who ran an iron foundry in St Philips, a business that had transferred to Bristol from Birmingham. This was one of the companies that young Tad Whitchurch dealt with frequently, for their main expertise was in manufacturing iron manhole and drain covers for the expanding water systems in the west country.

Tad now held a position of authority. He was completely in charge of a certain section of the city's water system and there were a dozen men working under him. His enthusiasm and hard work had been rewarded. He had married a young lady named Mary, daughter of a City Councillor. They had three fine young sons and two daughters and lived in a splendid house in the district of Knowle which was being built higher up the hill from St Philips and the district of Totterdown, where many small terraced houses had been erected for the railway workers, with easy access to Temple Meads station.

Whitchurch had also seen some more new buildings. In 1883 a very spacious vicarage was built on the main road which led to Bristol to the north and Wells to the south. The church was thriving at this time and with the new alterations and pews could compare favourably with any village church in Somerset. There was a good congregation, still mostly farmers and their families from the surrounding area. The gypsies still encamped periodically in the vicinity, although the boundaries of what had been Fyllwood Forest had shrunk considerably in the last century as generation after generation of farmers had acquired and worked the land below the Dundry hills which overlooked Whitchurch. The gypsies were no longer accepted as part of village life and many folk in the Victorian era had grown to be suspicious and even disapproving of the Romany folk. The boundaries of the forest were now as far away as the Smythe estate at Ashton Court and the lower reaches of Brunel's suspension bridge slopes at Abbots Leigh on the opposite side of the bridge to Clifton.

Tad and his wife Mary often took their children for a walk on a Sunday afternoon through Leigh Woods. The children particularly liked the long winding pathway known as Nightingale Valley which led down to the river. Sunday afternoon walks with the family had become a firm Victorian institution and the Whitchurch family often met many others following the same pursuit. On one such occasion they met a family known to Tad through his business connections. Tad was particularly impressed with one of their younger sons. He had met young Dick previously, a shy gentle lad of eighteen with an obvious appreciative eye for nature and beauty, who did not seem at all suitable for the cut and thrust of business life. As the two families paused to chat, a baby rabbit, obviously astray from its mother and as yet unused to human predators was spied sitting on the track watching them all with bright little eyes. It made a charming picture sitting there unafraid when suddenly Tad's younger daughter went to make a grab for it, but was restrained, albeit gently, by young Dick. 'It's only a babe lost from its mother,' he whispered to the little girl, 'Don't frighten it.'

At the same time an innate sense of alarm suddenly urged the baby rabbit to scuttle back into the bushes, the moment was gone, and everybody laughed. Dick talked to the children then about the wonders of nature and the joys of observing the beautiful things in the world.

Dick's uncle said to Tad, 'The boy Dick's clever enough, and works well enough, but he's a dreamer, too poetic. He's always got his head stuffed into books.'

Apparently young Dick had lost his father quite early in

his life and his uncle appeared to have taken over the reins for Dick's family.

In the following years Tad saw Dick quite often in the course of business, and Tad was to recall this moment in the woods with particular reason, over twenty years later. The occasion was the visit to Bristol of Queen Victoria, now an old lady, on 15 November 1899. Tad was nearing sixty at this time, and a grandfather. As the Queen, a small dumpy unimpressive figure dressed in black, was driven past College Green, a piece of land adjoining the cathedral in the centre of the city, he spotted Dick across the crowds and waved. Dick, now a mature man, had two little girls with him, obviously his daughters. A while later when the crowds had dispersed Tad was able to meet up with him. After an exchange of greetings Tad noticed that the elder of the two little girls was looking very despondent.

Dick said, 'She's quite disappointed. The Queen is not a bit like she expected – she was looking for a lady in a shiny satiny dress and a glittering crown and all she saw was this little old lady in black!'

'Oh dear dear dear,' said Tad jovially, 'We can't have this, can we?' He didn't know what else to say.

Dick continued thoughtfully, 'She's really disillusioned and unfortunately that's the way of it.' He added kindly, 'She'll get to learn about life and the way things sometimes turn out. I'll find a way to soften the disappointment.'

This was true, thought Tad. The younger man had remarkable insight for a Victorian father. Most children at this time were treated true to the tradition of 'Children should be seen and not heard', and most fathers would have told the child 'not to be silly' or ignored them, but it was obvious that Dick treated his children in a special way. He was a thinker like Tad. After a little more conversation they went their separate ways. As the new century approached the world was becoming different. Tad wasn't to know it, but it was very different from the world of four hundred years ago when another much-loved Queen, Elizabeth Tudor, had been driven regally through the streets of

Bristol, resplendent in her rich clothes and jewels to the house of Sir John Young, the House on the Quay. Where this house had stood there was now a school founded by Edward Colston, an ancestor of the farmers of the same name at Whitchurch, and a well-known benefactor to the city of Bristol. Soon Colston's school was to be moved to a more spacious country situation to the east of the city and the site of the old school was to become a splendid new concert hall to be named the Colston Hall. Change was everywhere as the new century was dawning.

12

The Wars of the Twentieth Century

After the ripples of the distant Boer War and in the early years of the twentieth century Whitchurch remained almost unchanged. The old Queen had died, succeeded by her son Edward, a jolly man, and purported to be fond of the ladies. His reign was comparatively brief.

The lads of the village at this time were a merry crowd, and on Sundays after morning service the choirboys and their friends would race out of the south door of St Nicholas church, over the fields and across the stream to lark around until Sunday lunch was ready. Sometimes if they were so minded they would climb right up to Maesknoll Tump, an ancient landmark from where there was a wonderful view across the fields to Bristol in the distance. These boys in later years were to remember these carefree moments. On one occasion, a very hot day in summer, a couple of the lads were resting from the heat in a little coppice on the slopes, taking advantage of the shade, when a young fox unguarded came through the trees. There was a momentary vision of startled eyes, a swish of body and then all that was to be seen was a bright bushy tail disappearing swiftly back through the trees. The boys were country-bred and used to the creatures of the land, for most of them were from families that had worked the land for centuries. The older lads who were in the habit of going out sometimes in the evenings often came across the badgers that lived there-abouts, and the baby badgers were a joy to watch, frolicsome tiny creatures making weird little noises, trembling and crawling all over each other, and occasionally jerked into place by a stern mother, used to the ways of the world and ever-watchful for danger.

In the spring and summer there were yellowhammers and magpies, and the blackbirds' bright songs in the sycamore trees. There were prickly hedgehogs and boxing hares and all the lads knew where to go to see their mad behaviour in the spring months. In May there was hawthorn blossom around the orchards scattered between the prolific apple blossom, and when autumn came there were the trees turning russet and beautiful. This then for these country lads was the England of pre-1914, carefree, uncomplicated and later to be idyllically and hungrily remembered by the same lads in the muddy trenches and war-torn wastelands of France.

When the Great War finally did come there was a great surge of patriotism throughout the land, and Whitchurch was no exception. Their ancestors had fought the Spanish Armada, braved the Napoleonic wars, survived Trafalgar; they were ready to fight for their country. Industrialization in the nation became even more intense, for this war was to be fought in a vastly different way from previous wars.

After the turn of the century the nation had been in optimistic mood, and most people looked forward to life becoming better and easier with all the new inventions that were taking hold, so before the great wave of patriotism there had been a kind of awakening surprise that the country was at war again – 'But not for long' was the general sentiment, and 'It'll soon be over!' They were not to know that this war, later dubbed 'The war to end all wars' would prove to be long, hard, fierce and very bloody.

Some of the young Whitchurch hopefuls who went off to war had sung in St Nicholas church choir together as boys; boys of the same ilk who had run over the fields in carefree fashion after church on Sunday mornings. It was on a Sunday morning too that they all marched off to war together, to the adulation of the entire village who had turned out to wave them off. The recruiting sergeant took them into Bristol first to be kitted out with their khaki uniforms. They were shown how to wind their puttees round their legs, and given basic training. Within weeks they were off with all the other recruits to France, the trenches, and the horrors that they would never forget, and a lot of them would not survive. The same story was repeated all over the country. Lads, friends and brothers, all volunteering together for what seemed to them like a great adventure, going off to fight together, and very often to die together. The slaughter and the suffering were unimaginable.

In Bristol quite a few railway apprentices joined up together, among them the grandson of Tad Whitchurch, Zachary, or Zac as he was affectionately called by his family. Being trainee engineers they were all put in the same regiment, the South Midland Royal Engineers.

In 1915 Tad was quite an elderly man, and the grief was very hard to bear when his family received news of Zac's death less than a fortnight after the lad had sailed for France. Some time later Tad ran into his old friend Dick, and told him of Zac's death. He learned that a young son of Dick's had also gone off to war, at the tender age of seventeen. The lad had been really keen to join up so had put his age on and joined the Royal Artillery with the horse-drawn guns. Dick's wife had tried hard to stop him and went determinedly to the barracks in Whiteladies Road Clifton to harangue the recruiting sergeant, who hadn't wanted to know about the boy's age. He had a willing recruit and that was all that mattered to him, so she had lost the argument. It was rumoured that this kind of situation was happening all over the country; if the lads were fit and willing then very often rules and regulations were conveniently overlooked. Dick also mentioned his elder daughter whose sweetheart, also a former railway apprentice with the South Midland Royal Engineers, had been severely wounded in the leg and sent home. Tad suddenly remembered vividly the occasion when this child, this elder daughter of Dick's, had been so bitterly disappointed over the visit of Queen Victoria, and her father's words of wisdom

205

about children learning to face up to life. How prophetic those words seemed now.

The two men sat and talked philosophically for a little while. It was the last time they were to meet. Tad died peacefully in his sleep three weeks before the Armistice was declared on 11 November 1918 at 11 a.m., the eleventh hour of the eleventh day of the eleventh month. So he was never destined to know the thrill of victory and the great joy of the nation when the boys eventually came marching home from the horror and mud of France and the wind-swept seas that surrounded their homeland, for many lads had volunteered to serve with the Royal Navy and had undergone endless hours, days, even sometimes over a week, suffering privation and exposure after their ships had been torpedoed by German submarines. They counted themselves the very lucky ones, lucky to have survived, for too many young men had gone to watery graves, from the merchant service also, the food and supply ships that had kept the lifelines open to an island nation. There had been other theatres of war in addition to France and the sur-rounding seas of the British Isles. This, then, was why those in authority had called this war The Great War and the World War. Some called it the war to end all wars.

Tad's two other grandsons survived the war, as did Dick's eager young lad who had put on his age. Another of the survivors was young Fred Slocombe, the Whitchurch village policeman's son. Fred had somehow survived the hell of many battles and had had numerous experiences including a meeting in the trenches with an idealistic young man named Lawrence. This young man was later to become very famous and a legend in his own time, Lawrence of Arabia.

There were many amazing tales of bravery under fire, and the lads of Whitchurch like many others had served their country well. Altogether fourteen young men from the village had died in the Great War. A roll of honour was placed near the font by the south door of St Nicholas church, a fitting place, for many of the young men whose names were displayed there had been baptized in the font. The plaque read as follows:

Alfred Henry Collins
Melville Franklin
Sidney Llewellyn Hall
Thomas Hendy
William Herbert Hilborne
Richard Raymond Knight
Clifford Nash
Percy William Parker
Thomas Page
William Page
Herbert George Rogers
Arthur James Stratton
Edward Whiteaway
Edward Wood
'Their name liveth for evermore'

The grieving family of one of these young men went a little further and had another separate brass memorial placed on the north wall where all could read the following inscription:

In loving memory of Richard Raymond dearly loved elder son of Richard and Clara Knight who was killed in action at Arras April 10th 1917 aged 19 years. 'Greater love hath no man than this that a man lay down his life for his friends.'

This somehow summed up the feelings of the whole community. A lad of nineteen years cut down so cruelly in the spring of his life.

During all these terrible times Whitchurch as a village had been slowly changing. In 1914 a brand new extensive village school was built on the main Bristol Road, just past the old toll gate on the other side, and the old one-roomed village school so ardently planned and built by Sarah Whip-

207

pie in the last century became the church hall to be used for social occasions.

About 1916 Lyons Court Farm, still regarded by some as the local manor house, which the Smyth family had owned for a considerable time, was sold to a family called George. This wonderful old building which had always been well cared for with no expense spared for repairs and alterations, had withstood the ravages of the centuries, and although weathered with time was still a good house for the farmer George and his family. Visitors were enchanted with the architecture. A main hall with a minstrel gallery and most rooms leading off from it, had in it a very unusual carving of a man with a book, and there had been many discussions with the family and some of their learned visitors on the identity of this man, but nobody could be certain about it. The old house like many ancient houses held its own secrets. Also in the building one stone archway had been uncovered which was distinctly Norman, and bore a remarkable likeness to the arched north porch of St Nicholas church.

Some years after the George family had established themselves at Lyons Court one of the sons discovered an old shoe wedged in the stones of an upper room which was being converted and decorated. It was quite tiny, very old, and had obviously lain hidden there for centuries. It could be suggested that it was a discarded shoe of Rachel, Sir Ralph de Lyon's adored bride who had run around the house barefoot, but as the shoe was very worn and patched and said by some to be of the Tudor era, it was more likely to have been the footwear of a servant girl of that period.

Maybe that shoe had danced in merriment at the celebrations for the defeat of the Spanish Armada! It will never be known, for again yet another explanation was put forth. The shoe could have been lodged in the wall deliberately, for it is a well-known fact that placing a shoe in the wall was an ancient custom, supposedly to bring good fortune to a house and its occupants and to keep away evil spirits. If this was the case it is feasible that a patched worn shoe would serve the purpose just as well as a good shoe in use!

Another mystery surrounding Lyons Court was connected with what was called the old "guardee room". This was a lower room facing east, and rumour had it that at one time this room held the entrance to a tunnel leading to the church. There had been talk of tunnels in the village for centuries, but nothing definite had ever come of it. It could be that the owners of properties like Lyons Court Farm and the custodians of the church were not in a hurry to publicize such facts, even if such tunnels did exist, for obvious reasons such as unwelcome intruders, not to mention the unsafe conditions of the said catacombs, neglected for centuries. Many people believed that the purported existence of these tunnels coincided with the hounding and hiding of priests and monks during the reign of Henry the Eighth, and some said it was all to do with Cromwell and the Civil War. Whatever the reasons for either or both of these rumours there was one reported fact of a tunnel entrance being found in the cellars when the Black Lion Inn was being renovated in later years. Unfortunately the whole area was later covered over to extend the car park, so any evidence disappeared for ever.

Whitecross Farm was still functioning in the earlier part of the twentieth century, as indeed was Filwood Farm, which, after centuries, was still being farmed by the Halls. The Halls had a long and interesting history as farmers in Whitchurch, from the original Ben Hall who had battled constantly to keep the forest at bay from his precious acres, and also Dorothy, the fiery female rebel who had defied and outwitted Cromwell's men. In 1924 Filwood Farm was eventually bought again by the Hall family, after being bought and rented out variously by the Smyths and the Gore-Langtons, relatives of the Smyths. Records also showed that Lyons Court Farm had been rented for a while by members of the Hall family, also from the Smythes, in 1861. These three farms, Lyons Court, Filwood and Whitecross were the oldest farms in the district, although like the church they had been renovated and rebuilt at various times through the centuries. They were and always had been part of the fabric of Whitchurch, the whole held together with the church. From the time of Davold the Blessed, Jean d'Arcy, Brother Luke, Will Potter, and all those who followed, these old buildings had witnessed a rich panorama of events in the life of Whitchurch.

The 1920s also produced the 'flappers'. These were the young women who, having gained the vote at last in 1921, advertised their new-found status by having their hair cut short, or 'bobbed' as it was called, to the horror of a lot of the older generation. 'A woman's hair is her crowning glory' had been a much-quoted Victorian saying. The flappers wore straight long-waisted dresses with hems at calf-length, which was considered very daring by their elders who had worn ankle-length skirts as generations of women had before them, and their favourite dance was 'The Charleston'. At one time only the gentry had indulged seriously in dancing at Hunt Balls and the like, with the graceful waltz, and before that the more stately gavotte. The lower classes had been content to dance their country dances around the maypole or Morris dancing at country fairs, but now this new dance, imported from America, became all the rage in most levels of society.

Whitchurch village was now linked up to the Great Western Railway and trains stopped regularly at Whitchurch Halt, a tiny platform serving the railway line to the south of the village. The Halt was used extensively by Whitchurch folk wishing to travel further afield. They were highly pleased with this addition and it was put to good use. It was very pleasant being conveyed through the surrounding countryside which boasted extremely pretty scenery, to neighbouring villages or perhaps greater distances. People could also travel into the city of Bristol if they so wished on business or for shopping. Whitchurch was becoming part of a greater world. At this time some motor-cars appeared in the district, owned by those who could afford them or were brave enough to drive them. Motor-driven charabancs, large vehicles to hold a score or more passengers, were also beginning to make an appearance, and they were very popular for people who wanted to go on group outings and the like. The older generation shook their heads – 'Horses have always been good enough for us!' – but the new century was already so saturated with invention and creative flair that the younger folk were totally inspired with the novelty of it all, and there was no stopping them.

Tad Whitchurch's youngest grandson Charles had not gone to war. He had trained as a chemist and successfully ran his own pharmacy and shop in Bristol. Tad had given all his children a good education, and they in turn educated their children well. Charles had married a country girl called Margaret and they had produced three children in quick succession, two sons Dennis and Clive and a daughter, Pamela. They all lived happily and comfortably in a newly-built house in Knowle. As the children grew up they did all the usual things that children and young people of that era did. The boys joined the local Boy Scout Troop and Pamela joined the Girl Guides. They went every year to Weston-Super-Mare, the local seaside resort on the Bristol Channel, with their local church's Sunday school outing. This was a treat for everyone large and small, and they would set off excitedly from Temple Meads railway station after travelling down the main Wells Road to the station by tram. The trams in the 1930s were numerous and efficient over most of Bristol. Charles, being quite prosperous, could also afford to take his family away for two weeks' holiday during August when the schools were closed, usually to Devon or Cornwall.

In 1938 when Dennis the elder son was just nineteen, Charles Whitchurch died very suddenly leaving his family quite lost and bewildered at this tragic turn of events. The Second World War was also threatening, although Neville Chamberlain the British Prime Minister had been to Munich, shaken the hand of the dictator Adolf Hitler and declared 'Peace in our time'. Suddenly to Margaret, Charles's widow, the world became a very insecure place. She decided to sell the house and the chemist's shop her husband had been so proud of. The children were all in their teens and not quite so dependent, and the money she received for the house and business would ensure security for them all. They moved out of the house at Knowle to buy a smaller newly-built bungalow at the top of the lane that led to the church at Whitchurch. The children were quite happy with their mother's plans, for she was country-bred and had always nursed a hankering to return to rural life. Another fact taken into account was that if there was a war they would be well away from the city which would surely be a target for the Nazi bombers. Several of Margaret's friends were dubious about this notion and pointed out that the next war would be a war in the air without a doubt, and Whitchurch airport was not far away. It was only a comparatively small landing field situated to the east of the village, adjacent to the lane which led to Bishopsworth, and it was frequented mostly by members of the local flying club, although occasionally there would be commercial aeroplanes using it from an air travel company called Imperial Airways. Margaret shrugged off the doubts of her friends and their fears seemed unimportant. The airport was not a Royal Air Force base.

In the 1930s there were all sorts of summer activities and air shows at Whitchurch airport. The nation's youth were becoming very air-minded and lots of young men were eager to learn to fly. The flying club and organizers at Whitchurch quite regularly took people up for what they called 'a flip' round the airfield, usually lasting about ten minutes, and the more daring, if they had the money, could extend the experience to flying higher and 'looping the loop'. It was considered quite the thing and an achievement to have looped the loop. This feat entailed flying upside down for a little time while the pilot flew a kind of aerial figure-of-eight. The air shows were a chance to show off some of the locally-built aeroplanes manufactured at the Bristol Aeroplane Company, a fast expanding business situated to the north of Bristol in a place called Filton, surprisingly the same name that Whitchurch had once been called

212

back in Saxon days. Some of the aeroplanes were war planes; fighters and bombers being built by the government, not on a large scale, but with an eye on Germany and the dictator Hitler, who was amassing quite a huge air force in addition to a large navy and army. Some of the demonstrations at the air shows involved the dropping of dummy bombs, in reality strong flour bags, on specified targets, and great were the cheers when a target was well and truly hit! Other skills to demonstrate flying prowesss involved dipping one wing and picking up a large white 'handkerchief'; quite an art as it meant that the pilot had to tilt one wing dangerously near the ground to achieve this. All these demonstrations and the squadrons of war planes flying in formation inspired the imagination of more than one fresh-faced youth who would eventually end up flying Spitfires or Hurricanes in the Battle of Britain that was to come.

The darkness of threatened conflict was gathering around Europe again, and before the war was even declared on 3 September 1939 some local citizens in Bristol and villagers in Whitchurch had been appointed as air-raid wardens, and were busy distributing and fitting the population with gas-masks in the event of gas attacks from the air. This war was going to be a very different one from the first World War. This war would be brought on a much larger scale to the very doorsteps of the civilian population.

When the war eventually did come Dennis went off to the army to 'do his bit' which was a common phrase of the era. Clive followed his example and joined the Royal Navy some months later. Margaret and her daughter Pamela were on their own.

The first real impact of war hit them personally in May 1940 with the collapse of France and the mighty evacuation from Dunkirk. Dennis had been posted to France with the B.E.F. – the British Expeditionary Force. For days which seemed like months Margaret was desperately anxious about her son, one of the thousands stranded on the beaches of Dunkirk. She had no way of knowing whether he was dead, wounded or taken prisoner, and then quite unexpectedly he had walked through the door one fine June morning, tired and quiet with what looked like the eyes of an old man, but sound enough in wind and limb. Margaret thanked God for his deliverance. It seemed to have been a miracle that so many men had survived such an ordeal, that the weather had stayed so fair in the Channel for the little ships to get into the shallow water to rescue them and ferry them back to the bigger craft. Dennis had seen so many horrific sights while he was waiting his turn to be rescued from the beach, some men being dive-bombed by the German Stukas and left wounded and struggling in the water and others being killed or drowned at the moment of rescue after being hauled on to the smaller craft. The beaches were continually raked with machine-gun fire as the planes swept down upon them, and many lads were killed or wounded before they even reached the water. Dennis had become separated from his squad when they had been ordered to abandon their vehicles and make for the beaches. When he got to the coast he had been particularly worried about his pal Johnny who he thought was close behind him. He later found out that Johnny had been killed.

The whole operation of rescue had taken six to eight days and Dennis was full of praise for the little ships, the pleasure-boats, the fishing-boats and privately owned boats from the Thames and the south coast of England, private citizens having answered the urgent call to assist the Royal Navy in the crisis. It had been absolutely vital to rescue what was left of the British Expeditionary Force, and it was indeed miraculous that so many were saved, together with quite a few French soldiers, all determined to return to the fight at the first possible opportunity. It was a wonderful but sad operation for now the country was alone and vulnerable against the might of Nazi Germany and the Battle of Britain was about to begin in earnest.

The L.D.V. (Local Defence Volunteers), were formed, a civilian army recruited from men, many of them ex-service-men from the 1914–1918 war, who were too old for active service but keen enough to defend their homeland and get to grips with any Nazi paratroopers who dropped from the skies. The country was full of stories and speculation about enemy paratroopers, for there had been reports from some countries in occupied Europe that the Nazis had adopted many forms of disguise when they invaded, and the most popular story was that they had even dressed up as nuns! The population was also on the lookout for enemy spies in their midst for there were also reports that prior to the outbreak of war Hitler had enrolled certain people, members of the Nazi Party, to infiltrate the country and gather information on troop movements and ship departures. The name given to these people was 'Fifth Columnists' and it was in very common use at the time. Anyone with even a hint of a continental accent or any strangers to a district were looked upon with a certain amount of suspicion until they were verified.

Everyone waited for the invasion which didn't come. Instead the skies of southern England were filled with deadly aerial combat every day in the beautiful summer of 1940. The young men of the Royal Air Force were constantly on call during those fateful months and many of them died defending their country and keeping the enemy at bay. Still Hitler did not invade. It was obvious that he had intended to invade only after he had 'softened up' the nation with numerous raids on its defences, but the Royal Air Force had put a stop to that strategy, and when in the middle of September it was announced that the Germans had lost a record number of aircraft (their losses had been growing steeper with each day that passed), it seemed that they had missed the chance of invasion, for the winter would soon be upon them. The Battle of Britain in the air had been won. It was then that the Nazis turned to the bombing of the nation's large cities, the Blitzkreig, or Blitz as it was generally known. By then Dennis had fully recovered from the hell of Dunkirk, and rejoined his regiment fully resolved to continue with his duties.

As soon as she was eighteen Pamela had joined the Red

Cross and was a V.A.D. nurse. She was stationed in Bristol so went home to Whitchurch quite regularly. Her mother, Margaret, was not too lonely for by this time she had become a member of the W.V.S., the Women's Voluntary Service, and was helping out in emergencies all over the district. When Bristol was bombed, Margaret Whitchurch became busier than she would ever have thought possible. Her heart went out to the survivors of the Blitz as they queued for water brought round by official Army water-carrying vehicles. The pipes and main water supplies were fractured and cut off in many places, and the authorities did not want to risk disease to add to the misery of death, injury and homelessness. Margaret went about whatever task was given to her, ably and cheerfully, whether it be helping in the soup kitchens, finding clothes for the bombed-out, comforting relatives, minding children and organizing the water queues. Whenever she undertook the latter she could not help but think of how her husband Charles used to tell the tales of his grandfather, proud old Tad, who had been instrumental in setting up the very waterwork network which was constantly being destroyed or damaged with every air raid, repaired and then damaged again. She wondered more than once what old Tad would have made of it all. It was at these times that Margaret was pleased that she had moved out to Whitchurch from the city. The green fields and rolling hills of Somerset were a real balm to the spirit whenever she had time to return to her bungalow, away from the shattered city.

If Margaret was busier than she had ever been, then her daughter Pamela was equally so. Pamela was rushed off her feet doing duty at several local hospitals, wherever the need was greatest. Even when the worst of the air-raids were over she was still very busy, but she loved nursing and had become very proficient with experience. It was during one of her spells on duty in a Casualty Department that she met Virgil Border, one of the many Americans newly stationed in the city. Virgil was not the casualty. He had been to the cinema with a friend to while away an hour or two during

216

some time off, and they were walking down the street to where their jeep was parked, when an old lady had stumbled and fallen in front of them. She had twisted her ankle, and was altogether in a very shaken state. The two Americans had loaded her gently into their jeep, enquired where the nearest hospital was, and brought her into Casualty. Pamela had dealt with the situation, all the while eyeing this young, blond, square American who reminded her so much of her brothers away at the war. She brought Virgil and his friend, his buddy as he called him, a cup of tea for their trouble, and there was the usual transatlantic banter common to the time about the virtues of coffee and tea. When they were ready to leave Virgil lingered behind.

'Say, ma'am, I hope you don't think I'm getting too fresh in saying that I'd very much enjoy the pleasure of your company whenever you're off duty. I know we've only just met but believe me I do know a proper lady when I see one, and I sure would like to know you better!'

Pamela hesitated, and then made up her mind. She'd heard tales about Yanks picking up girls, but this young man did seem to have a sense of rightness about him. The very fact of him being there, bothering about an old lady he didn't even know when he could have so easily have passed on by, commended him to her.

'All right, but you don't even know my name. I don't even know yours!'

His easy style stimulated her like a breath of fresh air. 'Well now that's simple enough!' He stood to mock attention and extended his hand 'Lieutenant Virgil Border of the U.S. Army Air Force at your service, ma'am! May I ask to whom I have the pleasure of speaking?'

Pamela laughed and shook his hand warmly in response, 'Pamela Whitchurch.'

'That sure is a funny thing,' said Virgil, 'I'm doing some temporary liaison work at a place called Whitchurch. There's a small airport there.'

Pamela really laughed then. 'I live there . . . when I can get home these days!'

'Gee, what a coincidence, that's great.'

So it was that on the occasions when they could both get time off, they looked forward to, and eagerly enjoyed, each other's company. Whenever Virgil was at Whitchurch airport he would try to drop into the bungalow, and even if Pamela was not there and Margaret was, she would make him very welcome. This enthusiastic broad-shouldered flaxen-haired young man reminded her very much of her absent sons Dennis and Clive, away at the war, and it was very pleasant to have a masculine presence about the house again. Margaret could tell that it had been an instant attraction between Virgil and Pamela, and the friendship which she knew was getting to be something deeper had her wholehearted approval.

These days the airport at Whitchurch was used mainly for repair services but it was also used for flights for V.I.P.s to places like Lisbon and other neutral areas of Europe. One of the V.I.P.s to fly from Whitchurch had been Leslie Howard the famous film star who was, alas, never to be seen in person again. Nothing was known of what had happened to his aeroplane and all kinds of rumours circulated that it had been shot down mistakenly by a German pilot with false information that some person of political importance was on board. It was whispered around that Winston Churchill, the Prime Minister, had used the airport on more than one occasion. Virgil's job was to ensure that things ran smoothly for certain U.S. diplomats using the airport, such as Wendell Wilkie, a top man in American politics, and Eleanor Roosevelt, the U.S. President's wife, who arrived on one occasion. She was immersed in war charity work and the Red Cross movement.

As Virgil became more involved with Pamela he told her something of his background. His ancestors had originally hailed from Plymouth, and he was descended from an English sea-captain, Captain Border, who had settled in the U.S. centuries before. Virgil's father, a Boston businessman, was very keen on tracing his forebears, and being quite a successful businessman he had the money to indulge his whim. If his father, or Virgil, had ever known, they would have been more than pleased to think that Virgil had landed right back in the original place of his true ancestors; indeed parts of Whitchurch airport were on the very site of the former Saxon village, the home of Gudrum and his son Davold the Blessed, even more previous ancestors of Virgil's family. However, fate did not stop its pattern there.

Virgil was greatly taken with the rolling beauty of the local countryside with its green hills and ancient farmsteads. The neat hedges, the streams, the quaint little village halt with its tiny platform and scalloped wooden awning, where the engines puffed and steamed through to other villages, so different from the great roaring siren-shrieking monsters that ploughed across the vastness of America. It was spring and the ground was muddy and churned, especially near the entrance to the airport. Virgil had enjoyed a couple of hours off duty and had been out walking the countryside late one afternoon. Just after he'd come through the entrance to the airport he caught sight of a glint of metal in the evening sun, near one of the surrounding hedges. Fascinated, he sloshed through the mud and was astonished to find himself looking down at some sort of medallion. It looked like gold and was fairly well-preserved, for the soil hereabouts was mostly clay. He was never to know it but it was, of course, the medallion that his ancestor, poor ill-fated Arnold Blessed, had lost on the cart-track on the way to morning service all those centuries ago. Virgil could see that the inscription on the medallion, still quite plain, was of some kind of dragon creature, and when he got back to his quarters he gave it a good clean. He didn't know much about antiquities but even to his inexperienced eye there was no doubt about it, this medallion was very very old. He told no one of his find; he just had the feeling that this precious article belonged to him and Pamela alone.

He could not have known how very right he was. It is a strange fact that there are some times in people's lives when such deep intuitive decisions are made without any conscious effort. Here was a young man with a precious possession that was truly his by right, and indeed it was Pamela's also, for they shared a common ancestor, a fact that they would never know. Virgil's name was Border, due to the fact that several hundred years before a drunken midwife had made a stupid mistake with the Blessed twin boys. And Pamela was not to know that her true name should have been Blessed, and not Whitchurch, the name of the foundling son of a young maid and Stephen Blessed, descendant of the other twin. She would never have found out the well-kept secret of Stephen and Sally, even if she had been keen to trace her ancestry. The only records available would have shown nothing. The name Blessed meant nothing to her, and there were no people around Whitchurch with that name any more.

The next time he saw Pamela, Virgil presented her with the medallion. He had painstakingly purchased a splendid gold chain for it in an antique shop in Bath. On his tour of the old shops in the back lanes he had been highly delighted to see the elderly mother of the King, Queen Mary, widow of George the Fifth, on a perusal of the same antique shops. Without being told he had known she was someone different, not only by the behaviour of the people fluttering around her but by the unusual way she was garbed. She was dressed entirely in pale blue from the queenly toque that graced the noble head right down to the shoes and stockings. This would be something to tell the folks back home, he had actually seen Royalty! Apparently Queen Mary was a fairly regular visitor to the antique shops of Bath, and sometimes Bristol, and the dealers in both cities had become quite accustomed to her visits since she had been living away from war-torn London in the nearby Gloucestershire countryside at Badminton House, the home of the Duke and Duchess of Beaufort.

Pamela was thrilled with the unusual gift and lovingly amused at Virgil's enthusiastic account of seeing Queen Mary. By this time both she and Virgil were sure of their feelings for each other and had decided to get married.

'I don't want an engagement ring at the moment,' she

said as he placed the medallion around her neck, 'this splendid necklet will suffice!'

Virgil had talked of buying her a ring and even looked at some antique varieties, as the rings available in wartime Britain were quite limited in design and quality. He agreed with her idea; when he got back to the States he would choose something really splendid. Pamela was a pretty, slender girl with small features and dark curls, very much like her mother – 'Not a Whitchurch at all!' her father had said when he'd first seen his newly-born daughter. Her brothers were both blond and square, very similar to Virgil. Maybe this was why her mother made such a fuss of him, for Margaret had missed her boys greatly. Then Virgil had come along with his cheerful presence, his easy American ways, and also his generosity in helping Margaret out with food and various other commodities to supplement the meagre wartime rations.

One thing Virgil could not provide, however, was a fully-iced wedding cake. When he and Pamela were married in St Nicholas church she wore a second-hand white damask wedding gown donated by an older female cousin who had been married in the carefree clothing-coupon-free days before the war. There were no bridesmaids and only a few relatives at the church, like so many service weddings of the time. They went back to the family bungalow for the reception, and although they had a beautiful wedding cake made from saved-up rations, there was no icing on it. On this occasion not even American ingenuity could produce the luxury of icing, or 'frosting' as Virgil called it. Like so many brides of the era, Pamela had to be content with a white cardboard mock cake cover, decorated magnificently for all that, with miniature bells and lovers' knots, concealing the cake beneath. Pamela did not mind. She was joyously happy. Virgil produced a wide golden wedding ring and she wore the medallion. Even her mother, who at first thought it was 'not proper' that Virgil had failed to give her an engagement ring, had to admit that the medallion was absolutely beautiful. 'Where did he get it?' she had asked her daughter several times with no adequate answer, and on one occasion she had said, 'If it was antique shop then you might as well have had an antique ring. I know that good engagement rings are in short supply.' Pamela had just smiled enigmatically. Virgil had been to Bath again several times and also he had taken her to Christmas Steps in Bristol, browsing through the antique shops, and had dearly wanted to buy his beloved a ring in spite of her protests, but Pamela was firm. 'When the war is over and things are back to normal you can buy me a proper ring then.'

This was not to happen. Shortly after their marriage Virgil was unexpectedly drafted back to active service and stationed just outside London. He was able to get back to see Pamela quite regularly, but of course not as often as when he had been stationed so near. When their little son was born their joy knew no bounds and Pamela gave up her nursing job with the V.A.D. to care for little Virgil. They had called him Virgil on Pamela's insistence because he looked so much like his father, and all agreed that as he grew into a toddler the resemblance was greater with each passing day. Pamela took great care to make sure that he received all the vitamins dished out by the Ministry of Food such as cod liver oil and orange juice. This was to ensure that the nation's children grew up as healthy as possible despite food rationing.

It was a sad day when Pamela heard that Virgil's aeroplane had been shot down. One morning when she was in the bungalow on her own with little Virgil, for Margaret had gone on duty, a grave-faced young fellow officer called with the news that was to change her life forever. The sun was shining and the blackbirds were singing brightly, but Pamela did not register any of this. Her usual world had stopped and she was in a different realm of consciousness as she went through the motions automatically of offering the young man refreshment and generally acting the hostess. It was all so surreal, and there was little Virgil toddling from chair to chair, burbling and chirping in his baby way, in just the same way as always.

There was no hope. The plane and crew had gone swiftly into the sea without a chance of anyone parachuting to safety, and there were no survivors although an extensive search had been carried out.

Pamela's whole being felt as if it was on hold for quite a long time. Her mother's deep concern, the kindness of relatives and friends did nothing to allay her deep sorrow. She went through the actions of living, eating, sleeping, caring for baby Virgil, and it was the child who gave her the strength gradually, very gradually, to face and eventually accept her situation. She realized that she had a great responsibility to their son, the child of their love, a minia-ture replica of his father with his blond curls, his merry little ways, his stocky little form. Little Virgil loved to play with the medallion which she always wore; it was a kind of strange comfort. She would sit with the child on her lap, his tiny fingers exploring and smoothing the gold, and now and again in an unusual moment she could almost feel content. It was a link. She would dream of the future when young Virgil became a man. When he met his true love she would give him the medallion for her, just as she had received it.

So it was that the everlasting cycle of life with its amazing twists and turns was working purposefully away, as it had been for nigh on nine hundred years in the village of Whitchurch, a place in time.